By Mary Higgins Clark

MARY HIGGINS CLARK

Where Are You Now?

POCKET BOOKS

New York   London   Toronto   Sydney

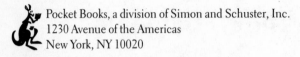
Pocket Books, a division of Simon and Schuster, Inc.
1230 Avenue of the Americas
New York, NY 10020

This Pocket Books export edition April 2008

POCKET and colophon
are registered trademarks of Simon & Schuster, Inc.

For information about special discounts for bulk purchases,
please contact Simon & Schuster Special Sales at
1-800-456-6798 or business@simonandschuster.com

Designed by Jan Pisciotta

Manufactured in the United States of America

10   9   8   7   6   5   4   3   2

Library of Congress Cataloging-in-Publication Data
Clark, Mary Higgins.
    Where are you now? : a novel / Mary Higgins Clark.
        p.   cm.
    1. Missing persons—Fiction.   2. Brothers and sisters—Fiction.
3. Manhattan (New York, N.Y.)—Fiction.   4. Domestic fiction.
5. Psychological fiction.   I. Title.
PS3553.L287W53 2008
813'.54—dc22   2007039251
ISBN-13: 978-1-4165-7655-6
ISBN-10:   1-4165-7655-X

Acknowledgments

Perhaps the question I am most frequently asked is, "Where do you get your ideas?" The answer is simple. I read an article in a newspaper or magazine, and for some reason it sticks in my mind. That's what happened when I read about a young man who disappeared thirty-five years ago from his college dorm and phones home every year or so, refusing to give any information about why he left or where he is.

His mother is now elderly, still hoping that one day before she dies she will see him again.

When a situation intrigues me, I ask myself three questions: Suppose? What if? Why?

I thought: *Suppose a college senior disappeared ten years ago; what if he calls only on Mother's Day; why did he disappear?*

And then all the *"supposes"* and *"what ifs"* and *"whys"* start to tumble around in my mind, and a new novel begins.

Writing is always a marvelous adventure for me. By its very nature, of course, it is a solitary one. Fortunately, I have the steadfast guidance and encouragement of my forever editor and friend, Michael Korda, this year with the assistance of Senior Editor Amanda Murray. Heartfelt thanks, Michael and Amanda.

Sgt. Stephen Marron, NYPD, Ret., and Detective Richard Murphy, NYPD, Ret., are my splendid experts in police procedure and criminal investigation. Cheers and thanks, Steve and Rich.

Associate Director of Copyediting Gypsy da Silva and I have worked together for more than three decades. Always, my thanks to her, Lisl Cade my publicist, and my agent, Sam Pinkus, and my readers-in-progress, Agnes Newton, Nadine Petry, and Irene Clark.

Blessings, cheers, and love unending to the home front: John Conheeney, "spouse extraordinaire," and all our children and grand-children. We are indeed blessed.

Blossoms of spring and heaps of good wishes to you, my cherished readers. I hope you enjoy reading this tale as much as I've enjoyed writing it. Same time next year? You bet.

In memory of Patricia Mary Riker,
"Pat,"
Dear friend and wonderful lady
With love

Where are you now
Who lies beneath your spell?

—"The Kashmiri Song,"
   Words by Laurence Hope,
   Music by Amy Woodforde-Finden

Where
Are You
Now?

1

It is exactly midnight, which means Mother's Day has just begun. I stayed overnight with my mother in the apartment on Sutton Place where I grew up. She is down the hall in her room, and together we are keeping the vigil. The same vigil we've kept every year since my brother, Charles MacKenzie Jr., "Mack," walked out of the apartment he shared with two other Columbia University seniors ten years ago. He has never been seen since then. But every year at some point on Mother's Day, he calls to assure Mom he is fine. "Don't worry about me," he tells her. "One of these days I'll turn the key in the lock and be home." Then he hangs up.

We never know when in those twenty-four hours that call will come. Last year Mack called at a few minutes after midnight, and our vigil ended almost as soon as it began. Two years ago he waited until the very last second to phone, and Mom was frantic that this slim contact with him was over.

Mack has to have known that my father was killed in the Twin Towers tragedy. I was sure that no matter what he was doing, that terrible day would have compelled him to come home. But it did not. Then on the next Mother's Day, during his annual call, he started crying and gasped, "I'm sorry about Dad. I'm really sorry," and broke the connection.

I am Carolyn. I was sixteen when Mack disappeared. Following in his footsteps, I attended Columbia. Unlike him, I then went on to Duke Law School. Mack had been accepted there before he disappeared. After I passed the Bar last year, I clerked for a civil court judge in the courthouse on Centre Street in lower Manhattan. Judge Paul Huot has just retired, so at the moment I'm unemployed. I plan to apply for a job as an Assistant District Attorney in Manhattan, but not quite yet.

First, I must find a way to track my brother down. What *happened* to him? Why did he disappear? There was no sign of foul play. Mack's credit cards weren't used. His car was in the garage near his apartment. No one of his description ever ended up in the morgue, although in the beginning, my mother and father were sometimes asked to view the body of some unidentified young man who had been fished out of the river or killed in an accident.

When we were growing up, Mack was my best friend, my confidant, my pal. Half my girlfriends had a crush on him. He was the perfect son, the perfect brother, handsome, kind, funny, an excellent student. How do I feel about him now? I don't know anymore. I remember how much I loved him, but that love has almost totally turned to anger and resentment. I wish I could even doubt that he's alive and that someone is playing a cruel trick, but there is no doubt in my mind about that. Years ago we recorded one of his phone calls and had the pattern of his voice compared to his voice from home movies. It was identical.

All of this means that Mom and I dangle slowly in the wind, and, before Dad died in that burning inferno, it was that way for him, too. In all these years, I have never gone into a restaurant or theatre without my eyes automatically scanning to see if just maybe, by chance, I will run into him. Someone with a similar profile and sandy brown hair will demand a second look and, sometimes, close scrutiny. I remember more than once almost knocking people over to get close to someone who turned out to be a perfect stranger.

All this was going through my mind as I set the volume of the phone on the loudest setting, got into bed, and tried to go to sleep. I guess I did fall into an uneasy doze because the jarring ring of the phone made me bolt up. I saw from the lighted dial on the clock that it was five minutes to three. With one hand I snapped on the bedside light and with the other grabbed the receiver. Mom had already picked up, and I heard her voice, breathless and nervous. "Hello, Mack."

"Hello, Mom. Happy Mother's Day. I love you."

His voice was resonant and confident. He sounds as though he doesn't have a care in the world, I thought bitterly.

As usual the sound of his voice shattered Mom. She began to cry. "Mack, I love you. I need to see you," she begged. "I don't care what trouble you may be in, what problems you have to solve, I'll help you. Mack, for God's sake, it's been ten years. Don't do this to me any longer. Please . . . please . . ."

He never stayed on the phone for as long as a minute. I'm sure he knew that we would try to trace the call, but now that that technology is available, he always calls from one of those cell phones with a pre-paid time card.

I had been planning what I would say to him and rushed now to make him hear me out before he hung up. "Mack, I'm going to find you," I said. "The cops tried and failed. So did the private investigator. But I won't fail. I *swear* I won't." My voice had been quiet and firm, as I had planned, but then the sound of my mother crying sent me over the edge. "I'm going to track you down, you lowlife," I shrieked, "and you'd better have an awfully good reason for torturing us like this."

I heard a click and knew that he had disconnected. I could have bitten my tongue off to take back the name I had called him, but, of course, it was too late.

Knowing what I was facing, that Mom would be furious at me for the way I had screamed at Mack, I put on a robe and went down the hall to the suite that she and Dad had shared.

Sutton Place is an upscale Manhattan neighborhood of town houses and apartment buildings overlooking the East River. My father bought this place after putting himself through Fordham Law School at night and working his way up to partner in a corporate law firm. Our privileged childhood was the result of his brains and the hard work ethic that was instilled in him by his widowed Scotch-Irish mother. He never allowed a nickel of the money my mother inherited to affect our lives.

I tapped on the door and pushed it open. She was standing at the panoramic window that overlooked the East River. She did not turn, even though she knew I was there. It was a clear night, and to the left I could see the lights of the Queensboro Bridge. Even in this predawn hour, there was a steady stream of cars going back and forth across it. The fanciful thought crossed my mind that maybe Mack was in one of those cars and, having made his annual call, was now on his way to a distant destination.

Mack had always loved travel; it was in his veins. My mother's father, Liam O'Connell, was born in Dublin, educated at Trinity College, and came to the United States, smart, well-educated, and broke. Within five years he was buying potato fields in Long Island that eventually became the Hamptons, property in Palm Beach County, property on Third Avenue when it was still a dirty, dark street in the shadow of the elevated train track that hovered over it. That was when he sent for and married my grandmother, the English girl he had met at Trinity.

My mother, Olivia, is a genuine English beauty, tall, still slender as a reed at sixty-two, with silver hair, blue-gray eyes, and classic features. In appearance, Mack was practically her clone.

I inherited my father's reddish brown hair, hazel eyes, and stubborn jaw. When my mother wore heels, she was a shade taller than Dad, and, like him, I'm just average height. I found myself yearning for him as I walked across the room and put my arm around my mother.

She spun around, and I could feel the anger radiating from her. "Carolyn, how *could* you talk to Mack like that?" she snapped, her arms wrapped tightly across her chest. "Can't you understand that there must be some terrible problem that is keeping him from us? Can't you understand that he must be feeling frightened and helpless and that this call is a cry for understanding?"

Before my father died, they often used to have emotional conversations like this. Mom, always protective of Mack, my father getting to the point where he was ready to wash his hands of it all and stop worrying. "For the love of God, Liv," he would snap at Mom, "he sounds all right. Maybe he's involved with some woman and doesn't want to bring her around. Maybe he's trying to be an actor. He wanted to be one when he was a kid. Maybe I was too tough on him, making him have summer jobs. Who knows?"

They would end up apologizing to each other, Mom crying, Dad anguished and angry at himself for upsetting her.

I wasn't going to make a second mistake by trying to justify myself. Instead I said, "Mom, listen to me. Since we haven't found Mack by now, he's not worrying about my threat. Look at it this way. You've heard from him. You know he's alive. He sounds downright upbeat. I know you hate sleeping pills, but I also know your doctor gave you a prescription. So take one now and get some rest."

I didn't wait for her to answer me. I knew I couldn't do any good by staying with her any longer because I was angry, too. Angry at her for railing at me, angry at Mack, angry at the fact that this ten-room duplex apartment was too big for Mom to live in alone, too filled with memories. She won't sell it because she doesn't trust that Mack's annual telephone call would be bounced to a new location, and of course she reminds me that he had said one day he would turn the key in the lock and be home . . . Home. *Here.*

I got back into bed, but sleep was a long way off. I started planning how I would begin to look for Mack. I thought about going to Lucas

Reeves, the private investigator whom Dad hired, but then changed my mind. I was going to treat Mack's disappearance as if it had happened yesterday. The first thing Dad did when we became alarmed about Mack was call the police and report him missing. I'd begin at the beginning.

I knew people down at the courthouse, which also houses the District Attorney's office. I decided that my search would begin there.

Finally I drifted off and began to dream of following a shadowy figure who was walking across a bridge. Try as I would to keep him in sight, he was too fast for me, and when we reached land, I didn't know which way to turn. But then I heard him calling me, his voice mournful and troubled. *Carolyn, stay back, stay back.*

"I can't, Mack," I said aloud as I awakened. "I can't."

2

Monsignor Devon MacKenzie ruefully commented to visitors that his beloved St. Francis de Sales Church was located so close to the Episcopal Cathedral of St. John the Divine that it was almost invisible.

A dozen years ago, Devon had expected to hear that St. Francis would be closed, and he could not in honesty have contested the decision. After all, it had been built in the nineteenth century and needed major repairs. Then, as more apartment buildings went up in the area and older walk-ups were renovated, he had been gratified to see the faces of new parishioners at Sunday Masses.

The growing congregation meant that in the past five years he had been able to carry out some of those repairs. The stained-glass windows were cleaned; years of built-up soil removed from the murals; the wooden pews sanded and refinished, the kneeling benches covered with soft new carpeting.

Then, when Pope Benedict decreed that individual pastors could decide to offer a Tridentine Mass, Devon, who was proficient in Latin, announced that henceforth the eleven o'clock Sunday Mass would be celebrated in the ancient tongue of the Church.

The response stunned him. That Mass was now filled to overflowing, not only with senior citizens but teenagers and young adults who reverently responded *"Deo gratias"* in place of "Thanks be to God," and prayed *"Pater Noster"* instead of "Our Father."

Devon was sixty-eight, two years younger than the brother he had lost on 9/11, and uncle and godfather of the nephew who had disappeared. At Mass, when he invited the congregation to silently offer their own petitions, his first prayer was always for Mack and that one day he would come home.

On Mother's Day, that prayer was always especially fervent. Today, when he returned to the rectory, there was a message waiting for him on the answering machine from Carolyn. "Uncle Dev—he called at five of three this morning. Sounded fine. Hung up fast. See you tonight."

Monsignor Devon could hear the strain in his niece's voice. His relief that his nephew had called was mixed with sharp anger. Damn you, Mack, he thought. Haven't you any idea what you're doing to us? As he tugged off his Roman collar, Devon reached for the phone to call Carolyn back. Before he could begin to dial, the doorbell rang.

It was his boyhood friend, Frank Lennon, a retired software executive, who served as head usher on Sundays and who counted, itemized, and deposited the Sunday collections.

Devon had long since learned to read people's faces and to know instantly if there was a genuine problem. That was what he was reading in Lennon's weathered face. "What's up, Frank?" he asked.

"Mack was at the eleven, Dev," Lennon said flatly. "He dropped a note for you in the basket. It was folded inside a twenty-dollar bill."

Monsignor Devon MacKenzie grabbed the scrap of paper, read the ten words printed on it, then, not trusting what he was seeing, read them again. "UNCLE DEVON, TELL CAROLYN SHE MUST NOT LOOK FOR ME."

3

Every year for the past nine years, Aaron Klein had made the long drive from Manhattan to the cemetery in Bridgehampton, to place a stone on the grave of his mother, Esther Klein. She had been a lively fifty-four-year-old divorcee, who died at the hands of a mugger as she was on her daily run early one morning near the Cathedral of St. John the Divine.

Aaron had been twenty-eight then, newly married, comfortably secure in his upward climb at Wallace and Madison Investment Bankers. Now he was the father of two sons, Eli and Gabriel, and a small daughter, Danielle, who bore a heartbreaking resemblance to her late grandmother. Aaron never visited the cemetery without once again experiencing anger and frustration at the fact that his mother's murderer was still walking the streets, a free man.

She had been struck in the back of the head with a heavy object. Her cell phone was on the ground beside her. Had she sensed danger and taken it out of her pocket to try to dial 911? That possibility was the only one that made sense.

She had to have been attempting to call. The records the police obtained showed she had neither made nor received a call at that time.

The cops thought it was a random mugging. Her watch, the only jewelry that she ever wore at that time of day, was missing, as was her house key. "Why take her house key if whoever killed her didn't know who she was and where she lived?" he had asked the cops. They hadn't had an answer to that one.

Her apartment had its own street-level entrance around the corner from the doorman-monitored main entrance of the building, but as the detectives who worked on the case pointed out, there was nothing missing from it. Her wallet, containing several hundred dollars, was in her pocketbook. Her jewelry box, open on the dresser, held the few pieces of valuable jewelry he knew her to own.

The intermittent rain began to fall again as Aaron knelt down and touched the grass over his mother's grave. His knees sank into the muddy ground as he placed the stone, and whispered, "Mom, I so wish you had lived to see the kids. The boys are finishing the first grade and kindergarten. Danielle is a little actress already. I can just see her in a dozen years auditioning for one of the plays you'd be directing at Columbia."

He smiled, thinking of what his mother's response would be. "Aaron, you're a dreamer. Do your math. By the time Danielle is in college, I'd have been seventy-five years old."

"You'd still be teaching and directing and you'd still be full of spunk," he said aloud.

4

On Monday morning, carrying the note Mack had dropped in the collection basket, I set off for the District Attorney's office in lower Manhattan. It was beautiful out, sunny and warm with a balmy breeze, the kind of weather that would have been appropriate for Mother's Day instead of the cold, wet day that had spoiled any hope of outdoor gatherings.

Mom and Uncle Dev and I had gone out to dinner Sunday night. Obviously the note that Uncle Dev handed us sent Mom and me into a tailspin. Mom's initial reaction was to be thrilled that Mack might be so near. She has always been convinced that he is far away in Colorado or California. Then she became fearful that my threat to find him had put him in some kind of jeopardy.

At first I simply didn't know what to think about it, but now I had a growing suspicion that Mack might be head over heels in trouble and trying to keep us away from it.

The lobby at 1 Hogan Place was crowded, and the security was as tight as it gets. Even though I had plenty of identification, without a specific appointment to see someone, I could not get past the guard. As the people on line behind me began to get restless, I tried to explain that my brother was missing, and we might finally have something to indicate where we could begin looking for him.

"Ma'am, you'll have to place a phone call to Missing Persons and make an appointment," the guard insisted. "Now, please, there are other people who need to get upstairs to their jobs."

Frustrated, I walked outside the building and pulled out my cell phone. Judge Huot had been in civil court, and I never had much contact with the Assistant D.A.s, but I did know one, Matt Wilson. I called the District Attorney's office and was connected to his phone. Matt wasn't at his desk and had recorded the usual answering machine instructions. "Leave your name, number, and a brief message. I'll get back to you."

"This is Carolyn MacKenzie," I began. "We've met a few times. I was Judge Huot's law clerk. My brother has been missing for ten years. He left a note for me yesterday in a church on Amsterdam Avenue. I need help to see if we can track him down before he disappears again." I finished by giving my cell phone number.

I was standing on the steps. A man was going past me, a square-shouldered guy in his midfifties with close-cropped gray hair and a purposeful stride. I could tell that he had overheard me because, somewhat to my dismay, he stopped and turned around. For a moment we eyed each other, then he said abruptly, "I'm Detective Barrott. I'll take you upstairs."

Five minutes later, I was sitting in a shabby small office that contained a desk, a couple of chairs, and stacks of files. "We can talk in here," he said. "Too much noise in the squad room."

He never took his eyes off my face as I told him about Mack, only interrupting me to ask a few questions. "Calls only on Mother's Day?"

"That's right."

"Never asks for money?"

"Never." I had put the note in a plastic sandwich bag. "I don't know if his fingerprints might be on it," I explained. "Unless, of course, he had someone else drop it in the basket for him. It seems so crazy that he would take a chance on Uncle Dev spotting him from the altar."

"Depends. He might have dyed his hair, could be twenty pounds heavier, be wearing dark glasses. It isn't hard to disguise yourself in a crowd, especially when people are wearing rain gear."

He looked at the scrap of paper. The writing was plainly visible through the plastic. "Do we have your brother's fingerprints on file?"

"I'm not sure. By the time we reported him missing, our house-keeper had dusted and vacuumed his room at home. He shared the student apartment with two of his friends, and like most of those places, there were at least a dozen others who were in and out every day. His car was washed and cleaned after the last time he used it."

Barrott handed it back to me. "We can run this paper through for prints, but I can tell you now we won't get anything. You and your mother handled it. So did your uncle, the monsignor. So did the usher who brought it to your uncle. My guess is that at least one other usher might have helped to add up the collection."

Feeling as though I needed to offer more, I said, "I'm Mack's only sibling. My mother and father and I came in to register with the familial DNA laboratory. But we've never heard from them, so I guess they've never found anyone who could be even a partial match."

"Ms. MacKenzie, from what you tell me, your brother had absolutely no reason to willingly disappear. But if he did that, there was and is a reason. You've probably watched some of these crime programs on television so you probably have heard that when people disappear, the reason usually ends up being an accumulation of problems caused by either love or money. The jilted suitor, the jealous husband or wife, the inconvenient spouse, the addict frantic for a fix. You have to reexamine all your preconceived notions about your brother. He was twenty-one. You say he was popular with the girls. Was there one special girl?"

"No one his friends told us about. Certainly no one who ever came forward."

"At his age, a lot of kids gamble too much. A lot more experiment with drugs and become addicted. Suppose he was in debt? How would your father and mother have reacted to that?"

I found myself reluctant to answer. Then I reminded myself that these were questions my mother and father had undoubtedly been asked ten years ago. I wondered if they had been evasive. "My father would have been furious," I admitted. "He had no use for people who threw away money. My mother has a private income from an inheritance. If Mack needed money he could have gotten it from her, and she wouldn't have told Dad."

"All right. Ms. MacKenzie, I'm going to be perfectly honest with you. I don't think we have a crime here, so we can't treat your brother's disappearance as a crime. You can't imagine how many people walk out of their lives every day. They're stressed. They can't cope, or even worse, they don't want to cope anymore. Your brother calls you regularly—"

"Once a year," I interrupted.

"Which is still regularly. You tell him you're going to track him down, and he responds immediately. 'Leave me alone' is his message to you. I know it sounds rough, but my advice is to make yourself realize that Mack is where he wants to be, and the most connection he wants to have with you and your mother is that one Mother's Day call. Do the three of you a favor. Respect his wishes."

He stood up. Clearly our interview was over. Clearly I should not waste the time of the police department any longer. I picked up the note and as I did, reread the message. "UNCLE DEVON, TELL CAROLYN SHE MUST NOT LOOK FOR ME."

"You've been very—honest, Detective Barrott," I said, substituting the word "honest" for "helpful." I didn't think he had been helpful in the least. "I promise I won't bother you anymore."

5

For twenty years, Gus and Lil Kramer, now in their early seventies, had been the superintendents of a four-story apartment building on West End Avenue that the owner, Derek Olsen, had renovated for student housing. As Olsen explained when he hired them, "Look, college kids, smart or dumb, are basically slobs. They'll have boxes of pizza piled up in the kitchen. They'll amass enough empty beer cans to float a battleship. They'll drop their dirty clothes and wet towels on the floor. We don't care. They all move out when they graduate.

"My point," he had continued, "is that I can raise the rent as much as I want, but only as long as the common areas look sharp. I expect you two to keep the lobby and hallways looking like Fifth Avenue digs. I want the heat and the air-conditioning always working, any plumbing problems fixed on the double, the sidewalk swept every day. I want a quick paint job when a space is vacated. When the new arrivals come with their parents to check out the place, I want all of them to be impressed."

For twenty years the Kramers had faithfully followed Olsen's instructions, and the building where they worked was known as upscale student housing. All the students who passed through it were fortunate enough to have parents with deep pockets. A number of those parents made separate arrangements for the Kramers to regularly clean the lodgings of their offspring.

The Kramers had celebrated a Mother's Day brunch at Tavern on the Green with their daughter, Winifred, and her husband, Perry. Unfortunately, the conversation had been almost completely a monologue from Winifred, urging them to quit their jobs and retire to their cottage in Pennsylvania. This was a monologue they'd heard before, one that always ended with the refrain, "Mom and Dad, I hate to think of you two sweeping and mopping and vacuuming after those kids."

Lil Kramer had long since learned to say, "You may be right, dear. I'll think about it."

Over rainbow sherbet, Gus Kramer had minced no words. "When we're ready to quit, we'll quit, not before. What would I do with myself all day?"

Late Monday afternoon, as Lil was knitting a sweater for the expected first child of one of the former students, she was thinking about Winifred's well-meant but irritating advice. Why doesn't Winifred understand that I love being with these kids? she fumed. For us, it's almost like having grandchildren. She certainly never gave us any.

The ring of the telephone startled her. Now that Gus was getting a little hard of hearing, he had raised the volume, but it was much too loud. You could wake up the dead with that racket, Lil thought as she hurried to answer it.

As she picked up the receiver, she found herself hoping that it wasn't Winifred following up on her retirement speech. A moment later, she wished it had been Winifred.

"Hello, this is Carolyn MacKenzie. Is this Mrs. Kramer?"

"Yes." Lil felt her mouth go dry.

"My brother, Mack, was living in your building when he disappeared ten years ago."

"Yes, he was."

"Mrs. Kramer, we heard from Mack the other day. He won't tell us where he is. You can understand what this is doing to my mother and me. I'm going to try to find him. We have reason to believe that he's living in the area. May I come and talk with you?"

No, Lil thought. No! But she heard herself answering the only way possible. "Of course, you can. I . . . we . . . were very fond of Mack. When do you want to see us?"

"Tomorrow morning?"

Too soon, Lil thought. I need more time. "Tomorrow's very busy for us."

"Then Wednesday morning around eleven?"

"Yes, I guess that's all right."

Gus came in as she was replacing the receiver. "Who was that?" he asked.

"Carolyn MacKenzie. She's starting her own investigation into her brother's disappearance. She's coming to talk to us Wednesday morning."

Lil watched as her husband's broad face reddened, and behind his glasses, his eyes narrowed. In two strides his short, stocky body was in front of her. "Last time, you let the cops see you were nervous, Lil. Don't let that happen in front of the sister. You hear me? *Don't let it happen this time!*"

6

On Monday afternoon, Detective Roy Barrott's shift was up at four P.M. It had been a relatively slow day, and at three o'clock he realized that he had nothing to command his immediate attention. But something was bothering him. Like his tongue roving through his mouth to find the source of a sore spot, his mind began to retrace the day searching for the source of the discomfort.

When he remembered his interview with Carolyn MacKenzie, he knew that he had found it. The look of dismay and contempt he had seen in her eyes when she left him made him feel both ashamed and embarrassed now. She was desperately worried about her brother and had hoped that the note he'd left in the collection basket at church might be a step toward finding him. Although she hadn't said it, she obviously thought he might be in some kind of trouble.

I brushed her off, Barrott thought. When she left she said she wouldn't bother me again. That was the word she used, "bother."

Now, as he leaned back in his desk chair in the crowded squad room, Barrott shut out the sounds of the ringing telephones that surrounded him. Then he shrugged. It wouldn't kill me to take a look at the file, he decided. If nothing else, to satisfy myself that it's nothing more than a guy who doesn't want to be found, a guy who will one day change his mind, and end up on *Dr. Phil* being reunited with his mother and sister while everybody has a good cry.

Wincing at a touch of arthritis in his knee, he got up, went down to the records department, signed out the MacKenzie file, brought it back to his desk, and opened it. Besides the pile of official reports, and the statements from Charles MacKenzie Jr.'s family and friends, there was a legal-sized envelope filled with pictures. Barrott pulled them out and scattered them on his desk.

One immediately caught his eye. It was a Christmas card with the MacKenzie family standing in front of their Christmas tree. It reminded Barrott of the Christmas card that he and Beth had sent in December, the two of them with the kids, Melissa and Rick, standing in front of their Christmas tree. He still had that card in his desk somewhere.

The MacKenzies got a lot more dolled up for their picture than we did, Barrott thought. The father and son were in tuxedos, the mother and daughter in evening gowns. But the overall effect was the same. A smiling, happy family wishing their friends the joys of Christmas and greetings for the New Year. It had to be the last one they sent before the son disappeared.

Now Charles MacKenzie Jr. had been missing for ten years, and Charles MacKenzie Sr. had been dead since 9/11.

Barrott rummaged through some personal papers in his desk and pulled out his family's card. He rested his elbows on the desk and held up the two Christmas cards, comparing them. I'm lucky, he thought. Rick has just finished his freshman year at Fordham on the dean's list, and Melissa, another straight-A kid, is finishing her junior year at Cathedral High and going to a prom tonight. Beth and I are more than lucky. We're blessed.

The thought crossed his mind, suppose something happened to me on this job, and Rick walked out of his dorm and disappeared. What if I wasn't around to find him?

Rick wouldn't do that to his mother and sister, not in one hundred thousand years, he told himself.

But that, in essence, is what Carolyn MacKenzie wants me to believe about her brother.

Slowly, Barrott closed the Charles MacKenzie Jr. file and slid it into the top drawer of his desk. I'll look it over in the morning, he decided, and maybe drop in on some of those people who gave statements at that time. Can't hurt to ask some questions and see if their memories got refreshed along the way.

It was four o'clock. Time to shove off. He wanted to be home in time to take pictures of Melissa in her prom dress with her date, Jason Kelly. A nice enough kid, Barrott reflected, but so thin that if he drank a glass of tomato juice, it would be as visible as mercury in a thermometer. I also want to have a little chat with the limo driver who's picking up the kids. Just to get a look at his license and let him know that he'd better not even think of driving one mile over the speed limit. He stood and put on his jacket.

You take all the precautions you can to protect your children, Barrott thought, as he turned and yelled, "See you," to the guys in the squad room and walked down the corridor. But sometimes no matter what you do, something goes wrong and your kid becomes involved in an accident or is the victim of foul play.

Please God, he prayed as he pushed the button for the elevator, don't let it ever happen to us.

7

Uncle Dev had told Elliott Wallace about the note Mack left in the collection box, and on Monday evening Elliott met us for dinner. Only a flicker of anxiety showed through his typically unruffled exterior. Elliott is the CEO and chairman of Wallace and Madison, the investment firm on Wall Street that handles the family finances. He'd been one of my father's best friends, and Mack and I have always considered him a surrogate uncle. Divorced for years, Elliott is in love with my mother, I think. I also believe that her lack of interest in him in the years since Dad died is one more casualty of Mack's disappearance.

As soon as we were settled at his favorite table in Le Cirque, I handed Elliott Mack's note and told him it made me more determined than ever to find him.

I had really hoped that Elliott would side with me in my decision to try to find Mack, but he disappointed me. "Carolyn," he said, slowly, as he read and reread the note, "I don't think you're being fair to Mack. He calls every year so that you'll know he's all right. You've told me yourself that he sounds confident, even happy. He responds immediately to your promise—or threat—to find him. In the most direct means at his disposal, he orders you to leave him alone. Why don't you go along with his wishes, and, more important, why don't you refuse to allow Mack to remain the center of your existence?"

It was not the kind of question I'd expected from Elliott, and I could see the effort it took for him to make it. His eyes were troubled, his forehead creased, as he turned his gaze from me to my mother, whose own expression had become unreadable. I was glad we were at a corner table where no one else could observe her. I was afraid she would flare up at Elliott as she had at me after Mack's call on Mother's Day, or even worse, break into a storm of weeping.

When she didn't answer him, Elliott urged, "Olivia, give Mack the space he wants. Be satisfied that he's alive, even take comfort in the fact that he's obviously close by. I can tell you right now that if Charley were here, that's exactly what he would be telling you."

My mother always surprises me. She picked up a fork and in an absentminded way, traced something on the cloth with the prongs. I would bet anything it was Mack's name.

As soon as she began to speak, I realized I had been completely wrong in evaluating her response to Mack's note.

"Since Dev showed us that message from Mack last night, I've been thinking somewhat in the same vein, Elliott," she said. The pain in her voice was evident but there was no hint of tears there. "I lashed out at Carolyn because she became angry at Mack. That wasn't fair to her. I know that Carolyn worries about me all the time. Now Mack has given us an answer, not the answer I wanted, but that's the way it is."

Here Mom tried to smile. "I am going to try to consider him an AWOL son—absent without leave. He may live in this area. As you say, he did respond quickly, and if he doesn't want to see us, Carolyn and I are going to respect his wishes." She paused, then added firmly, "So there."

"Olivia, I hope you stick to that decision," Elliott said fervently.

"I'm surely going to try. As a first step, my friends the Clarences are leaving for a cruise on their yacht, starting at the Greek islands this Friday. They've been trying to persuade me to join them. I'm going to do it." She put her fork down in a gesture of finality.

I sat back and pondered this unexpected turn of events. I had planned to talk to Elliott about my appointment with the superintendents of Mack's building on Wednesday. Now, of course, I wouldn't. Ironically, Mom had finally come to accept Mack's situation, as I had begged her to for years, and now I didn't welcome it. As every hour passed, I was more and more convinced that Mack was in serious trouble and facing it alone. I was about to raise that possibility but then clamped my lips together. With Mom away, I could search for Mack without having to cover up what I was doing, or worse yet, lying to her about it.

"How long is the cruise, Mom?" I asked.

"At least three weeks."

"I think it's a great idea," I said honestly.

"So do I." Elliott agreed. "Now, what about you, Carolyn? Still interested in becoming an Assistant District Attorney?"

"Absolutely," I said. "But I'll wait a month or so to apply. If I'm lucky enough to be hired, I won't have any time off for quite a while."

The evening progressed pleasantly. Mom, lovely in a pale blue silk shirt and matching slacks, became animated and smiling, far more than I had seen her for years. It was as though coming to terms with Mack's situation was giving her peace.

Elliott's mood brightened as he watched her. Growing up, I used to wonder if Elliott wore a shirt and tie to bed. He is always terribly formal, but when Mom turns on the charm, he simply melts. He's a few years older than Mom, which makes me wonder if his head of charcoal brown hair can possibly be natural, but I think it may be. He carries himself with the erect posture of a career military officer. His expression is usually reserved, even aloof until he smiles or laughs, and then his whole appearance lightens up, and you can catch a glimpse of a more spontaneous person hiding behind his ingrained formality.

He jokes about himself. "My father, Franklin Delano Wallace, was named after his distant cousin, President Franklin Delano Roosevelt, who remained Father's hero. Why do you think my name is Elliott? That was the name the president chose for one of his sons. And despite all he did for the common man, remember that Roosevelt was first and foremost an aristocrat. I'm afraid my father was not only an aristocrat but a downright snob. So when I come across too stuffy, blame it on the stuffed shirt who raised me."

By the time we finished coffee, I had decided that I absolutely would not even hint to Elliott that I was going to actively search for Mack. I offered to stay at Mom's apartment while she was away, a fact that pleased her. She isn't impressed with the studio in Greenwich Village that I rented last September when I started my clerkship with the judge. She certainly didn't know that my reason for staying at Sutton Place was to be available if Mack learned that I was still looking for him and tried to reach me there.

Outside the restaurant I hailed a cab. Elliott and Mom chose to walk to Sutton Place. As the cab pulled away, I watched with mixed feelings as Elliott took Mom's arm, and, their shoulders brushing, they went down the street together.

8

Sixty-seven-year-old retired surgeon Dr. David Andrews did not know why he had felt so uneasy after putting his daughter back on the train to Manhattan where she was completing her junior year at NYU.

Leesey and her older brother, Gregg, had come up to Greenwich to be with him on Mother's Day, a tough day for all of them, only the second one without Helen. The three of them had visited her grave in St. Mary's cemetery, then gone out for an early dinner at the club.

Leesey had planned to drive back to the city with Gregg, but at the last minute decided to stay overnight and go back in the morning. "My first class is eleven o'clock," she had explained, "and I feel like hanging around with you, Dad."

Sunday evening, they had gone through some of the photograph albums and talked about Helen. "I miss her so much," Leesey had whispered.

"Me, too, honey," he had confided.

But Monday morning when he dropped her at the station, Leesey had been her usual bubbly self, which was why David Andrews could not understand the gnawing sense of worry that undermined his golf game both Monday and Tuesday.

On Tuesday evening, he turned on the 6:30 news and was dozing in front of the television when the phone rang. It was Kate Carlisle,

Leesey's best friend, with whom she shared an apartment in Greenwich Village. Her question, and the troubled voice in which she asked it, caused him to bolt up from the easy chair.

"Dr. Andrews, is Leesey there?"

"No, she isn't, Kate. Why would she be here?" he asked.

As he spoke he glanced around the room. Even though he had sold the big house after Helen's death, and she'd never been in this condo, when the phone rang, he instinctively looked around for her, her hand outstretched to take the receiver from him.

When there was no answer, he demanded sharply, "Kate, why are you looking for Leesey?"

"I don't know, I just hoped . . ." Kate's voice broke.

"Kate, tell me what happened."

"Last night she went out with some of our friends to the Woodshed, a new place we've been talking about trying."

"Where is it?"

"It's on the border of the Village and SoHo. Leesey stayed after the others left. There was a really good band, and you know how she loves to dance."

"What time did the others leave?"

"It was about two o'clock, Dr. Andrews."

"Had Leesey been drinking?"

"Not much. She was fine when they left but she wasn't here when I woke up this morning, and no one has seen her all day. I've been trying to reach her on her cell phone, but she doesn't answer. I've been calling everyone I could think of who might have seen her, but no one has."

"Did you call that place where she was last night?"

"I spoke to the bartender there. He said that Leesey stayed till they closed at three o'clock and then left alone. He swore that she absolutely wasn't drunk or anywhere near it. She just stayed till the end."

Andrews closed his eyes, trying desperately to sort out the steps he needed to take. Let her be all right, God, he prayed. Leesey, the un-expected baby born when Helen was forty-five years old and they had long since given up hope of having a second child.

Impatiently, he pulled his legs off the hassock, pushed it aside, stood up, brushed back his thick white hair from his forehead, then swallowed to activate the salivary glands inside his suddenly dry mouth.

The commuter traffic is over, he thought. It shouldn't take more than an hour to get down to Greenwich Village.

"From Greenwich, Connecticut, to Greenwich Village," Leesey had joyfully announced three years ago when she decided to take early acceptance at NYU.

"Kate, I'll start down right away," Andrews said. "I'll call Leesey's brother. We'll meet you at the apartment. How far is this bar from your place?"

"About a mile."

"Would she have taken a cab?"

"It was nice out. She probably would have walked."

Alone on dark streets, late at night, Andrews thought. Trying to keep his voice from breaking, he said, "I'll be there in an hour. Keep calling anyone you can think of who might have an idea where she is."

Dr. Gregg Andrews was showering when the phone rang, and he de-cided to let the answering machine pick it up. He was off duty and had a date with someone he had met the night before at a cocktail re-ception for the launching of a novel by a friend. Now a cardiac sur-geon at New York–Presbyterian Hospital, as his father had been until his retirement, he toweled dry, walked into his bedroom, and consid-ered the fact that the May evening had begun to turn cool. From his closet, he chose an open-necked long-sleeve light blue shirt, tan slacks, and a navy blue jacket.

Leesey tells me I always look so stuffy, he remembered, thinking with a smile of the little sister who was twelve years his junior. She says I should get some cool colors and mix them up.

She also says I should get contact lenses and get rid of my crew cut, he thought.

"Gregg, you're really cute, not handsome, but cute," she had told him matter-of-factly. "I mean women like men who look as though they have a brain in their heads. And they always fall for doctors. It's kind of a 'Daddy' complex, I think. But it doesn't hurt to look a little zippy."

The message light was blinking on the phone. He debated whether he should bother to check it now but then pressed the play button.

"Gregg, it's Dad. Leesey's roommate just called me. Leesey is missing. She left a bar alone last night, and no one has seen her since. I'm on my way to her apartment. Meet me there."

Chilled, Gregg Andrews stopped the machine, and pushed the numeral that rang his father's car. "Dad, I just got your message," he said when his father answered. "I'll meet you at Leesey's apartment. On the way I'll call Larry Ahearn. Just don't drive too fast."

Grabbing his cell phone, Gregg rushed out of his apartment, caught the elevator as it was descending from an upper floor, ran through the lobby, and, ignoring the doorman, rushed out into the road to flag down a cab. As usual at this hour, there was none to be seen with the light on. Frantically he looked up and down the street, hoping to spot one of the gypsy limos that were often available on Park Avenue.

He spotted one that was parked halfway down the block and rushed to get in it. He barked Leesey's address to the driver, then opened his cell phone to call his college roommate at Georgetown, who was now Captain of detectives in the Manhattan District Attorney's office.

After two rings, he heard Larry Ahearn's voice instructing the caller to leave a message.

Shaking his head in frustration, Gregg said, "Larry, it's Gregg. Call me on my cell. Leesey is missing."

He checks his calls all the time, Gregg reminded himself as the car threaded its way downtown with agonizing slowness. When they were passing Fifty-second Street, he remembered that in fifteen minutes the young woman he had met last night would be waiting for him in the bar of the Four Seasons.

He was about to leave a message for her when Ahearn called back. "Tell me about Leesey," he ordered.

"She was in a bar or club or whatever you want to call those places in the Village and SoHo last night. She left alone when it closed and never got home."

"What's the name of the bar?"

"I don't know yet. I didn't think to ask Dad. He's on his way in."

"Who would know?"

"Leesey's roommate, Kate. She's the one who just called Dad. I'm meeting him at the apartment she and Leesey share."

"Give me Kate's phone number. I'll get back to you."

Larry Ahearn's private office was adjacent to the squad room. He was glad that at this moment no one could see the expression on his face. Leesey had been six years old when he visited the Andrews home in Greenwich the fall of his freshman year in Georgetown. He had seen her grow up from a pretty kid to a strikingly beautiful young woman, the kind any guy, never mind a predator, would zone in on.

She left the bar alone when it closed. Dear God, that crazy kid.

They just don't get it.

Larry Ahearn knew that soon he would have to tell Gregg and Leesey's father that in the last ten years, three young women had disappeared in that same SoHo-Village area after spending an evening in one of those bars.

9

On Wednesday morning, as eleven o'clock drew near, Lil Kramer became increasingly uneasy. Ever since the call came from Carolyn MacKenzie on Monday, Gus had been constantly warning her to say only what she knew about Mack's disappearance ten years ago. "Which is nothing," he kept reminding her. "Absolutely *nothing*! Just do your usual stuff about what a nice young man he was, period. No nervous-Nelly glances at me to help you out."

The apartment was always immaculate, but today the sun was especially bright and, like a magnifying glass, exposed the worn areas on the arms of the couch and the chip on the corner of the glass coffee table.

I never wanted that glass table, Lil thought, glad to find an object to blame for her distress. It's too big. It doesn't go with this old-fashioned furniture. When Winifred redecorated her own apartment, she insisted that I take it and get rid of my nice leather-top table that was Aunt Jessie's wedding gift to me. This glass thing is too big, and I'm always bumping my knees on it, and it doesn't match the end tables like the other one did, she thought.

Her mind jumped to another source of concern. I just hope that Altman's not here when the MacKenzie girl comes in.

Howard Altman, the real estate agent and manager for the nine small apartment buildings owned by Mr. Olsen, had arrived an hour ago for one of his unscheduled visits. Gus called him "Olsen's Gestapo." It was Altman's job to make sure that the individual superintendents were keeping everything up to snuff. He never even has the slightest complaint about us, Lil thought; what scares me is that whenever he comes into this apartment, he always says it's a waste of money to have two people living in a big five-room corner unit.

If he thinks I'll ever switch to a pokey one-bedroom, he has another think coming, she told herself indignantly as she adjusted the leaves in the artificial plant on the windowsill. Then she stiffened as she heard voices in the hall and realized that Gus was coming in with Altman.

Even though it was warm outside, Howard Altman, as usual, was wearing a shirt, tie, and jacket. Lil could not see him without thinking of Winifred's scornful description of him. "He's a wannabe, Mom. He thinks getting all dolled up to inspect apartment buildings will make people think he's hot stuff. He was a superintendent just like you and Dad until he started kissing the feet of old man Olsen. Don't let him bother you."

But he *does* bother me, Lil thought. He bothers me because of the way he looks around as he walks in the door. I know that someday he's going to try to make us switch apartments so that he can tell Mr. Olsen he's figured out a new way to make more money for him. He bothers me because as Mr. Olsen got older, he practically turned over the running of all the buildings to Altman.

The door opened, and Gus and Altman came in. "Well, hello, Lil," Howard Altman said heartily, as he crossed the living room with long strides and an outstretched hand to greet her.

Today he was wearing trendy sunglasses, a light tan jacket and brown slacks, a white shirt, and striped green and tan tie. His sandy hair was too short in Lil's opinion, and it was too early in the season to have such a deep tan. Winifred was sure he spent half his spare time in a tanning salon. But all of the above considered, she grudgingly admitted, he was a good-looking man, with even features, dark brown eyes, an athlete's build, and a warm smile. If you didn't know how petty he could be, he could fool you, she thought. He took her hand in a firm grip. He claims he hasn't hit forty yet. I say that he's forty-five if he's a day, Lil thought as she gave him a tight smile.

"I don't know why I even bother to stop by here," Howard said, jovially. "If I could only have the two of you in all our buildings, we could make a fortune."

"Well, we try to keep everything nice," Gus said in the fawning voice that drove Lil crazy.

"You do more than try. You succeed."

"It was good of you to stop by," Lil said, glancing at the clock on the mantel. It was five minutes of eleven.

"Couldn't pass by without popping my head in to say hello. I'll be on my way now."

The intercom rang from the foyer, and Lil was sure it was Carolyn MacKenzie. She and Gus exchanged glances, and he went to the phone on the wall. "Yes, of course, come right in. We're expecting you . . ."

Don't say her name, Lil prayed. Don't say her name. When Howard sees her on his way out, he'll probably think she wants to inquire about an apartment.

". . . Ms. MacKenzie," Gus finished. "Apartment 1B. To the right as you come into the foyer."

Lil watched as the good-bye smile on Howard Altman's face disappeared. "MacKenzie. Wasn't that the name of the guy who disappeared just before I came to work for Mr. Olsen?"

There was no answer except, "Yes, Howard."

"Mr. Olsen told me how upsetting that publicity was. He felt it really tarnished the image of this building. Why is she coming to see you?"

As Gus walked to the door, he said, flatly, "She wants to talk about her brother."

"I'd like to meet her," Howard Altman said, quietly. "If you don't mind, I'll stay."

10

I'm not really sure what I expected when I walked into that building on West End Avenue. I remember Mack showing me the apartment after he moved out of the dorm at Columbia. He was beginning his junior year then, so I was just turning fifteen.

Because he lived in the city there was no need for our parents or me to visit him there. Instead, he dropped in at home or met us at a restaurant regularly. I know that after he vanished, my mother and father went up to talk to his roommates and other people in the building, but they never let me come with them. That first summer, they made me go back to camp even though all I wanted to do was to help look for my brother.

As it turned out, I was glad that the Kramers couldn't meet me until now. Yesterday, my mother had me out all day with her, doing some last-minute shopping for her cruise. Then the eleven o'clock news last night carried the story of an NYU student who vanished early yesterday morning after leaving a bar in SoHo. There was a shot of her father and brother leaving her apartment building in the Village, and I realized with a jolt that it was right next door to mine. I ached for them.

No amount of money can convince Mom that living in the Village is every bit as safe as living on Sutton Place. For her, the Sutton Place apartment is a haven, a home she and my father joyfully bought when she was pregnant with me. At first it was a large six-room, one-floor apartment, but then as my father became more and more successful, he bought the apartment above us, turned the two into a duplex, and doubled its size.

Now, to me, it seems like a prison where until now my mother has been listening, always listening for the key to turn in the door and Mack to call out, "I'm home." For me, that belief that he might return has become a frustration, a sadness that won't ever go away. I feel so terribly selfish. I loved Mack, my big brother, my pal. But I don't want to have my life on hold any longer. Even the decision to wait before I apply for a job in the DA's office isn't about the fact that being hired means no time off for awhile. It's all about trying to find Mack and, if I fail, promising myself that then I'll get on with my own life at last. I'll spend most of these three weeks in Sutton Place while Mom's away, but that's not to feel safe — it's just in case Mack has some way of knowing I'm beginning to talk to everyone who was ever close to him and tries to call me.

This building where Mack had lived was old, the façade that gray stone that was so popular in New York in the early twentieth century. But the sidewalk and steps were clean, the handle of the outer door polished. That door was unlocked and opened into a narrow foyer where one can either dial an apartment number and be buzzed in, or use a key to open the door to the lobby.

I had spoken to Mrs. Kramer, and I don't really know why, but somehow I expected to hear her voice on the intercom. Instead, a man responded and directed me to their ground-floor apartment.

When I got inside, the door of 1B was already open, and a man was waiting for me who introduced himself as Gus Kramer, the superintendent. As I was going over the file this morning, I remembered what my father had said about him: "That guy is more worried that he'll be blamed for Mack's disappearance than he's concerned that something happened to Mack. And his wife is worse. She had the gall to say that Mr. Olsen would be upset. As if we have to be concerned about the owner of that renovated tenement!"

It's funny that when I was dressing for this appointment, I kept changing my mind about what to wear. I had actually laid out a lightweight pantsuit, the kind I wore to court when I was working for the judge, but somehow it seemed too businesslike. I wanted the Kramers to feel comfortable with me. As much as possible I wanted them to see me as Mack's kid sister, to like me, to want to help. That was why I decided to wear a long-sleeve cotton sweater, jeans, and sandals. As a portent for success, I wore the chain Mack gave me on my sixteenth birthday. There were two gold charms on it, one of ice skates, the other a soccer ball, in honor of my two favorite sports.

After Gus Kramer introduced himself and invited me in, it was like stepping back in time. Despite Daddy's success, he could never budge my grandmother from her apartment in Jackson Heights, Queens. This one had the same velour furniture, machine-made Persian carpet, and leather-top end tables as hers. The only thing that seemed out of place was the glass coffee table.

My first impression of Gus and Lil Kramer was that they were the kind of people who grow to look alike after years together. Her steel-gray hair was exactly the same shade as his. They were a little shorter than average height, with sturdy bodies. Their eyes were a matching pale blue, and there was no mistaking the wary expression in both faces as they offered me a begrudging smile.

Actually, it was the third person in the room who took over as host. "Ms. MacKenzie, I'm so pleased to meet you. I am Howard Altman, the district manager of Olsen Properties. I wasn't here at the time of your brother's disappearance but I know how concerned Mr. Olsen was—and has been—about it. Why don't we all sit down and let you tell us how we can be of assistance to you."

I could sense the resentment the Kramers had to Altman taking over, but for me it made it easier to deliver my planned speech. I sat on the edge of the nearest chair and addressed myself to him. "As you obviously have heard, my brother, Mack, disappeared ten years ago. There simply hasn't been a trace of him since then. But he does call us every Mother's Day as he did a few days ago. I got on the phone while he was talking to my mother and vowed to find him. Later that day he went to St. Francis, a church in this neighborhood where my uncle is the pastor, and left a note for me to warn me away. I'm so afraid Mack may be in some kind of trouble and ashamed to ask for help."

"A note!" Lil Kramer's exclamation silenced me. I was astonished to see the way her cheeks became flushed and the unconscious gesture with which she reached over and grasped her husband's hand. "You mean he went to St. Francis and left a note for you?" she asked.

"Yes, at the eleven o'clock Mass. Why would that surprise you, Mrs. Kramer? I know over the years that there have been articles about my brother's disappearance and the fact that he contacts us."

Gus Kramer answered for his wife. "Ms. MacKenzie, my wife has always felt terrible about your brother. He was one of the nicest, politest kids we ever had here."

"That's what Mr. Olsen said," Howard Altman told me. Then he smiled. "Ms. MacKenzie, let me explain. Mr. Olsen is so aware of the pitfalls that occur in this day and age with young people, even intellectually gifted young people. He was always around to greet new students. He's up there in years now, but he's told me about how impressed he was with your parents and your brother. And I can tell you, the Kramers have always kept a sharp eye out for heavy drinking, or worse, drug use. If your brother had encountered some kind of problem, it didn't begin or continue under this roof."

This from a man who didn't know Mack, who only knew about him. The message was loud and clear. Don't look here for your brother's problem, lady.

"I don't mean to suggest that anything about Mack residing here triggered his disappearance. But you can understand that it makes sense for me to start searching for him in the last place where he was seen. The brother I knew would never willingly cause my mother and father and me the grief and anxiety we have been living with for ten years." I felt the tears that were always too close to the surface shining in my eyes as I corrected myself. "I mean the anxiety my mother and I experience constantly. I think you may already know that my father was a 9/11 victim."

"Your brother never seemed like the kind of young man who would just disappear without a mighty important reason," Gus Kramer agreed.

His tone was sincere, but I did not miss the glance he shot at his wife or the fact that she was nervously biting her lips.

"Did you ever consider the possibility that your brother may have experienced a cerebral hemorrhage or any other physical condition that might have given him an attack of amnesia or even partial amnesia?" Howard Altman asked.

"I'm considering everything," I told him. I reached into my shoulder bag and took out a notebook and pen. "Mr. and Mrs. Kramer, I know it's been ten years but could I just ask you to tell me what you remember about anything Mack did or said that might have some significance? I mean, sometimes we think of something that didn't occur to us at the time. Maybe as Mr. Altman just suggested, Mack had some kind of amnesia attack. Did he seem in any way troubled or worried, or as though he wasn't feeling well physically?"

As I asked these questions, I thought of how, after the police gave up on trying to find Mack, my father then hired private investigator Lucas Reeves to continue the search. For the last few days I've been reviewing every word of his files. Everything the Kramers told him was in my notes.

I listened as Mrs. Kramer hesitantly, then enthusiastically, told me how Mack was the kind of young man who always held the door open for her, who put his laundry in his hamper, who always picked up after himself. "I never saw him look troubled," she said. The last time she had seen him was when she tidied up the apartment he shared with two other seniors. "Both of the other boys were out. He was working on his computer in his bedroom and told me the vacuum wouldn't bother him. That's the way he always was. Easy. Nice. Polite."

"What time was that?" I asked her.

She pursed her lips. "About ten o'clock in the morning, I would guess."

"That would be right," Gus Kramer confirmed quickly.

"And you never saw him again?"

"I saw him leave the building at about three o'clock. I was on my way home from the dentist. I was putting my key in the lock of our apartment. Gus heard me and opened the door. We both saw Mack come down the stairs. He waved as he went through the lobby."

I watched her glance at her husband for approval.

"What was Mack wearing, Mrs. Kramer?"

"What he had on in the morning. A T-shirt and jeans and sneakers and . . ."

"Lil, you're mixed up again. Mack was wearing a jacket and slacks and an open-necked sport shirt when he left," Gus Kramer interrupted sharply.

"That's what I meant," she said hurriedly. "It's just I keep seeing him in the T-shirt and jeans because that's when I had a little talk with him that morning." Her face convulsed. "Gus and I had nothing to do with his disappearance," she cried. "Why are you torturing us?"

As I stared at her I thought of what Lucas Reeves, the private investigator, had written in his file, that the Kramers were nervous that they might lose their jobs because of Mack's disappearance. Now, nearly ten years later, I didn't accept that reasoning.

They were nervous because they had something to hide. Now

they were trying to keep their stories straight. Ten years ago Mrs. Kramer had told Reeves that Mack was just coming out of the building when she saw him and that her husband was in the lobby.

At that moment I would have bet my life that neither one of them ever saw Mack leave this building. Or *did* he ever leave it? That question rushed into my mind and was immediately dismissed.

"I know how long it's been," I said. "But would it be possible to see the apartment where my brother lived?"

I could see that my request startled them. This time both Kramers looked to Howard Altman for guidance.

"Of course, the apartment has been rented," he said, "but since it's the end of the term many of the students have already left. What is the situation in 4D, Lil?"

"The two who shared the larger bedroom are gone. Walter Cannon has Mack's old room but he's leaving today."

"Then perhaps you could phone and ask if Ms. MacKenzie might stop in?" Altman suggested.

A moment later we were climbing the stairs to the fourth floor. "The students don't mind stairs," Altman told me. "I must say I'm glad I don't go up and down them every day."

Walter Cannon was a six-foot-four twenty-two-year-old who waved aside my apologies for the interruption. "I'm just glad you weren't here an hour ago," he said. "I had stuff all over the place." He explained that he was on his way home to New Hampshire for a summer vacation and was starting law school in the fall.

He's at the same point in time Mack was when he disappeared, I thought sadly.

The apartment coincided with my vague memory of it. A small foyer now stacked with the luggage Cannon would be carrying, a kitchen directly opposite the outer door, a hall to the right with a sitting room and bedroom off it, a bathroom at the end. To the left of the foyer, a second bath and, beyond it, the bedroom where Mack had lived. Not listening to Altman's comments about how well the apartments were maintained, I walked into what had been Mack's bedroom.

The walls and ceilings were off-white. A light flowered cotton spread was tossed on the bed. Matching drapery panels framed the two windows. A dresser, desk, and easy chair completed the furnishings. A wall-to-wall blue-gray carpet covered the floor.

"This apartment, like all the others after they've been vacated, will have a fresh coat of paint immediately," Altman was saying. "The carpet and spread and drapes will be cleaned. Gus Kramer will make sure the kitchen and baths are spotless. We're very proud of our units."

Mack lived here for two years, I thought. I imagined him feeling about it the way I feel about my apartment. It was his own space. He could get up early or late, read or not read, answer the phone or not answer the phone. The closet door was open, and of course it was empty now.

I thought about the Kramers' claim that he was wearing a jacket and open-necked shirt and slacks when he left that afternoon.

What was the weather like that day? I wondered. Was it one of those chilly May afternoons like last Sunday? Or, if it was very warm, and Mack did leave at three o'clock, would wearing a jacket have any significance? A date? A drive to a girl's house in Connecticut, or Long Island?

It's funny but in that room, ten years later, I had a sense of his presence. He was always so laid back. Dad had been competitive, quick to size up a situation, and, with lightning accuracy, appraise and judge it. I know I'm like that, too. Mack was more like Mom. He was always giving everyone a break. Like her, if he ever realized he was being used or treated shabbily, he wouldn't have a confrontation, he'd simply withdraw from the situation. And that, I think, is what Mom is doing now—she views Mack's note in the collection basket as a slap in the face.

I moved to the window, trying to see what he had seen. Knowing how Mack loved to stand at the windows of the Sutton Place apartment and study the panorama, the East River with boats and barges, the lights of the bridges, the air traffic heading in and out of La-Guardia Airport, I was sure he'd often gazed out these windows, overlooking West End Avenue, the sidewalks constantly streaming with people, the vehicle traffic bumper to bumper in the street.

The dream I had had of him after his predawn phone call on Mother's Day replayed itself in my mind. Once again I was walking along a dark path, desperate to find Mack.

And once again he was warning me to stay back.

11

In a weary voice, Dr. David Andrews said, "Detective Barrott, Leesey left that bar at three o'clock yesterday morning. It is now one o'clock Wednesday afternoon. She has already been missing thirty-four hours. Shouldn't you check the hospitals again? If anyone knows how busy emergency rooms are, God knows it's me."

Leesey's father was sitting at the small kitchen table in his daughter's college apartment, his hands folded, his head bowed. Heartsick, sleep-deprived, and despairing, he had refused his son's plea to go back with him to his apartment and wait for word there. After being here all night, Gregg had gone home to shower and change before stopping at the hospital to see his postoperative patients.

Roy Barrott was sitting opposite Leesey's father at the table. The night my daughter went to a prom, his daughter went to that joint, then disappeared, Roy thought, with a sudden guilty feeling at his own good fortune. "Dr. Andrews," he said, "you have to hold on to the possibility that Leesey may be perfectly all right. She *is* an adult, and has the right to privacy."

Barrott saw the expression on the doctor's face harden into anger and scorn. I sound like I'm suggesting that she's an easy pickup, he thought, and hurried to add, "Please don't think I believe that this is the case with Leesey. We're treating her disappearance as a serious problem." Barrott's boss, Captain Larry Ahearn, had made the urgency of this case perfectly clear already.

"Then what are you doing to find her?" The anger drained from David Andrews's face. His voice was low and halting.

He's only one degree from going into shock, Barrott thought. "We've reviewed the security cameras of the Woodshed, and she *did* leave alone. The only people left in the bar were the band that was playing, the bartender, and the security guard. They all swear that none of them left for at least twenty minutes after Leesey, so we presume none of them followed her. So far, they all check out as okay guys. Right now our people are going over every frame in the security camera at that bar Monday night to see if we can identify any potential troublemakers."

"Maybe someone who was there earlier waited outside for her." David Andrews knew that his voice was a monotone. Is this detective trying to reassure me? he asked himself. Then the same thought crossed his mind for the thousandth time: I *know* something terrible has happened to Leesey!

He pushed his chair away from the table and stood up. "I'm going to offer a twenty-five-thousand-dollar reward to anyone who helps us find her," he said. "I'm going to put her picture and a description of what she was wearing on posters. You've met my daughter's roommate, Kate. She'll get Leesey's friends to tack them up on every street between that bar and this building. Somebody has to have seen *something*."

As a father that's exactly what I would do, if I were in his shoes, Roy Barrott thought as he got to his feet, too. "Dr. Andrews, that's a very good idea. Give us the picture from your wallet and her height, weight, and hair color. We'll take care of having the posters made. It will be a big help if those posters are up when the bar crowd comes out tonight. I can promise you our undercover people will be in the Woodshed and every other dive around here, talking to people. With any luck we might find a person who saw someone paying a lot of attention to her. But I would suggest, sir, you go to your son's apartment and get some rest. I'll have an officer drive you there."

I'm only in the way, David Andrews thought bleakly. But he's right—I *do* have to sleep. Without speaking, he nodded.

The door from the bedroom was open. Kate Carlisle had spent a sleepless night, and now after napping briefly, she saw them leaving, with Barrott's hand firmly under the doctor's arm. "Dr. Andrews, are you all right?" she asked anxiously.

"Dr. Andrews is going to his son's apartment," Barrott explained. "I'll be back and forth. Kate, do you by any chance have a more recent photo of Leesey? The one I've seen that was in Dr. Andrews's wallet is more than a year old."

"Yes. I have a good one. I took it only last week. Angelina Jolie and Brad Pitt were walking in SoHo with their kids, and the paparazzi were all around them. I told Leesey to pretend she was a movie star, and I snapped a couple of pictures of her with my cell phone camera. One of them is a terrific shot. She was planning to have it framed for you, Dr. Andrews." Her voice broke. Flustered, Kate ran back into the bedroom, opened a drawer in a night table, grabbed a print from it, and hurried back to them.

In the photo, Leesey had struck a model's pose, her smiling face turned to the camera, her long hair tossed by the breeze, her slender body almost slouching, her hands buried deep in the pockets of her denim jacket.

Barrott's eyes traveled from the lovely girl in the center to the passers-by in the background. None of the faces was clear. Was it possible one of them had noticed Leesey? he wondered. A predator on the prowl?

I'll get this enlarged, he thought, as he took it from Kate. "This is a very clear picture of Leesey," he said. "I also want you to give me a print of the other picture you took of her. From what I understand, she was wearing a denim jacket the night she went to the club. She's wearing a denim jacket in this picture."

"She was wearing that same jacket," Kate said.

"She bought it two years ago, just before her mother died," David Andrews said. "It has a skirt she wore with it. Her mother laughed and told her that the skirt had strings hanging off it. Leesey told her that was the style. Her mother said if that was considered style, it was time to bring back the hoopskirt."

I sound maudlin, David Andrews told himself. I'm holding up this detective from finding Leesey. I've got to get out of the way here. "Kate, that's a good picture of Leesey. Anyone who saw her could identify her from it. Thank you very much."

Without waiting for her to answer, he started for the door, grateful for the strong hand under his arm. In silence he walked down the three flights of stairs. He was vaguely aware of a camera flashing and someone shouting questions at him as he crossed the sidewalk and was helped into a squad car. He did remember to ask Detective Barrott what else he would do to try to find Leesey. Barrott closed the car door and then leaned down to the window.

"Dr. Andrews, we've already canvassed the people in this building. We know from the security camera here that Leesey didn't get to this door but these houses all look alike. She might have gone to the wrong one. We're going to start door to door, working the whole neighborhood. It will help to have her picture."

"Why on earth would she go to the wrong door? She didn't have too much to drink, you told me that yourself. The bartender and all those other people in the Woodshed swear she was fine when she left that place," David Andrews reminded him sharply.

It was on the tip of Barrott's tongue to reply that, unless it can be proven otherwise, ninety-nine percent of bartenders will swear that a missing patron left the bar sober. Instead he said, "Doctor, no stone unturned. That's my promise to you."

The single reporter on the scene stuck a microphone in Barrott's face as he turned from the squad car. "Look," Barrott said, impatiently, "Captain Ahearn is holding a press conference at five o'clock. He's authorized to give a statement. I'm not."

He walked back into the lobby of the building, waited till he saw the reporter and cameraman get into their van and drive away, then came back out and walked to the next building. Like most of them on this block, the outer door was unlocked, and admittance was gained either by a key or being buzzed in by a tenant.

Barrott's eyes moved up and down the tenant list, then they widened as he spotted one name, "Carolyn MacKenzie." Six degrees of separation? he asked himself. Maybe.

Roy Barrott stood perfectly still, then traced his index finger over Carolyn MacKenzie's name.

The unerring instinct that made him such a superb detective was telling him that somehow, someway there was a connection between the two cases.

12

After I left the apartment building where Mack had lived, I went back to Sutton Place. In the day and a half since Mom had made the decision to go on the cruise, she had been energized, as if after living so long in limbo, she was trying to make up for lost time. She told me she was planning to go through closets and pull out clothing to give away, and then this evening she would be meeting Elliott and some other friends for dinner.

I wondered why she would bother to clean out closets just before she went on vacation, but that became evident. Over a quick lunch, a sandwich and a cup of tea in the breakfast room, she told me that she was listing the apartment with a broker and that as soon as she came back she was going to look for something smaller. "You're never going to move back in," she said, "I know that. I will have call forwarding, just in case Mack decides to phone next Mother's Day, but on the other hand, if I miss his call, so be it. I just may not hang around and wait for it."

I looked at her, astonished. When she said she was going to clean out closets, I was thinking that she meant her own. But now, without asking, I was sure that it was the closets in Mack's room that were going to be emptied.

"What are you going to do with Mack's things?" I asked, trying to sound casual.

"I'll have Dev send someone to get them and deliver them to a place where they'll be put to good use." Mom looked at me for approval and, finding something missing in my expression, said quickly, "Carolyn, you're the one telling me to move on. The fact remains that even if Mack walked through the door today, and even if his clothes still fit him, they'd probably be out of style."

"Don't misunderstand me," I told her. "I think it's a good idea, but I also think that it's the last thing in the world you should be worrying about two days before you're getting on a plane to fly to Greece. Look, Mom, do yourself a favor. Let *me* go through Mack's clothes and sort them out." Even as I spoke, it occurred to me that it was possible that ten years ago, no one had ever carefully explored the pockets of slacks and jackets that Mack had left in this apartment. Lucas Reeves had indicated in his case report that nothing of importance was found in the clothing Mack had left behind in his student apartment.

Without much hesitation, even with relief, Mom agreed. "I don't know what I'd do without you, Carolyn," she said. "You've been my rod and staff through all this. But I know you. You only stopped working two weeks ago, and I can tell you're restless. What will you do while I'm gone?"

She had inadvertently furnished me with a response that was at least partly honest. "We know someone will snap up this place in a heartbeat," I said. "I never intended to stay in the studio indefinitely. I'm going to look around for a bigger place myself. You'll let me have my pick of any furniture you don't take with you, right?"

"Of course. Let Elliott know. A decent one-bedroom is an expenditure he'll certainly approve." Elliott was the trustee of the money my grandfather had left me.

Mom took the last gulp of tea and stood up. "I'd better rush. Helene will have a fit if I'm late for my hair appointment. For the kind of money she charges, she could stand to possess a little more humility." She gave me a quick kiss on my cheek, then added, "If you find an apartment you like, make sure it has a doorman. I never have been comfortable with you living in a place where you have to let yourself in. I've been checking the news. There's no sign of that girl who lived next door to you who disappeared. God help her family."

I was glad Mom had the salon appointment. Now that I was determined to find Mack, I had the sense that I must not lose a minute in my search for him. Geographically, he had been so close to us when he left that note on Sunday. The meeting with the Kramers had left me desperately uneasy. Memories do fade, but when I spoke to them, they had contradicted each other about what Mack was wearing and exactly where they had seen him last. Also, Lil Kramer had been absolutely shocked when I told her he had been at the Mass. Why? Was Mack a threat to them? What did they know that scared them so much?

I had taken the report of Investigator Reeves from the file drawer in Dad's desk. Now I wanted to get the addresses of Mack's former roommates, Bruce Galbraith and Nicholas DeMarco. Nick had kept in touch with Dad regularly, in the beginning. Naturally, as time passed he heard from him less and less frequently. The last time I saw him was when he attended Dad's memorial Mass, but that day is a complete blur to me.

Dad's study isn't large, but as he used to say, it was big enough for what he needed. His big desk dominated the paneled room. To my mother's horror, the faded nine-by-twelve carpet that had been in his mother's living room was on the floor. "Reminds me of where I came from, Liv," he would say after one of her periodic efforts to get rid of it. A worn leather chair with a hassock was his favorite spot in the morning. He always got up very early, made himself coffee, and settled in that chair with the morning papers before showering and getting dressed to go to the office.

Bookcases covered the wall opposite the windows. Scattered on them were framed pictures of the four of us from those happy days when we had been together. Dad had a presence that showed through even in casual pictures: the determined jaw, softened by the wide smile, the keen intelligence in his eyes. He had done everything possible to trace Mack and would still be trying if he were alive. I'm sure of that.

I opened the top drawer of his desk and took out his phone book. On a slip of paper I wrote down Bruce Galbraith's phone number. I remembered he had gone into the family real estate business in Manhattan. I copied both his home and business numbers.

Nick DeMarco, the son of immigrant parents who owned a small storefront restaurant in Queens, had been a scholarship student at Columbia. I remembered that after he got his MBA from Harvard, he went into the restaurant business and, I understand, has been very successful. Both his home and business phone numbers and addresses were in Manhattan.

I sat at Dad's desk and picked up the receiver. I decided to call Bruce first. There was a reason for that. When I was sixteen, I had a fierce crush on Nick. He and Mack were particularly close friends, and Mack regularly brought him home for dinner. I lived for those dinners. But then one night he and Mack brought a girl with them. Barbara Hanover was a senior at Columbia and lived in the same student apartment building, and it was immediately clear to me that Nick was crazy about her.

Even though I was absolutely crushed, I thought I had kept up a good front that evening, but Mack could read me like a book. Before he, Nick, and Barbara left, he pulled me aside, and said, "Carolyn, I know you have big eyes for Nick. Forget it. He's got a different girl-friend every week. Stick to guys your own age."

My angry denial only caused Mack to smile. "You'll get over it," were his parting words to me that night. That was about six months before he disappeared, and it was the last time I stayed home when Nick was coming. I was embarrassed and didn't want to be there. The fact that it was obvious to Mack that I had a crush on Nick made me sure it had been obvious to everyone else. I was grateful neither of my parents ever referred to it.

I got through to Bruce's secretary at Galbraith Real Estate and was told that he was on a business trip until next Monday. Did I care to leave a message? I gave the secretary my name and phone number, hesitated, then added, "It's about Mack. We just heard from him again."

Then I called Nick. His office is at 400 Park Avenue. That's about a fifteen-minute walk from Sutton Place, I thought, as I dialed. When I asked for him, his secretary picked up and crisply told me that if I was from the media, any statement would be coming from Mr. DeMarco's lawyer.

"I'm not from the media," I said. "Nick was a friend of my brother's at Columbia. I'm sorry, I didn't realize he was having legal troubles."

Maybe the sympathy in my voice and the use of his first name was the reason his secretary was so frank. "Mr. DeMarco is the owner of the Woodshed, the place where a young woman was last seen before she disappeared the other night," she explained. "If you give me your telephone number, I'll have him return your call."

13

Aaron Klein had been working for Wallace and Madison for fourteen years. He had started there directly after receiving his MBA degree. At that time Joshua Madison was chief executive of the privately held wealth-management company, but when he died suddenly two years later, his partner, Elliott Wallace, had taken over as chairman and CEO.

Aaron had loved the gruff Josh Madison, but initially he had been intimidated by Wallace, whose formal manner was completely the opposite of his own easygoing style. Then as Aaron continued to rise steadily through the ranks, working with higher and higher-profile clients, Elliott had begun to invite him to lunch in the executive dining room of their office on Wall Street, a clear sign that he was being groomed for a top job.

Ten years ago their relationship had taken a giant leap forward when Elliott let down his guard and confided to Aaron the grief and pain he was experiencing at the disappearance of Charles MacKenzie Jr. Elliott had been managing the MacKenzie money for years, and after Charles Sr. died on 9/11, he spoke of Olivia MacKenzie and her children with an air of fierce protectiveness. From everything Elliott had ever said about the missing young man, Aaron knew that he looked on Mack as a surrogate son. The fact that Aaron's mother, Esther, had taught Mack in one of her drama classes at Columbia only strengthened the bond between them.

Then, a year later, when Aaron's mother was murdered during what was determined to be a random mugging, the bond had tightened further still. Now, it was generally accepted in the company that Aaron Klein was the chosen successor of Elliott Wallace.

Aaron had been away visiting clients in Chicago on Monday and Tuesday. Late Wednesday morning he received a call from his boss. "Aaron, do you have plans for lunch?"

"None that I can't change," Aaron said promptly.

"Then please meet me at twelve thirty in the dining room."

I wonder what's up, Aaron asked himself as he replaced the receiver. Elliott isn't usually this last-minute about lunch. At 12:15 he got up from his desk, went into his private bathroom, ran a comb through his sparse head of hair, and straightened his tie. Mirror, mirror, on the wall, he thought sardonically, who's the baldest of us all? Thirty-seven years old, in good shape, not bad-looking, but at the rate I'm going, by the time I'm fifty I'll be lucky if I have six hairs left on my head. He sighed and put away the comb.

Jenny tells me that's part of the reason I've done so well, he told himself. She says I look ten years older than I am. Thanks, honey.

Friendly as they had become, Aaron was always aware that to the blue-blooded Elliott Wallace, the fact that he, his chosen successor, was the grandson of immigrants had to be disappointing. That thought was in his mind as he walked toward the dining room. The kid from Staten Island approaches the privileged descendant of one of the first settlers of New Amsterdam, he thought. Never mind that the immigrants' grandson graduated from Yale in the top ten percent of his class and has a master's degree from Wharton; it still isn't the same as having classy ancestors. I wonder if I'll hear the "cousin Franklin" story again.

Aaron acknowledged that he both hated and was bored by Elliott's oft-repeated anecdote of FDR's having invited a Republican woman to host an event at Hyde Park when his wife, Eleanor, was away. When he was chided by the Democratic chairman, an astonished FDR replied, "But of course I asked her to be my hostess. She is the only woman in Hyde Park who is my social equal."

"That was my father's favorite story about his cousin Franklin," Elliott would chuckle.

As he reached the table and a waiter pulled out a chair for him, Aaron immediately sensed that anecdotes about his revered relatives were the last thing on Elliott's mind today. He looked thoughtful and concerned—in fact, *preoccupied.*

"Aaron, good to see you. Let's order quickly. I have a couple of meetings. I assume you'll have your usual?"

"Cobb salad, no dressing, and iced tea, Mr. Klein?" the waiter asked, smiling.

"You've got it." Aaron did not mind letting his boss think that his salad luncheon was a sign of self-discipline. The fact was that his wife, Jenny, loved to cook, and even her most casual dinners far surpassed the sterile menu of the executive dining room.

Elliott ordered, and when the waiter was out of earshot he got right to the point: "We heard from Mack on Sunday," he said.

"The usual Mother's Day call?" Aaron asked. "I was wondering if he'd stick to form and phone this year."

"He did that, and more."

Aaron did not take his eyes off Elliott Wallace's face as he listened to the account of the written communication from Mack.

"I've advised Olivia to respect Mack's wishes," Elliott said. "But oddly enough, she seems to have come to that conclusion on her own. She referred to Mack as 'absent without leave.' She's going to join some mutual friends of ours for a cruise around the Greek islands. I've been invited to be with them and may go for the last ten days."

"You *should*," Aaron said promptly. "You don't give yourself nearly enough time off."

"And on my next birthday I'll be sixty-five. In a lot of companies I'd be pushed out at that age. That's the benefit of owning this one—I'm not going anywhere for a long time." He paused, as if preparing himself, then said, "But I didn't ask you to join me to discuss vacation plans."

Surprised, Aaron Klein watched as Wallace's eyes clouded with worry.

"Aaron, you've gone through the experience of losing your mother in a random crime. If the positions were reversed, if your mother was the one who had disappeared and then kept in contact, would you respect her wishes or would you feel that you should keep on trying to find her? I find myself absolutely uncertain and troubled. Did I give Olivia the right advice, or should I have told her to renew and redouble her efforts to find Mack?"

Suppose Mom had disappeared ten years ago, Aaron asked himself. Suppose she phoned once a year, then, when I told her I needed to find her and was going to track her down, she sent me a note telling me to leave her alone, what would I do?

The answer was not hard to reach. "If my mother did to *me* what Mack has done to his family and to you, I would say, 'If that's the way you want it, Mom, so be it. I have other fish to fry.' "

Elliott Wallace smiled. " 'Other fish to fry'? That's a strange way to put it. But thank you, Aaron. I needed to be reassured I'm not failing Mack or Olivia . . ." He paused, then corrected himself: "I mean his mother and sister, of course."

"You're not failing them," Aaron Klein said emphatically.

That night, as he was sipping a predinner glass of wine with his wife, Aaron said, "Jenny, today I realized that even stuffed shirts are like schoolboys when they fall in love. Elliott can't mention Olivia MacKenzie's name without getting stars in his eyes."

14

Nicholas DeMarco, owner of the trendy club the Woodshed, as well as an upscale restaurant in Palm Beach, was notified of the disappearance of the NYU coed Leesey Andrews late Tuesday evening while on a golf outing in South Carolina.

On Wednesday morning, he flew home, and by three o'clock Wednesday afternoon he was following a secretary down a long corridor on the ninth floor of 1 Hogan Place to the section where the detectives assigned to the District Attorney of Manhattan worked. He had an appointment with Captain Larry Ahearn, the commanding officer of the squad.

Tall, with the lean figure of a disciplined athlete, Nick walked with long strides, a worried frown on his forehead. Absentmindedly, he passed a hand through his short hair, which, despite his best efforts, curled when it was damp.

I should have stopped home long enough to change, he chided himself. He was wearing an open-necked checkered blue and white sport shirt, which felt too casual, even with a light blue jacket and dark blue slacks.

"This is the detectives' squad room," the secretary explained, as they entered a large room in which rows of desks were haphazardly clustered. Only a half dozen of them were occupied, although piles of papers and ringing telephones testified to the fact that all of the others were active workstations.

The five men and one woman who were there looked up as he crossed the room, threading his way between the desks after the secretary. He was keenly aware of being the object of sharp scrutiny. Ten to one, they all know who I am and why I'm here, and they resent me. They have me pegged as the owner of one of those raunchy bars where underage kids get drunk, he thought.

The secretary knocked on the door of a private office to the left of the squad room and, without waiting for an answer, opened it.

Captain Larry Ahearn was alone in the room. He got up from behind the desk and offered his hand to DeMarco. "Thank you for coming in so promptly," he said briskly. "Please sit down." He turned to the secretary. "Ask Detective Gaylor to join us."

DeMarco took the chair nearest Ahearn's desk. "I'm sorry that I wasn't available last night. Early yesterday morning I flew to South Carolina to meet some friends."

"I understand from your secretary that you flew your own private plane from Teterboro Airport," Ahearn said.

"That's right. And I flew back this morning. I couldn't get an early start because of the weather down there. They had heavy storms in Charleston."

"When did your staff notify you that Leesey Andrews, a young woman who left your club at closing time early Tuesday morning, had disappeared?"

"The call came to my cell phone about nine o'clock last night. I was out to dinner with friends and hadn't carried it with me. Quite frankly, as a restaurant owner, I consider people who make or take calls in restaurants pretty insufferable. When I got back to the hotel at about eleven, I checked my messages. Is there any word about Ms. Andrews? Has she called her family?"

"No," Ahearn said briefly, then looked past DeMarco. "Come in, Bob."

Nicholas DeMarco had not heard the door open. He stood up and turned as a trim man with graying hair who looked to be in his late fifties crossed the room with a quick stride. He smiled briefly as he reached out his hand.

"Detective Gaylor," he said, then pulled up a chair and turned it, facing Nick at a right angle to the captain's desk.

"Mr. DeMarco," Ahearn began, "we are very concerned that Leesey Andrews may be the victim of foul play. Your employees tell us that you were in the Woodshed at approximately ten o'clock on Monday evening and were speaking with her."

"That's right," Nick answered promptly. "Because I was leaving for South Carolina, I worked late at my office at 400 Park Avenue. Then I stopped at my apartment, changed to casual clothes, and went down to the Woodshed."

"Do you visit your club frequently?"

"I would say I *drop in* frequently. I no longer do, nor want to do, hands-on management. Tom Ferrazzano runs the Woodshed for me as both host and manager. And I might add he does an excellent job of it. In the ten months we've been operating, we've never had one single incident caused by an underage drinker being served or an adult being served too much for his or her own good. Our employees are thoroughly checked out before they're hired, as are the bands we book to perform."

"The reputation of the Woodshed is good," Detective Gaylor agreed. "But your own employees tell us that you spent quite a bit of time talking to Leesey Andrews."

"I saw her dancing," Nick said promptly. "She's a beautiful girl and a really excellent dancer. To look at her you would think she was a professional. But she also looks very young. I know her ID had been checked, but if I had to bet on it, I'd have sworn she was underage. That's why I had one of the waiters bring her over to my table and asked to see it myself. She had just turned twenty-one."

"She joined you at your table," Gaylor said flatly. "You bought her a drink."

"She had a glass of pinot grigio with me, then returned to her friends."

"What did the two of you talk about while she was sipping that glass, Mr. DeMarco?" Captain Ahearn asked.

"The usual social-type conversation. She told me she was graduating from NYU next year and still deciding what she wanted to do. She said her father and brother were doctors but becoming a medical doctor wasn't right for her. She said that more and more she was thinking of going for a master's in social work but she wasn't sure. She was going to take a year off after college and then figure out the next step."

"Didn't that seem to you to be a lot of personal information to impart to a stranger, Mr. DeMarco?"

Nicholas DeMarco shrugged. "Not really. Then she thanked me for the drink and went back to her friends. I would say she was at my table for less than fifteen minutes."

"What did you do then?" Ahearn asked.

"I finished dinner and went home."

"Where do you live?"

"My apartment is on Park Avenue and Seventy-eighth Street. However I recently bought a building in TriBeCa and have a loft apartment there. That was where I stayed Monday night."

Nick had debated about furnishing that information to the police and decided it was wiser to put it on the table immediately.

"You have a loft in TriBeCa? None of your employees told us that."

"I don't share my personal investments with my employees."

"Is there a doorman in your building in TriBeCa?"

He shook his head. "As I told you, my apartment is a loft. The building is five stories high. I own it and have bought out the leases of the tenants. The other floors are now unoccupied."

"How far is it from your bar?"

"About seven blocks." Nicholas DeMarco hesitated, then added, "I am very sure you must have most of this information already. I left the Woodshed shortly before eleven o'clock. I walked to the TriBeCa place and went to bed immediately. My alarm went off at five A.M. I showered, dressed, and drove to Teterboro Airport. I took off at six forty-five, and landed in Charleston at Charleston Airport. I teed off at the club at noon."

"You did not invite Ms. Andrews to stop in for a nightcap?"

"No, I did not." Nicholas DeMarco looked from one to the other of the detectives. "From the news reports I heard driving in from the airport, I know that Leesey's father has posted a twenty-five-thousand-dollar reward for any information leading to her whereabouts. I intend to match that sum. More than anything, I want Leesey Andrews found alive and well, primarily because it would be horrifying if anything happened to her . . ."

"*Primarily?*" Ahearn said, taken aback momentarily. "What other reason do you have to want her found?"

"My second very selfish reason is that a great deal of money has been spent buying the property on which the Woodshed is situated, renovating the premises, furnishing and staffing it. I wanted to create a safe, fun place for young people and not-so-young people to enjoy. If Leesey's disappearance is traced to an encounter she had in my club, the media will hound us, and within six months our doors will be closed. I want you to investigate our employees, our customers, and me. But I can promise you that you're wasting your time if you think I had anything to do with that girl's disappearance."

"Mr. DeMarco, you are one of the many people we are and will be interviewing," Ahearn said calmly. "Did you file a flight plan at Teterboro?"

"Of course. If you check the records, the flying time down yesterday morning was excellent. Today, because of the nearby storms, it was somewhat slower."

"One last question, Mr. DeMarco. How did you get back and forth to the airport?"

"In my car, I drove myself."

"What kind of car do you drive?"

"I usually drive a Mercedes convertible unless for some reason I'm carrying a lot of baggage. Actually my golf clubs were in my SUV, so that was what I drove back and forth to the airport yesterday and today."

Nicholas DeMarco did not need to catch the glance the two detectives exchanged to know that he had become a person of interest in the disappearance of Leesey Andrews. I can understand why, he thought. I was talking to her a few hours before she disappeared. No one can verify that she didn't meet me later at the apartment. I took off early the next morning in a private plane. I can't blame them for being suspicious—that's their job.

With a brief smile, he offered his hand to both men and told them that he was going to make public immediately his offer to match the twenty-five-thousand-dollar reward for information leading to Leesey's whereabouts.

"And I can assure you, we'll be working 24/7 to find her, or if something has happened to her, find the person who did it," Ahearn said, in a tone of voice that Nicholas DeMarco correctly interpreted as a warning.

15

As I was leaving the Sutton Place apartment, my cell phone rang. The caller identified himself as Detective Barrott, and though my pulse quickened, I kept my response to him deliberately cool. He had brushed me off on Monday, so what possible reason did he have for calling me now?

"Ms. MacKenzie, as you may be aware, a young woman, Leesey Andrews, who disappeared last night, lives next door to you on Thompson Street. I am there now, interviewing the neighbors on the block. I saw your name listed on the directory in your building. I'd very much appreciate an opportunity to speak with you again. Is it possible to set up an appointment with you soon?"

Holding the phone to one ear, I signaled to the doorman to hail a cab for me. There was one nearby just discharging a passenger. As I waited for an elderly lady to get out, I told Barrott that I was on my way back to my own apartment and, depending on traffic, would be there in about twenty minutes.

"I'll wait for you," he said flatly, giving me no opportunity to let him know whether that was convenient for me or not.

Some days a cab ride between Sutton Place and Thompson Street takes fifteen minutes. Other days the traffic simply crawls. This was one of those crawling days. It wasn't as though I was in any rush to see Detective Barrott—it's just that once I'm on my way anywhere, I'm

impatient to get there, another characteristic inherited from my father.

And that made me think of my father's anxiety when Mack disappeared and the anxiety Leesey Andrews's father must be feeling now.
Last night on the eleven o'clock news, holding back tears, Dr. Andrews had held up his daughter's picture and pleaded for assistance
in finding her. I thought I could imagine what he was going through,
then wondered if that was really true. Bad as it had been for us, Mack
had after all seemingly walked out of his life in midafternoon. Leesey
Andrews was surely more vulnerable, alone at night, and certainly no
match for a strong predator.

All that was whirling through my mind as the cab made its way
slowly to Thompson Street.

Barrott was sitting on the steps of the brownstone, an incongruous
sight, I thought, as I paid the driver. The afternoon had turned warm
again, and he had opened his jacket and loosened his tie. When he
spotted me, in a fluid movement he stood up quickly, tightened the
tie, and buttoned the jacket again.

We greeted each other with reserved courtesy, and I invited him
inside. As I turned the key in the entrance door, I noticed a couple of
vans with TV markings parked outside the building next door, the
building where Leesey Andrews lived—or had lived.

My studio apartment is in the rear of the building and is the only
one on the lobby floor. I took it on a year's lease last September when
I started working for Judge Huot. In these past nine months it has become, for me, a peaceful haven from Sutton Place, where my sense
of loss over my father and anxiety over Mack are never totally absent.

Mom was appalled at the size of this place. "Carolyn, nine hundred square feet, you won't be able to turn around," she had
lamented. But I have been thrilled by the womblike space. It is a
cheery cocoon and I think has been greatly responsible for helping
me evolve from a chronic state of inner sadness and anxiety to a surg-

ing desire, even a *need*, to have done with it, to get on with life. Thanks to Mom's good taste, I grew up in a home that was beautifully decorated, but I've taken a certain joy in shopping for my studio at bargain sales in home furnishings departments.

My spacious bedroom on Sutton Place has a separate sitting area. On Thompson Street, I have a pullout couch, which, remarkably, has a very comfortable mattress. As Detective Barrott followed me into the apartment, I caught the way he surveyed the room, with its black enamel side tables and bright red modern lamps, small black enamel coffee table, and two armless chairs upholstered in the same stark white of the couch. He let his eyes slide over the white walls and the rug with its checkered black and white and red pattern.

The kitchen is a narrow unit off the living room. An ice cream parlor table and two padded wrought iron chairs under the window are the full extent of the dining facilities. But the window is wide, lets in a lot of light, and plants and geraniums on the sill bring the outdoors in.

Barrot took everything in, then politely refused my offer of water or coffee and sat down opposite me on one of the side chairs. He surprised me by starting with an apology. "Ms. MacKenzie," he said, "I'm pretty sure you feel that I dismissed your concerns when you came to see me on Monday."

I let my silence tell him that I agreed.

"I started to look over your brother's file yesterday. I'll admit that I didn't get very far. The call came in about Leesey Andrews and of course that took precedence, but then I realized it would also give me another chance to talk to you. As I told you, we're canvassing the neighborhood. Do you know Leesey Andrews?"

The question surprised me. Maybe it should not have, but I thought to myself that when he phoned and asked to meet me, if I had known her even slightly, I would have said so immediately. "No, I don't know her," I said.

"Did you see her picture on television?"

"Yes, I did, last night."

"And you didn't have any sense of ever having seen her around?" he persisted as though he wasn't sure that I wasn't being evasive.

"No, but of course, living next door, I may have passed her in the street. There are a number of young women students in that building." I knew I sounded irritated and I was. Surely Barrott wasn't suggesting that because my brother was missing I might have some kind of link to this girl's disappearance?

Barrott's lips tightened. "Ms. MacKenzie, I hope you realize that I'm asking you the same questions I, and other detectives, are asking everyone in this neighborhood. Because we already know each other, and because you of all people understand the agony her father and brother are going through, I'm hoping that somehow you can help us. You're an extremely attractive young woman, and as a lawyer you're trained to be very observant." He leaned slightly forward, his hands clasped. "Do you ever walk around this area alone at night, let's say after dinner or a movie, or do you ever go out very early in the morning?"

"Yes, I do." I knew my tone had softened. "Most mornings I jog around six o'clock, and if I'm meeting friends locally in the evening, I often walk home alone."

"Have you ever had a sense of being watched, of someone following you?"

"No, I haven't. On the other hand, I would say I'm rarely out later than midnight, and the Village is still pretty lively at that time."

"I understand. But I'd appreciate it if you'd keep your eyes open for us. Predators, like arsonists, sometimes enjoy watching the excitement they've created. Something else. There *is* another way you might be able to help us. Your neighbor on the second floor, Mrs. Carter, is very fond of you, isn't she?"

"I'm very fond of her. She's terribly arthritic and terrified of going out if the weather is bad," I explained. "She's had a couple of nasty falls. I check on her and pick up odds and ends from the grocery store if she needs them." I leaned back in my chair, wondering where he was going with this.

Barrott nodded. "She told me that. In fact she was singing your praises. But you know how it is with some old people. They're afraid of getting in trouble themselves if they talk to police. My own aunt was like that. She wouldn't admit it when she saw a neighbor dent another neighbor's car. 'It's none of my business,' was the way she put it." He paused thoughtfully. "I could tell that Mrs. Carter was nervous about talking to me," he continued. "But she *did* tell me she enjoys sitting at the window. She claims she didn't recognize Leesey's picture, but I have a hunch she did. It may only be that she has noticed Leesey walking by and doesn't want to get involved with the investigation in any way, but maybe if you have a cup of tea with her, she might open up to you."

"I'll do that," I said willingly. Mrs. Carter may be old, but she doesn't miss a trick, and she is a window sitter, I thought. She certainly has all the dirt on the neighbors who live on the three floors above her. I considered the irony that I was now investigating for Barrott, when my intention had been to have *him* investigate for *me*.

Barrott stood up. "Thank you for letting me stop in, Ms. MacKenzie. As you can understand, we're working round the clock on this case, but when it's resolved, I'm going to get back to reviewing your brother's file and see if we can come up with some new avenues to follow."

He had given me his card on Monday but probably suspected that I had torn it up, which I had. As I accepted another one from him, he said he'd keep in touch with me. I saw him out, locked the door behind him, and realized that I suddenly felt weak-kneed. Something about his manner made me suspect that Detective Roy Barrott had not been honest. To him, I was not just someone who happened to be a neighbor of a missing young woman. He was trying to create reasons to keep in contact with me.

But why?

I simply didn't know.

16

Lil Kramer had been nervous from the moment Carolyn MacKenzie phoned on Monday requesting a meeting, but on Wednesday, shortly after Carolyn left, had gone into the bedroom, laid down, closed her eyes, and begun to cry silently, tears running down her cheeks.

Lil could hear Gus saying his good-byes to Howard, then he walked into the bedroom and stood over her. At her husband's impatient demand to know what her problem was, her eyes had flown open. "My problem? I'll tell you what it is! Gus, I was in St. Francis de Sales Church at the Latin Mass last Sunday. I've been thinking about going ever since they began saying it again last year. Don't forget, my father was a Catholic and used to take me to church once in a while, back when all the Masses were in Latin."

"You never told me you went there Sunday," Gus snapped.

"And why would I have told you? You have no use for any religion, and I didn't need to hear you ranting that all clergymen are con men."

Gus Kramer's expression changed. "All right, all right. You were there. Hope you said a prayer for me. So what?"

"It was so crowded. You wouldn't believe it. People were standing in the aisles. You heard what Carolyn MacKenzie just told us. *That Mack was there!* I know you won't believe me, but at Mass I had the feeling that I saw someone familiar, just for a moment. But as you know, I'm blind as a bat if I don't have my bifocals with me, and I forgot them when I changed my purse."

"I repeat, so what?"

"Gus, don't you understand what I'm saying? Mack was there! Suppose he does decide to come back! You know," she finished in a whisper, "you know."

As she had expected, Gus had immediately become angry. "Damn it, Lil, that guy must have had his own reasons for pulling the disappearing act. I'm sick of seeing you wringing your hands over him. Knock it off. Stop it. You told his sister just enough to satisfy her. Now keep your mouth shut. Look at me." Roughly he leaned over the bed and raised her chin so that she could not avert her gaze from him. "You're half-blind without your distance glasses. You're jumping to conclusions because of that note Mack supposedly left in the collection. You didn't see him there. So forget all about it."

Lil would not have believed she had the courage to ask her husband why he was so sure. "How can you be so positive that Mack wasn't there?" she demanded in a tense whisper.

"Just trust me," Gus said, his face darkening with anger.

It was the same rage she had seen ten years ago when she told Gus what she had found in Mack's room while she was cleaning. It was that rage that had made her wonder despairingly all these years if Gus could have been responsible for Mack's disappearance.

In a clumsy gesture of affection, Gus ran his calloused hand over Lil's forehead, then, with a heavy sigh, said, "You know, Lil, I'm beginning to think it may be a good idea after all for us to retire to Pennsylvania. If that sister of Mack's starts dropping around here, sooner or later she's going to get you so upset, you'll say too much."

Lil, who loved living in New York and who had dreaded moving to an idle retired life, whimpered, "I want to go right away, Gus. I'm so afraid for us."

17

Bruce Galbraith always checked in with his secretary at the end of the business day. Unlike most of the people he knew, he did not carry a BlackBerry and often turned off his cell phone. "Too many distractions for my taste," was his explanation. "It's like watching a juggler with too many balls in the air."

Thirty-two years old, average height, with sandy hair and rimless glasses, he joked about himself that he was so average he wouldn't even be noticed by a security camera. On the other hand, he was not so self-effacing that he did not know his own worth. He was a superb deal-closer and was considered by his colleagues to have a near-psychic ability to foresee the trends in the real estate market.

The result was that Bruce Galbraith had multiplied the value of the family real estate business to the point where his sixty-year-old father had simply turned over the reins to him. At his retirement dinner his father had said, "Bruce, my hat's off to you. You're a good son and a far better businessman than I ever was, and I was good. Now, you keep making money for us, and I'll pursue my goal of becoming a scratch golfer."

Bruce was in Arizona on Wednesday when he made his daily late-afternoon call to his secretary. She told him that a Carolyn MacKenzie had phoned and left a message that Mack had been in contact again and would Bruce please call her.

Carolyn MacKenzie? Mack's kid sister? These were not names he wanted to hear.

Bruce had just returned to his suite in the hotel he owned in Scottsdale. Shaking his head, he walked over to the minibar and reached into it for a cold beer. It was only four o'clock, but he had been outside in the heat most of the day and deserved it, he assured himself.

He settled in the big armchair facing the floor-to-ceiling window that overlooked the desert. At any other time it was his favorite view, but at this moment he was seeing only the college apartment he had shared with Mack MacKenzie and Nick DeMarco, and reviewing again what had happened there.

I don't want to see Mack's sister, he told himself. All that happened ten years ago, and even then Mack's parents knew I was never close to him. He never once asked me home to Sutton Place for dinner, although he was always taking Nick with him. It didn't even cross Mack's mind that I might enjoy going, too. To him, I was just an unobtrusive guy who happened to be sharing an apartment with him.

Nick the lady-killer; Mack, everyone's choice for the nicest guy in the world. So nice that he apologized for beating me out by a fraction to be one of the top ten graduates of our class. I'll never forget the look on Dad's face when I told him I hadn't made it. Four generations at Columbia, and I was the first not to be in the top ten. And Barbara, God, the crush I had on her in those days. I worshipped her. . . . She never even glanced in my direction, he thought.

Bruce tilted his head and finished the beer. I'll have to call Carolyn, he decided. But I'll tell her what I told her parents. Mack and I lived together, but we never hung out together. I didn't even see him the day he disappeared. I got out before he and Nick were awake. So, leave me alone, little sister.

He stood up. Forget it, he told himself impatiently. Just forget about it. The quote that often ran through his head whenever he happened to think about Mack jumped into his mind again. He knew the quote wasn't completely accurate, but it worked for him: "But *that* was in another land, and besides the king is dead."

He went back to the phone, picked it up, and dialed. When his wife answered, he knew his face lit up at the sound of her voice. "Hi, Barb," he said. "How are you, sweetheart? And how are the kids?"

18

After his luncheon with Aaron Klein, Elliott Wallace went back to his office and found himself thinking about Charles MacKenzie Sr. and the friendship they had forged in Vietnam. Charley had been in the army's ROTC and was a second lieutenant when they met. Elliott had told Charley that he was born in England of American parents and had spent most of his childhood in London. He had moved back to New York with his mother when he was nineteen. He had then enlisted in the army, and four years later he had earned his own commission and was side by side with Charley in some of the fiercest fighting of the war.

We liked each other from day one, Elliott thought. Charley was the most competitive person I've ever met and probably the most ambitious. He was planning to go to law school the minute he was discharged. He swore that he was going to be a very successful lawyer and a millionaire. He was actually pleased that he had grown up in a family that didn't have two nickels to rub together. He used to kid me about my background. "And what was the butler's name, Ell?" he would ask me. "Was it Bertie, or Chauncey, or Jeeves?"

As he leaned back in his leather chair, Elliott smiled at the memory. I told Charley that the butler was William, and he was gone by the time I was thirteen. I told him that my father, God rest him, was the most cultivated human being and the worst businessman in the history of the civilized world. That was why my mother finally threw in the towel and brought me home from England.

Charley didn't believe me back then, but I swore to him that in my own way I was just as ambitious as he was. He wanted to become wealthy because he'd never known that world. I was one of the haves who became a have-not and wanted it all back. While Charley was in law school, I went to college and then got my MBA.

We both succeeded financially, but our personal lives were so different. Charley met Olivia, and they had a wonderful marriage. God, how like an outsider I felt when I saw the way they looked at each other! They had twenty-three good years, until Mack disappeared, and after that they didn't have a day that wasn't filled with worry about him. And then 9/11, and Charley was gone. My marriage to Norma was never fair to her. What was it Princess Diana told an interviewer—that there were three people in her marriage to the Prince of Wales? Yes, that's the way it was with Norma and me, only less glamorous.

Grimacing at the memory, Elliott picked up his pen and began to doodle on a pad. Norma didn't know it, of course, but the way I felt about Olivia was always between us. And now that my marriage is a distant memory, after all these years, maybe Olivia and I can plan a future together. She recognizes that she can't live her life around Mack anymore, and I can see that her feeling about me has changed. In her eyes, I've become more than Charley's best friend and the trusted family advisor. I could tell that when I kissed her good night. I could tell when she confided that Carolyn needs to be free to stop worrying about her, and most of all I can tell because she's planning to sell the Sutton Place apartment.

Elliott got up, walked over to the section of the mahogany bookcase that housed a refrigerator, and opened the door. As he reached for a bottle of water, he wondered if it was too soon to suggest to Olivia that a penthouse on Fifth Avenue, down the block from the Metropolitan Museum, might be a wonderful place to live.

My penthouse, he thought with a smile. Even twenty-five years ago, when I bought it after Norma and I were divorced, I dreamed I was buying it for Olivia.

The telephone rang, then the crisp British voice of his personal secretary sounded on the intercom. "Mrs. MacKenzie is calling, sir."

Elliott rushed back to his desk and picked up the receiver.

"Elliott, it's Liv. June Crabtree was coming for dinner and at the last minute she can't make it. I know Carolyn is meeting her friend Jackie. By any chance would you like to take a lady to dinner?"

"I would be delighted. How about having a drink at my place around seven and then going over to Le Cirque?"

"Perfect. See you then."

When he replaced the receiver, Elliott realized there was a slight bead of perspiration on his forehead. I've never wanted anything more in my life, he thought. Nothing must spoil it for us, and I'm so afraid something might. Then he relaxed and laughed aloud as he thought of what his father's reaction would be to that kind of negative thinking.

As dear cousin Franklin said, he thought, the only thing we have to fear is fear itself.

19

Late Wednesday afternoon and long into the night, grim-faced NYU students, scattered throughout Greenwich Village and SoHo, were taping posters on storefronts and telephone poles and trees in the hope that someone might recognize Lisa "Leesey" Andrews and provide information that would lead to her recovery.

The photo that her roommate had taken only a few days earlier of a smiling Leesey, the statistics of her height and weight, the address of the Woodshed, the time she left it, her home address where she was presumed to have been heading, and the fifty thousand dollars reward offered by her father and Nicholas DeMarco were all included on the poster.

"More information than we usually give, but we're pulling out all the stops," Captain Larry Ahearn told Leesey's brother at nine o'clock Wednesday night. "But, Gregg, I'm going to be fair with you. Truth is, if Leesey was abducted, every hour that passes lessens our chances of finding her alive and safe."

"I know that." Gregg Andrews had gone down to headquarters after giving his father a strong sedative and making him go to bed in the guest room of his apartment. "Larry, I feel so damn helpless. What can I do?" He slumped in his chair.

Captain Ahearn leaned across his desk toward Gregg, his expression sober. "You can be a crutch for your father and take care of your patients in the hospital. Leave the rest of it to us, Gregg."

Gregg did his best to look reassured. "I'll try." He got up slowly, as if every move was an effort. He reached for the door of Ahearn's office, then turned back. "Larry, you said, '*if* Leesey was abducted.' Please don't waste your time thinking that she would deliberately put us through this agony."

Gregg opened the door and came face-to-face with Roy Barrott, who was about to knock on the door of his boss's office. Barrott had heard Andrews's statement and realized it echoed what Carolyn MacKenzie had said about her brother in this same office two days earlier. Pushing aside that comparison, he greeted Andrews, then stepped into Ahearn's office.

"The tapes are finished," he said briefly. "Want to look at them now, Larry?"

"Yes, I do," Ahearn said, looking at Gregg's retreating figure. "Do you think there's any benefit in having her brother look at them with us?"

Barrott turned swiftly to follow Ahearn's line of sight. "Maybe there is. I'll grab him before he gets to the elevator."

Barrott caught Gregg as he was punching the elevator button and asked if he'd accompany them down the hall to the tech room. Barrott explained, "Dr. Andrews, the tapes taken Monday night by the security cameras at the Woodshed have been enhanced, frame by frame, to try to pick out anyone who seemed particularly close to Leesey on the dance floor or who was among the last to leave the club."

Without speaking, Gregg nodded, then followed Barrott and Ahearn into the tech room and took a chair. As the tape ran, Barrott, who had already studied it twice, briefed him and Captain Ahearn on the contents.

"Except for the friends she was sitting with all night, nothing we have seems to show anything significant. The friends all agree that Leesey was with them except for the fifteen minutes she was with De-Marco at his table or when she was on the dance floor. After the rest of her group left at two A.M., the only time she sat at a table was when the band started to pack up. The place had thinned out by then, so we have a couple of pretty clear shots of her until she exited alone."

"Can you go back to that shot of her at the table?" Gregg asked. Watching his sister on tape sent a wave of sadness through him.

"Sure." Barrott rewound the tape in the VCR. "Do you see anything that we've missed, Doctor?" he asked, trying to keep his voice noncommittal.

"Leesey's expression. When she was dancing, she was smiling. Look at her now. She looks so pensive, so sad." He paused. "Our mother died two years ago, and Leesey's had a hard time struggling with that grief."

"Gregg, do you think that her state of mind would cause her to have a temporary amnesia or anxiety attack that would make her run away?" Ahearn's question was penetrating and demanded a straight answer. "Is that a possibility?"

Gregg Andrews raised his hands and pressed his temples as though trying to stimulate his thought processes. "I don't know," he said finally. "I just don't know." He hesitated, then continued, "But if I had to stake my life, and Leesey's life, on it, I would say it didn't happen that way."

Barrott fast-forwarded the VCR. "All right. In that last hour, whenever the camera scans her, she never has a glass in her hand, which backs up what the waiter and bartender told us, that she only had a couple of glasses of wine all night and wasn't drunk when she left." He turned off the VCR. "Nothing," he said in disgust.

Gregg Andrews got up. His voice strained, he said, "I'll go home now. I have surgery in the morning and I need to catch some sleep."

Barrott waited till he was out of earshot, then stood and stretched. "I wouldn't mind catching some sleep myself, but I'm going to the Woodshed."

"Do you think DeMarco will show up there tonight?" Ahearn asked.

"My guess is that he will. He knows our guys are going to be swarming all over the place. And he's smart enough to know that it will be a big night for him. Plenty of customers will want to get in, out of curiosity, and of course the minor-league so-called celebrities will flock to the place knowing the media will be around. Trust me. The maggots will gather."

"Of course they will." Ahearn stood up. "I don't know if you've checked since you got back, but the track we have on Leesey's cell phone shows whoever has it has been moving around in Manhattan all day. DeMarco only got back from South Carolina late this morning, so if he did it, he has someone in New York working with him."

"It would be nice to think that girl went off the deep end, and she's the one who's running around Manhattan," Barrott commented, as he reached for his jacket. "But I don't think that's the way it's going to turn out. I think whoever grabbed her has already dumped her somewhere and is smart enough to know that when the cell phone is on, we can target that area and start searching there."

"And smart enough to know that by moving her cell phone around, it leaves open the door that she's alive." Ahearn looked thoughtful. "We've checked out DeMarco so thoroughly that we know when he lost his baby teeth. Nothing in his background suggests he'd try something like this."

"Did our guys find anything in the files of the other three girls who disappeared?"

"Nothing that we haven't investigated into the ground. We're checking out the credit card receipts from Monday night to see if we can match any patrons of the Woodshed to the names we have of the people who were in the bars in those cases."

"Uh-huh. Okay, see you, Larry."

Ahearn studied Barrott's face. "You've got someone in mind besides DeMarco, haven't you, Roy?"

"I'm not sure. Let me think about it," Barrott said vaguely. But Ahearn could see that Barrott was focused on something.

20

Jackie Reynolds has been my closest friend since the first grade, when we attended the Academy of the Sacred Heart together as six-year-olds. She's one of the smartest people I know, as well as a gifted athlete. Jackie can hit a golf ball so hard that it would make Tiger Woods blink. The September after we graduated from Columbia, we drove to Duke together. While I was studying law, she was working for a doctorate in psychology.

She has that unmistakable look of the born athlete, tall and firm-bodied, with long chestnut hair that, as often as not, is held together at the nape of her neck with a rubber band. Her extraordinary brown eyes are her dominant feature. They exude warmth and sympathy and make people want to confide in her. I always tell her that she should give cut rates to her patients. "You don't have to drag their problems out of them, Jackie. They walk through your door and spill their guts."

We talk frequently on the phone and get together every few weeks. It used to be even more often, but now Jackie is getting pretty serious about the guy she's been dating for the past year. Ted Sawyer is a lieutenant in the fire department and a genuinely top-drawer person. He intends to be fire commissioner of New York someday, then run for mayor, and I'd bet my bottom dollar that he'll do both.

Jackie has always been worried about how little interest I've shown in dating. She correctly attributed my lack of interest to the fact that I've felt emotionally burned out. Tonight, if the subject came up, I intended to reassure her that I am now actively working to put all that inertia behind me.

We met at Il Mulino, our favorite pasta place in the Village. Over linguine with clam sauce and a glass of pinot grigio, I told her about Mack's phone call and the note he left in the collection basket.

" 'Uncle Devon, tell Carolyn she must not look for me,' " Jackie repeated. "I'm sorry, Carolyn, but if Mack *did* write that note, it suggests to me that he may be in some kind of trouble," she said quietly. "If he weren't under stress and just wanted to be left alone, I think he would have written, 'Please don't look for me,' or simply, 'Carolyn, leave me alone.' "

"That's exactly what I'm afraid of. The more I look at the note and think about it, the more I sense desperation."

I told Jackie about going to see Detective Barrott. "He practically showed me the door," I said. "He wasn't interested in the note. He gave me the impression that if Mack wanted to be left alone, I should respect his wishes. So I started my own investigation by meeting with the superintendents of Mack's apartment building."

She listened to my description of the meeting, interrupting only to query me about Mrs. Kramer. "You say she seemed nervous when you talked to her?"

"She *was* nervous, and she kept looking over to her husband for approval, as if she wanted to make sure she had given the right answers. Then they both changed their story in midstream about the last time they saw Mack and what he was wearing."

"Memory is notoriously inaccurate, especially after ten years," Jackie said slowly. "If I were you, I'd try to see Mrs. Kramer when her husband isn't around."

I made a mental note, then told her about my second conversation with Detective Barrott. Jackie hadn't realized that my studio is right next door to the building where Leesey Andrews lived. I told her about Detective Barrott meeting me there and that I felt there was something behind his wanting to stay in touch with me.

The expression in Jackie's eyes changed. I could read deepening concern in them. "I'll bet Detective Barrott wishes he had taken that note from you," she said vehemently. "I'll bet he'll get around to asking you for it soon."

"What are you getting at?" I asked.

"Carolyn, have you forgotten about the missing persons cases that were in the news just before Mack disappeared. That a bunch of Columbia guys, including Mack, were in the bar in SoHo where that first girl who disappeared had been hanging out? That was just a few weeks before Mack himself vanished."

"I hadn't thought of that," I admitted. "But why would that be relevant now?"

"Because you've handed the D.A.'s office a possible suspect. Mack doesn't want you to find him, which, as I just suggested, could mean that he may be in some kind of trouble. Or it could mean that he *is* the trouble. He called your mother on Sunday and left the note in the collection basket later in the morning. Suppose Mack decided to check out where you now live, maybe to warn you away again. Your address at the apartment is listed in the phone book. Suppose he came by early Tuesday morning and spotted Leesey Andrews on the street walking home. I'll bet that's the way your Detective Barrott is adding things up."

"Jackie, are you crazy?" I began, but the words died in my throat. I was desperately afraid that she had analyzed Barrott's thinking process correctly. In his eyes, and because of me, my missing brother may have become a person of interest in the disappearance of Leesey Andrews, and perhaps of the young woman who vanished ten years ago, only weeks before he did.

Then, in utter dismay, I remembered that not one but three young women had vanished in these ten years before Leesey Andrews failed to return home.

In his wildest dreams, could Barrott possibly be beginning to believe that if Mack is alive he may have become a serial killer?

21

Sometimes the best thing about the moment he took a life was when the scent of fear reached his nostrils. They knew they were going to die, and at that point they stammered out a few words.

One of them asked, "Why?"

Another whispered a prayer, "Lord, receive . . . me . . ."

A third tried to break away, then spat an obscenity at him.

The youngest pleaded with him, "Don't, please don't."

He ached to go back to the Woodshed tonight, to listen to everything they were saying there. It was amusing to watch the plain-clothes detectives at work. He could spot them a mile away. Their eyelids always had a hooded look because they were trying to conceal the fact that their bright little eyes were darting around the room.

An hour ago in Brooklyn, he had phoned the number they had on the poster, using one of his unsubscribed phones and prepaid phone cards. He'd made his voice sound excited, and said, "I just left Peter Luger's Restaurant. I saw that girl, Leesey Andrews, having dinner with some guy there." Then he turned off both that cell phone and Leesey's cell phone and hurried into the subway.

He could just imagine the way the cops must have swarmed over there, disrupting the place, annoying the diners, querying the waiters. . . . By now they've probably decided that it was just another nutcase calling. I wonder how many crazies have called in to say they've seen Leesey, he wondered. But only one person saw her. *Me!*

But the family wouldn't be sure that it was a crank call. The family never *is* sure until they see a body. Don't count on it, family. If you don't believe me, have a chat with the relatives of the other girls.

He turned on the television to catch the eleven o'clock news. As he'd expected, the breaking news story was being reported opposite the Woodshed. There were crowds of people lined up trying to get into the place. A reporter was saying, "The tip that police received that Leesey Andrews was seen having dinner at a restaurant in Brooklyn has been largely discounted."

He was disappointed that the police had not released the information about the tracking of her cell phone in Brooklyn. But later on, I'll take Leesey's cell phone to Thompson Street for a quick visit, he thought. That will really drive them crazy—thinking she might be being held so near her home.

He almost laughed out loud.

22

It was Friday afternoon before I heard from Nick DeMarco. As luck would have it, when my cell phone rang, I was standing just inside the open door of the Sutton Place apartment, saying good-bye to Mom.

Elliott had just arrived to take her to Teterboro Airport, where she would join the Clarences to fly on their private jet to Corfu, in the Greek islands, where their yacht was anchored.

Elliott's chauffeur had carried the luggage down the hall and was pressing for the elevator. In another thirty seconds they all would have been gone, but I flipped open the phone automatically. I could have bitten off my tongue after I said, "Hello, Nick." Instantly alert, there was no question that both Mom and Elliott guessed it was Nick DeMarco. The statement he gave at a news conference, expressing his deep regret that Leesey Andrews may have met a predator at his club, had been broadcast and rebroadcast in the forty-eight hours since he had made it late Wednesday afternoon.

"Carolyn, I'm sorry I didn't get back to you sooner," Nick said. "As you can understand it's been pretty hectic these past few days. What's your schedule? Are you free to get together this evening or sometime tomorrow?"

I turned slightly away, taking a step back toward the living room. "This evening would be fine," I said quickly, aware that Elliott and

Mom were staring at me. They reminded me of the game "Statues" that we used to play when I was about ten years old. Whoever was the leader swung the others around by the hand, and after she let go, you had to stay frozen in exactly the position you were in when you stopped spinning. The one who could last the longest without twitching a muscle was the winner.

Mom's body was rigid, her hand on the doorknob, and Elliott, holding Mom's carry-on bag, was standing statuelike in the vestibule. I wanted to tell Nick I'd call him back but was afraid to let the chance pass to confirm a meeting with him.

"Where will you be?"

"The Sutton Place apartment," I told him.

"I'll pick you up there. Seven o'clock, okay?"

"Fine." We both clicked off.

Mom had a worried frown on her face. "Was that Nick DeMarco? Why on *earth* is he calling you, Carolyn?"

"I called *him* on Wednesday."

"Why would you do that?" Elliott asked, his tone puzzled. "You haven't had any contact with him since your father's funeral, have you?"

I combined a couple of truths and twisted them into an untruth. "I had a serious crush on Nick years ago. Maybe it's still lingering a bit. When I saw him on TV, I thought it wouldn't hurt to phone him and express my concern that Leesey Andrews disappeared after leaving his club. Result—he phoned!"

I saw an expression of cautious relief on my mother's face. "I always enjoyed Nick when he came to dinner with Mack. And I know he's been *very* successful."

"He certainly seems to have done very well these past ten years," Elliott agreed. "As I remember, his parents had some sort of store-front restaurant. But I must say I don't envy him the publicity he's getting now." Then he touched my mother's arm. "Olivia, we must get started. As it is, we're going to hit all the rush hour traffic, and the Lincoln Tunnel will be a nightmare."

My mother is famous for leaving at the last minute and counting on all the traffic lights to be turning green to make smooth her path. At this moment, I found myself comparing Elliott's gentle reminder with my father's reaction, if he had been here.

"Liv, for God's sake, we're getting a free ride to Greece. Let's not miss it!" would have been his way of hurrying her out.

With a final flurry of farewell kisses and admonitions, Mom got into the elevator with Elliott, her final words, "Call me if you need anything, Carolyn," muffled by the closing door.

I'll admit that I was flustered about this date with Nick, if you can call it a date. I put on fresh makeup, brushed my hair, decided to leave it loose, then, at the last minute, I put on a new Escada suit my mother had insisted on buying for me. Both jacket and slacks were a pale shade of green, and I knew they brought out the red tones in my brown hair.

Why bother? Because after ten years I was still embarrassed by Mack's candid statement that it was obvious I had a crush on Nick. I'm not dolling up for him, I told myself; I'm satisfying myself that I don't look like a gawky adolescent fainting over her idol. But when the concierge phoned from the lobby to tell me that Mr. DeMarco was here, I have to admit that for a nanosecond, I did feel like the sixteen-year-old who had been foolish enough to wear her heart on her sleeve.

Then, when I opened the door for him, what struck me immediately was that the boyish, seemingly carefree Nick I remembered was gone.

When I saw him on television, I had noticed that his jawline had tightened and that at thirty-two, he already had strands of gray in his dark hair. But face-to-face, there was more. His dark brown eyes had always had a teasing, flirtatious look, but now the expression in them was serious. Even so, his smile, when he took my hand, was the one I remembered, and he seemed genuinely pleased to see me. He gave me a social peck on the cheek but spared me the "little Carolyn, all grown up" routine.

Instead he said, "Carolyn MacKenzie, Juris Doctoris! I heard somewhere that you had passed the bar and were clerking for a judge. I meant to call to congratulate you but never quite got around to it. I'm sorry."

"The road to hell is paved with good intentions," I said matter-of-factly. "Or at least that's what Sister Patricia told us in the fifth grade."

"And Brother Murphy told us in the seventh grade, 'Never put off till tomorrow what you can do today.' "

I laughed. "They were both right," I said. "But clearly you didn't listen." We grinned at each other. It was the kind of banter we used to exchange at the dinner table. I picked up my shoulder bag. "I'm all set," I told him.

"Fine. My car is downstairs." He glanced around. From where he was standing, he could see a corner of the dining room. "I have such good memories of coming here," he said. "When I went home for an occasional weekend, my mother wanted to know every detail of what we ate, and I had to describe the color of the tablecloth and napkins, and what kind of flowers your mother used in the centerpiece."

"I assure you we didn't do that every night," I said, as I fished my key from my bag. "Mom enjoyed fussing when you and Mack were coming home."

"Mack didn't mind showing off this place to his friends," Nick commented. "But I reciprocated, you know? I took him to our place in Astoria for the best pizza and pasta in the universe."

Was there an edge in Nick DeMarco's voice, as though he still resented the comparison? Maybe not, but I wasn't sure. In the elevator on the way down, he noticed that Manuel, the elevator operator, was wearing a class ring and asked about it. Manuel proudly told him that he had just graduated from John Jay College and was scheduled to start at the police academy. "I can't wait to become a cop," he said.

Of course I haven't really lived at home since I started Duke Law, but even so, Manuel and I often exchanged pleasantries. He's worked in our building for at least three years, yet in seconds Nick knew more about him than I ever did. I realized that Nick had the ability to make people open up to him immediately and that that might be why he is so successful in the restaurant business.

Nick's black Mercedes-Benz was parked in front of the building. I was surprised to see a chauffeur jump out to hold the back door open for us. I don't know why, but I never would have visualized Nick as having a chauffeur. This one was a big, heavyset man in his midfifties with the face of a retired prizefighter. His broad nose seemed to have lost most of the cartilage, and there was a scar along his jaw.

Nick introduced us. "Benny worked for Pop for twenty years. Then when Pop retired five years ago, I inherited him. My very good fortune. Benny, this is Carolyn MacKenzie."

Despite his brief smile and pleasant "Nice to meet you, Ms. MacKenzie," I had the feeling that Benny was giving me a very thorough once-over. He obviously knew where we were going, because he set off without waiting for instructions.

As we pulled away from the curb, Nick turned to me. "Carolyn, I'm assuming and hoping that you're free for dinner."

And I was assuming and hoping you'd want to have dinner, I thought. "That would be nice," I told him.

"There's a place in Nyack, just a few miles from the Tappan Zee Bridge. The food is excellent, and it's quiet. At this point, I'm pretty anxious to stay away from the media." He rested his head back on the leather seat.

On the way up the FDR Drive, he told me that he had been asked to stop at the District Attorney's office again yesterday afternoon, to answer more questions about the conversation he had with Leesey

Andrews the night she disappeared. "It was unfortunate that I stayed in the loft apartment that night," he said frankly. "There's only my word that I didn't invite her to stop by on her way home, and I think for lack of anyone else to focus on, I'm in the spotlight."

You're not the *only* one, I thought, but decided not to share with him my certainty that, thanks to me, Detective Barrott also had his sights on Mack as a suspect. I noticed that Nick did not mention Mack's name in the car, and I wondered about that. From the message I gave to his secretary, that I wanted to see him because I had heard from Mack again, he certainly knew we were going to talk about my brother. I wondered if perhaps he didn't want Benny to hear that conversation. My suspicion was that Benny was gifted with very keen hearing.

The restaurant Nick had chosen, La Provence, was everything he had promised. It had been a private home and retained that atmosphere. The tables were far apart. The centerpieces on them were made up of a candle surrounded by budding flowers, and each table had different flowers. Paintings that I guessed to be of the French countryside were hung on the paneled walls. It was obvious from the warm greeting the maitre d' extended to Nick that he was a regular customer. We followed him to a corner table with a window that looked over the Hudson. The night was clear, and the view of the Tappan Zee Bridge spanning the river was splendid.

I thought of my dream of trying to follow Mack as he crossed a bridge. Then I tuned it out.

Over a glass of wine, I told Nick about Mack's usual Mother's Day call and then about the note he left in the collection basket. "The fact that he wrote that I must not try to find him makes me feel that something is very wrong in his life," I said. "I'm just afraid that Mack needs help."

"I'm not so sure about that, Carolyn," Nick said, quietly. "I was witness to how close he was to you and your parents. He would know that if he needed anything in a financial way, your mother would provide it on the spot. If he's sick, I would think he'd want to be around you and your mother. I never saw Mack touch drugs, but I don't know, maybe he had started and knew it would crush your father if he found out about it. Don't think I haven't tried all these years to figure out what would make him vanish."

I guess it's what I expected to hear, but even so, I felt as if every door I tried to open was being slammed in my face. When I didn't respond, Nick waited me out for a minute, then said, "Carolyn, you said yourself that Mack sounded pretty chipper when he called on Mother's Day. Why don't you look at that message not as a plea for help, but as a firm request, or even a command? You can certainly read it that way, too. 'Tell Carolyn she must not look for me!' "

He was right. I know he was. But in a much bigger sense he was wrong. Every instinct in my body told me that.

"Let it go, Carolyn," Nick said. Now his voice was gentle. "When and if Mack decides to surface, I am going to give him one swift kick for the way he's treated you and your mother. Now, tell me about yourself. I guess your clerkship with the judge expires soon. Isn't that the way it works?"

"I'll tell you about that," I said. "But just a little more about Mack first. I went to see the Kramers Wednesday morning."

"The Kramers? You mean the superintendents of the building where Mack and I lived?"

"Yes. And Nick, you may not believe me, but Mrs. Kramer was nervous. She kept looking over at her husband to make sure whatever she told me was all right. I swear to you, she was afraid of making some kind of mistake. What did you think of them when you lived there?"

"To be honest, it's not what I thought *of* them, it's more that I didn't think *about* them. Mrs. Kramer cleaned the apartment, thanks to your mother's generosity, and did our wash once a week. Otherwise it would probably have been a pigsty. She was a good cleaning woman but downright nosey. I know Bruce Galbraith was furious at her. He came in one day and she was reading the mail on his desk. If she was reading his, I figured she was probably reading mine, too."

"Did you challenge her on it?"

He smiled. "No. I did something dopey. I typed a letter, signed her name to it, and stacked it with my mail so that she would find it. It read something like this: 'Darling, it is such a pleasure for me to wash your clothes and make your bed. I feel like a young girl when I look at you. Sometime will you take me dancing? All my love, Lilly Kramer.' "

"You *didn't!*" I exclaimed.

The boyish twinkle I remembered appeared in Nick's eyes for a brief moment. "When I thought it over, I threw it out before she could see it. Sometimes I wish I hadn't."

"Do you think Mack might have had a problem with her going through his mail?"

"He didn't say it, but I have a feeling he was upset about her, too. But he never said why, then he was gone."

"Do you mean it was just before he disappeared?"

Nick's expression changed. "Carolyn, surely you don't think the Kramers had anything to do with Mack's disappearance?"

"Nick, just talking about them to you brought up something that obviously never came up at the time of the investigation, that Bruce caught her snooping, and that Mack may have been upset with her, too. Give me your assessment of Gus Kramer."

"Good superintendent. Nasty temper. I heard him yelling at Mrs. Kramer a couple of times."

"Nasty temper?" I asked, raising my eyebrows, then said, "You don't have to answer, but think about it. Suppose he and Mack had some kind of confrontation."

The waiter then came to take our orders, and Nick never did answer my question. After that we kept the conversation to catching up on the past ten years. I told him that I was going to apply for a job in the District Attorney's office.

" 'Going to apply'?" Now it was Nick who raised his eyebrows. "As Brother Murphy said, 'Never put off till tomorrow what you can do today.' Any special reason for waiting?"

I answered vaguely about taking a little time to find an apartment. After dinner, Nick opened his BlackBerry discreetly and checked it for messages. I asked him to see if there was any update about Leesey Andrews.

"Good idea." He pushed a button, scanned the news briefs, then turned off the BlackBerry. " 'Hope is fading that she'll be found alive,' " he said soberly. "I wouldn't be surprised if I'm asked to drop in to the DA's Office again tomorrow."

And I may get a call from Barrott, I thought. We finished our coffee, and Nick signaled to the waiter for a check.

It was only later, when he was dropping me at the door of Sutton Place, that he brought up the subject of Mack again. "I can read you, Carolyn. You're going to keep trying to find Mack, aren't you?"

"Yes."

"Who else are you going to talk to?"

"I have a call in to Bruce Galbraith."

"You won't get much help or sympathy from him," he said wryly.

"Why not?"

"Do you remember Barbara Hanover, the girl who came with Mack and me to dinner at your house?"

And how, I thought. "Yes, I remember her," I said, but then I couldn't help adding, "I also remember that you had a big crush on her."

Nick shrugged. "Ten years ago I had a crush on someone different every week. Anyhow, it wouldn't have done me any good. If she cared about anyone, my guess is that it was Mack."

"Mack?" Could I have been so focused on Nick that I didn't notice?

"Couldn't you tell? But Barbara was looking for a ticket to medical school. Her mother had a catastrophic illness that ate up all the money that had been earmarked for Barbara's education. That is why she married Bruce Galbraith. They eloped that summer, remember?"

"That's something else that never came out during the investigation," I said slowly. "Was Bruce jealous of Mack?"

Nick shrugged. "You never knew what Bruce was thinking. But what's the difference? You talked to Mack less than a week ago. You certainly don't think Bruce sent him into hiding, do you?"

I felt like a fool. "Of course not," I said. "I really don't know anything about Bruce at all. He never came here with you and Mack."

"He's a loner. That last year at Columbia, even the nights he'd hit the clubs in the Village and SoHo with a crowd of us, he always seemed to be by himself. We called him 'the Lone Stranger.' "

I searched Nick's face, eager for more detail. "After Mack disappeared, when the investigation started, did the police question Bruce at all? The only thing I found about him in the file was his statement about the last time he saw Mack in the apartment."

"I don't think they did. Why would they? He and Mack never hung out together."

"I was just reminded by an old friend that a week or so before he disappeared, Mack and some other guys from Columbia were in a club the same night as the first girl who went missing. Do you remember if Bruce was there?"

Nick looked pensive. "Yes, he was. I remember because the club had recently opened, and we decided to check it out. But it seems to me that he left early. He certainly was never the life of the party. Anyhow, it's getting late, Carolyn. I've enjoyed it a lot. Thank you for coming."

He gave me a quick peck on my cheek, and opened the door to the lobby for me. There was no mention of getting together again. I walked through the lobby to the elevator then glanced back.

Nick was already in the car, and Benny was standing on the sidewalk, holding a cell phone to his ear, his expression unreadable. For some reason there was something sinister about the way Benny smiled as he snapped the cell phone closed, got back in the car, and drove away.

23

Every Saturday morning. Howard Altman took his boss Derek Olsen out for brunch. They met at exactly ten o'clock in the Lamplighter Diner, near one of the apartment buildings Olsen owned on Amsterdam Avenue.

In the decade during which he had been working for the increasingly testy Olsen, Altman had become very close to the elderly widower, a relationship he carefully nurtured. Lately the eighty-three-year-old Olsen made no bones about the fact that he was becoming more and more disgruntled with the nephew who was his only close relative. "Do you think Steve gives a damn whether I live or die, Howie," he asked rhetorically, as he wiped the last of the egg yolk from his plate with a piece of toast. "He should call me more often."

"I'm sure Steve gives more than a damn, Derek," Howard said lightly. "I certainly give a damn about you, but I still can't persuade you not to order two fried eggs, bacon, and sausage when we get together on Saturdays."

Olsen's eyes softened. "You're a good friend, Howie. It was my lucky day when you came to work for me. You're a good-looking guy. You dress nice. You handle yourself well. I can play bridge with my friends and play golf and know you're out there doing a good job for me. So what's going on in the buildings? Everything up to snuff?"

"I would say so. We've got a couple of kids in 825 behind in their rent, but I stopped in to see them and reminded them that your list of favorite charities doesn't have their names on it."

Olsen chuckled. "I'd have put it a little more crudely. Keep an eye on them." He tapped his cup on the saucer, signaling to the waitress that he wanted more coffee. "Anything else?"

"Something that really surprised me. Gus Kramer phoned me yesterday and gave me two weeks' notice."

"What?" The genial expression vanished from Derek Olsen's face. "I don't want him to go," he said flatly. "He's the best super I ever had, and Lil is like a mother hen to the students. The parents like her, too. They feel good about her. Why do they want to leave?"

"Gus said they're ready to retire."

"They weren't ready last month when I dropped in over there. Howie, I've got to tell you something. There are times when you push to cut corners when it don't make sense. You think you're doing me a favor by trying to kick them out of a big apartment so that you can get good rent for it. I know all about that, but for what I pay them, letting them have more space is a bargain. Sometimes you overstep yourself. This is one of them. Make nice with them. Give them a raise, but make *sure* they stay! And now that we're on the subject, when you deal with them and with the other supers, keep something in mind. You represent me, but you're *not* me. Clear? Very clear?"

"Of course." Howard Altman's vocal cords started to form the name "Derek." Instead he said humbly, "Very clear, Mr. Olsen."

"I'm glad to hear it. Anything else?"

Howard had planned to tell his boss that Carolyn MacKenzie had been in the Kramers' apartment on Wednesday asking questions about her missing brother, but he realized it would be a mistake. In his present mood, Olsen would decide that he should have been told at once, that Howie didn't understand what was important. Besides that, over the past decade whenever Olsen talked about the MacKenzie disappearance, he went ballistic — red in the face, his voice raised sharply.

"That kid takes off in May," he would rant. "The apartments were all rented for the next September. Half of them were canceled. The last place MacKenzie was seen was in my building, so his parents thought there might have been some nut hanging out in the stairwell . . ."

Howard realized that his boss was studying him intently.

"Howie, you look like you have more on your mind. Do you?"

"Nothing at all, Mr. Olsen," Howard said firmly.

"Good. You been reading about that missing girl? What's her name, Leesey Andrews?"

"Yes, I have. It's very sad. I was watching the news before I left this morning. I don't think they expect to find her alive."

"These young women should stay out of these clubs. In my day, they sat home with their mothers."

Howard reached for the check as the waitress placed it beside Olsen. It was a ritual they went through every week. Ninety percent of the time Olsen let him pick it up. When he was annoyed, he did not.

Olsen grabbed the check. "I don't want the Kramers to leave, Howie, understand? Remember last year you stepped on the toes of the super on Ninety-eighth Street? His replacement stinks. If the Kramers leave, maybe you should look for another job. I hear my nephew is out of work again. He's not stupid, in fact, he's pretty damned smart. Maybe if he had your cushy apartment and salary, he'd pay a little more attention to me."

"I hear you, Mr. Olsen." Howard Altman was furious at his employer, but much more so at himself. He had played it all wrong. The Kramers had been as nervous as cats on a hot tin roof when Carolyn MacKenzie showed up the other day. Why? He should have been smart enough to find out what was upsetting them. He made a silent vow to get what it was out of them before it was too late. I want my job, he thought. I *need* it.

Neither the Kramers nor Carolyn MacKenzie were going to cause him to lose it!

24

"Hope is fading that Leesey Andrews will be found alive," Dr. David Andrews read as the latest news report scrolled across the bottom of the television screen. He was sitting on the leather couch in the den of his son's Park Avenue apartment. Unable to sleep, he had gone in there sometime in the predawn hours. He knew he must have dozed off at some point, because shortly after he heard Gregg leave to make his rounds at the hospital, he became aware that a blanket was tucked around him neatly.

Now, three hours later, he was still there, alternately dozing and watching television. I should get showered and dressed, he thought, but he was too weary to move. The clock on the mantelpiece showed that it was quarter of ten. I'm still in pajamas, he thought—that's ridiculous. He looked up at the television screen. What had he just seen on it? I must have read it because the setting is on mute, he realized.

He groped for the remote control, which he remembered placing on the cushion so that he could adjust the volume in an instant if something came on about Leesey.

It's Sunday, he thought. It's been more than five days now. What do I feel right at this minute? Nothing. Not fear, nor grief, nor that murderous anger at whoever has taken her. Right now, at this minute, I just feel numb.

It won't last.

Hope is fading, he thought. Is that what I just read in the news tape on the screen? Or did I make it up? Why does that sound familiar?

A mental image of his mother, playing the piano at family parties and everyone joining in the singing, burst into his mind. They loved the old vaudeville songs, he thought. One of them began with the words, "Darling I am growing old."

Leesey won't ever grow old. He closed his eyes against the tidal wave of pain. The emotional numbness was gone.

Darling, I am growing old . . . Silver threads among the gold . . . Shine upon my brow today . . . Life is fading fast away . . .

Hope is fading . . . Those were the words that made me think of that song.

"Dad, are you okay?"

David Andrews looked up and saw the concerned face of his son. "I didn't hear you come in, Gregg." He rubbed his eyes. "Did you know that life is fading fast away? Leesey's life." He stopped, tried again. "No, I'm wrong. It's hope that's fading that she'll be found alive."

Gregg Andrews crossed the room, sat next to his father, and put an arm around his shoulders. "My hope isn't fading, Dad."

"Isn't it? Then you believe in miracles. Why not? I used to believe in them myself, too."

"Keep believing in them, Dad."

"Remember how your mother seemed to be doing so well, then overnight the picture changed and we lost her? That's when I stopped believing in miracles."

David shook his head, trying to clear it, and patted his son's knee. "You'd better take good care of yourself for me. You're all I have." He stood up. "I feel as if I'm talking in my sleep. I'll be okay, Gregg. I'm going to shower and dress and go home. I'm absolutely useless here. With your schedule at the hospital, you need downtime when you're here, and at home I'll be better able to keep a grip on myself, I hope. I'll try to get back into some kind of routine while we're waiting to see what develops."

Gregg Andrews looked at his father with the clinical eye of a doctor, observing the deep circles under his eyes, the bleak expression in them, the way in these four days his trim frame suddenly seemed extremely thin. He hasn't eaten a thing since he heard about Leesey, Gregg thought. In one way he wanted to object to his father leaving, in another he sensed that he'd be better off in Greenwich where he volunteered at the urgent care center three days a week and where he was among close friends.

"I understand, Dad," he said. "And maybe you *think* you've given up hope, but I don't believe you."

"Believe me," his father said simply.

Forty minutes later, showered and dressed, he was ready to leave. At the door of the apartment, the two men embraced. "Dad, you know you'll have a dozen people wanting to have dinner with you. Go out to the club with some of them tonight," Gregg urged.

"If not tonight, I will very soon."

After his father left, the apartment felt empty. We've been trying to keep up appearances for each other's sake, Gregg thought. I'd better take my own advice and stay busy. I'll take a long run in Central Park, then try to nap. He had already planned to go back and forth between the Woodshed and Leesey's apartment tonight at three A.M., the same time she had started to make that walk. Maybe I'll find someone to talk to, someone the cops have missed, he thought. Detective Barrott had told him that plainclothes detectives were doing that every night, but the need to help in the search had been building to a fever pitch in Gregg.

While Dad was here I couldn't do it, he thought. He'd have insisted on coming with me.

The day had started overcast, but when he went outside at eleven, the sun had broken through the clouds, and Gregg felt his own spirits lift a bit. Surely on a beautiful spring morning like this, his kid sister, funny, pretty Leesey, could not be gone. But if she wasn't dead, then where was she? Let it be an emotional breakdown or a spell of amnesia, Gregg prayed, as he covered the three blocks to the park with long strides. There, he decided to head north and swing back around the Central Park Boathouse.

Right foot, left foot, right foot, left foot. Let . . . us . . . find . . . her . . . Let . . . us . . . find . . . her . . . He prayed in cadence to the rhythm of the run.

An hour later, tired but somewhat less tense, he was walking back to his apartment when his cell phone rang. With conflicting emotions of hope and dread, he grabbed it from the pocket of his jacket, flipped it open, and saw that the call was from his father.

The words, "Hello, Dad," died on his lips as he listened despairingly. He heard uncontrollable sobbing. Oh, God, he thought, they've found her body.

"Leesey," David Andrews managed to say. "Gregg, it's Leesey. She *phoned!*"

"She *what?*"

"She left a message on the answering machine less than ten minutes ago. I just walked in. I can't believe it. I just missed her call."

Again, Gregg Andrews heard his father's sobs.

"Dad, what did she *say*? Where is she?"

The sobs suddenly stopped. "She said . . . that . . . she loves me but has to be by herself. She asked me to forgive her. She said . . . she said . . . that she'll call again on Mother's Day."

25

I spent Saturday morning in Mack's room in the Sutton Place apartment. I won't say it had a Sunset Boulevard quality to it, but I do know that it no longer held any sense of his presence for me. After Mack had been missing a few days, Dad ransacked his desk, hoping to find some clue as to where he might have gone, but the only things he found were the usual trappings of a college student—notes for exams, postcards, blank personal stationery. One file contained a copy of Mack's application to Duke Law School and his letter of acceptance from them. On it he had scrawled an exuberant "YES!"

But Dad didn't find what he was looking for—Mack's daily calendar—which might have given us a clue to any appointments he had made prior to his disappearance. Years ago, Mom had our housekeeper take down the banners Mack had tacked on the wall and the corkboard covered with group pictures of him and his friends. Everyone in those pictures had been questioned by the cops, and later by the private investigator.

The brown and beige coverlet, matching pillows, and contrasting window treatments were the same, as was the cocoa brown carpet.

There was still a picture of the four of us on top of the dresser. I found myself studying it and wondering if by now Mack had any strands of gray on his temples. It was hard to imagine. He'd had such a boyish face ten years ago. Now he was not only long past being a college student, was probably a suspect in absentia in more than one kidnapping and/or murder case.

There were two closets in the room. I opened the doors of both of them and detected that faint musty odor that grows when no fresh air circulates into a relatively small space.

I took a stack of jackets and slacks from the first closet and laid them on the bed. They all had plastic cleaners' bags over them, and I remembered that when Mack had been missing about a year, Mom had everything he owned cleaned and put back in the closet. I remember at the time Dad had said, "Livvy, let's give them all away. If Mack comes back I'll take him shopping. Let somebody else get some use out of all this stuff."

His suggestion had been rejected.

There was nothing to be found in this sterile clothing. I didn't want to just dump everything in large trash bags. I knew that would make it easier to carry them to the donation center, but it would be a shame if anything got wrinkled. Then I remembered that a couple of Mack's large suitcases, the ones he'd used on our last family trip, were in the storeroom behind the kitchen.

I found them there and brought them back to his room, hauling them up on the bed. I opened the first one and as a matter of habit, ran my fingers through the pockets to see if there was anything in them. There wasn't. I filled the suitcase with neatly folded suits and jackets and slacks, lingering over the tuxedo Mack wore in our family photo that last Christmas.

The second suitcase was a size smaller. Again I ran my hand through the side pockets. This time I felt something I guessed to be a camera. But when I pulled it out, I was surprised to see that it was a tape recorder. I never remembered seeing Mack using one. There was a tape in it and I pushed the play button.

"What do you think, Ms. Klein? Do I sound like Laurence Olivier or Tom Hanks? I'm recording you, so be kind."

I heard a woman's laugh. "You sound like neither of them, but you sound good, Mack."

I was so shocked that I pushed the stop button as tears welled in my eyes. Mack. It was as though he were in the room bantering with me, his voice lively and animated.

These yearly Mother's Day calls and the ever-increasing resentment that was my reaction to them had made me forget the way Mack used to sound, funny and energetic.

I pushed the play button again.

"Okay, here I go, Ms. Klein," Mack was saying. "You said to select some passage from Shakespeare? How about this one? Then he cleared his throat and began, "When, in disgrace with Fortune and men's eyes . . ."

His tone had changed drastically, had suddenly become ragged and somber.

" . . . I all alone beweep my outcast state, and trouble deaf heaven with my bootless cries—"

That was all that was on the tape. I rewound it and played it again. What did it mean? Was it a random selection or had it been chosen deliberately because it suited Mack's frame of mind? When was it made? How long before he disappeared had it been made?

Esther Klein's name was in the file of people the cops spoke to about Mack, but obviously she had offered nothing of consequence. I vaguely remembered that Dad and Mom had been surprised that Mack had been taking private acting lessons with her on the side. I can understand why he didn't tell them. Dad was always afraid that Mack was becoming too interested in his theatre electives.

Then Esther Klein had been fatally mugged near her apartment on Amsterdam Avenue, nearly a year after Mack went missing. The thought occurred to me that there might have been other tapes that he made while he studied with her. If so, what happened to them after her death?

I stood in Mack's room, holding the recorder, and realized it would be easy enough to find that out.

Esther Klein's son, Aaron, was a close associate of Uncle Elliott. I would call him.

I put the recorder in my shoulder bag and began packing Mack's clothes. When I was finished, the drawers in the dresser were empty, as were the closets. Mom had let Dad give Mack's heavy coats away one particularly cold winter, when the charities were pleading for them.

As I was about to close the second suitcase, I hesitated, then took out the formal black tie I had tied for Mack just before we posed for our Christmas picture that last year. I held it in my hands thinking back to how I had told him to lean down because I couldn't reach high enough to tie it tight.

As I wrapped it in tissue and put it in my shoulder bag to take back to Thompson Street with me, I remembered Mack's laughing response, " 'Blest be the tie that binds.' Now, please don't make a mess of it, Carolyn."

26

He wondered if her father had heard the message yet. He could just imagine his reaction when he listened to it. His little girl was alive and didn't want to see him! She said she would call on Mother's Day! Only fifty-one weeks to wait!

Daddy must be twisting in the wind, he thought.

By now the cops undoubtedly had a wiretap on Dr. Andrews's phone in Greenwich. He could just imagine the frenzy they were in. Would they throw up their hands and decide that Leesey has a right to her privacy and drop the search for her? Maybe. It was just the kind of thing people did.

It would be safer for him if they did.

Would they tell the media she had phoned?

I like the headlines, he thought. And I like reading about Leesey Andrews. They've known since Tuesday that she's missing. She's been in all the headlines the last three days. But today the story about her was buried on page four, which was disappointing.

It had been the same thing with the other three girls—within two weeks the story was dead.

As dead as they were.

I'll play around with what to do to keep Leesey on everybody's mind, but for now, he thought, I'll have my fun moving her cell phone around. That must be driving them crazy. "Goosey, Goosey, Gander," he whispered. "Wither do you wander? Upstairs? Downstairs? In my lady's chamber?"

He laughed. All three places, he thought.

All three.

27

"Doctor, you're sure that it *is* your sister's voice on the answering machine?"

"*Absolutely* sure!" Unconsciously, Gregg kneaded his forehead with his thumb and forefinger. I never get headaches, he thought. I don't need one to start now. Three hours after his father called he was downtown in the detective squad section of the District Attorney's office. The message Leesey had left on the answering machine in his father's Greenwich, Connecticut, home had been taken from the wiretap and amplified. In the tech room, Detective Barrott had already played it several times for him and Larry Ahearn.

"I agree with Gregg," Ahearn told Barrott. "I've known Leesey since she was a little girl, and I would swear that's her voice. She sounds nervous and agitated, but of course she may have had some sort of breakdown or . . ." He looked at Gregg. "Or she was forced to leave that message."

"You mean by someone who abducted her?"

"Yes, Gregg, that's exactly what I mean."

"You've confirmed that that call was made from her cell phone?" Gregg asked, trying to keep his voice steady.

"Yes, it was," Ahearn said. "It was bounced from the tower at Madison and Fiftieth. That's why she may be being held somewhere in that area. On the other hand, if she did choose to disappear, I don't see how she can walk outside in that location even to buy groceries without worrying about being spotted. Her picture has been all over the newspapers, television, and the Internet."

"Unless she has some kind of disguise like a burka, that would hide everything except her eyes," Barrott pointed out. "But even that would draw attention in Manhattan." He began to rewind the tape of Leesey's call. "Our tech guys are working on the background sound. Let's concentrate on listening to that."

Larry Ahearn caught the bleak expression on Gregg's face. "I don't think we need to hear it again, Roy."

"What happens now?" Gregg asked him. "If you decide Leesey *did* leave voluntarily, do you give up looking for her?"

"No," Ahearn said emphatically. "Not for one minute. Knowing Leesey as well as I do, even if she disappeared on her own, something is terribly wrong. We're staying on this 24/7 until we find her."

"Thank God for that." There's something else I need to ask them, Gregg thought. Oh, I know. "How about the media? Are you going to tell them that she's contacted us?"

"We don't want anyone to know," Larry said, shaking his head. "That was the first thing I told your father when we spoke to him."

"You told me the same thing, but I thought you meant you wanted to be sure it wasn't a crank call, or someone just imitating Leesey's voice."

"Gregg, we don't want a *hint* of this to get out," Larry Ahearn said urgently. "Awful as this is, it's good to know that as of a few hours ago Leesey was alive."

"I guess I agree. But where *is* she if she's alive? What may be happening to her? The other young women who disappeared after being at one of those clubs in SoHo were never found."

"But neither did any of them call a member of the family, Gregg," Ahearn reminded him.

"Dr. Andrews, there's something else . . ." Barrott began.

"Make it Gregg, please." A hint of a smile crossed Gregg Andrews's lips. "After I got my M.D., if anyone called me at home and asked for Dr. Andrews, it took Leesey months before she didn't automatically hand the phone to my father."

Barrott smiled briefly. "That's the way it is in my house. If my son gets great marks or some kind of achievement award, his sister thinks it was a mistake. All right, Gregg," he continued, "the last time you saw your sister was a week ago on Mother's Day. Was there anything unusual about that day?"

"That's what absolutely bewilders me," Gregg told him. "My mother's been dead only two years, so naturally it's a pretty low-key day for us. The three of us went to church together, visited her grave, then had dinner at the club. Leesey had planned to drive back to the city with me but at the last minute decided to stay overnight with Dad and take the train home in the morning."

"Before your mother died, was Mother's Day in any way symbolic for all of you, other than the usual sentiment that's attached to it?"

"No, not at all. We celebrated it together, but it wasn't a big deal. When my grandparents were alive, they were with us. There was nothing extraordinary at all about it." Gregg caught the way the two detectives glanced at each other and then the way Larry Ahearn nodded to Roy Barrott. "There's something you haven't told me," he said. "What is it?"

"Gregg, do you know Carolyn MacKenzie?" Ahearn asked.

Now his temples were beginning to pound. Gregg searched his memory, then shook his head. "I don't think so. Who is she?"

"She's a lawyer," Ahearn volunteered. "Twenty-six years old. Her studio is on Thompson Street in the building next door to where your sister lives."

"Does she know Leesey?" Gregg asked quickly. "Does she have any idea where she might be?"

"No. She doesn't know her, but maybe you remember a case ten years ago, when a college student walked out of his apartment and disappeared? His name was Charles MacKenzie Jr. Everyone called him Mack."

"I remember that case. They never found him, did they?"

"No," Ahearn said. "But he calls his mother every year on Mother's Day."

"*On Mother's Day!*" Gregg jumped up. "He's been gone ten years and calls his mother on Mother's Day. Are you suggesting that Leesey might be planning to follow a crazy pattern like that?"

"Gregg, we're not suggesting anything," Ahearn said, soothingly. "Leesey was eleven years old when Mack MacKenzie disappeared, so there's no reason to think that she might have known him. But we thought it's possible you or your father might know the family. My guess is that you travel in some of the same circles."

"Whatever that means." He looked perplexed. "Did Mack MacKenzie call his mother last Sunday?"

"Yes, he did." Ahearn decided not to immediately share the fact that Mack had left a message in the collection basket. "We don't know what that guy is doing or why he had to go underground. It certainly isn't widespread knowledge that he still phones his family on that one day. It makes us wonder if at some point Leesey might have met him, maybe at one of those clubs in SoHo, and, if she decided to disappear on her own, as he seems to have done, whether she'll stay in touch the same way."

"What do you know about MacKenzie, Larry? I mean if he disappeared voluntarily, was he in some kind of trouble?" Gregg looked pointedly at Larry, searching for answers.

"We couldn't find anything that added up. He had everything going for him and just walked out of his life."

"The same thing could be said about Leesey," Gregg snapped. "Are you starting to think that if she's come across this guy, the next time we'll hear from her is Mother's Day next year?" He looked from one to the other of them. "Wait a minute, do you think that this Mack guy might be a weirdo and has something to do with Leesey's disappearance?"

Larry looked across the table at his college roommate. It's not just his father who aged this week, he thought. Gregg looks ten years older than he did when we played golf last month. "Gregg, we are exploring everyone and every situation that may give us a lead to follow. Most of them will be dead ends. Now do me a favor and take my advice. Go home, get a decent dinner, and go to bed early. Take some comfort in the fact that we know Leesey was alive this morning. You've got a lot of patients who depend on your skill to give them a new lease on life. You can't fail them, and you will if you don't eat and sleep properly."

Not unlike the advice I gave Dad, Gregg thought. I will go home. I will get a couple of hours sleep and eat something. But tonight I'm going to walk back and forth between that SoHo club and Thompson Street. Leesey was alive this morning. But that doesn't mean that if she's with some kind of nut, she'll *stay* alive.

He pushed back his chair and stood up. "You're absolutely right, Larry," he said.

With a brief wave, he started to leave, but spun around when Ahearn's cell phone rang. Ahearn grabbed it from his pocket and raised it to his ear. "What's up?"

Gregg saw the angry frown before he heard Larry's muttered profanity. For the second time that day, he despairingly thought that Leesey's body had been found.

Ahearn looked at him. "Someone called the *New York Post* a few minutes ago and said that Leesey Andrews left a message for her father today and said she'd call again on Mother's Day. The *Post* wants confirmation." Spitting out the words, he shouted, "Absolutely no comment!" and slammed down the phone.

"Did Leesey make the call?" Gregg demanded.

"The reporter who took it couldn't be sure. Said it was a muffled whisper. There was no caller ID."

"That means that the call wasn't made from Leesey's phone," Gregg said. "She has caller ID."

"That's exactly what I mean. Gregg, I'm going to be brutally honest. Either Leesey had some kind of breakdown and wants publicity, or she's in the hands of a dangerous, game-playing nut."

"Who only calls home on Mother's Day," Roy Barrott said quietly.

"Or who has a loft apartment near the Woodshed and a longtime chauffeur who would do anything for him," Ahearn said bitterly.

28

Howard Altman gave careful thought about how he would approach the Kramers to persuade them to stay on as superintendents. *Olsen is right*, he admitted. *The guy I got him to fire last year in the Ninety-eighth Street apartment house* was *saving us a lot of money. I just didn't get it. Olsen doesn't want to do major repairs there. The property next door is for sale, and when it goes, he's sure they'll make a big offer for his building, too. The old super was keeping things together with chewing gum and kite string. The new one has a list of all the repairs that are needed and keeps telling Olsen it's criminal negligence not to do them immediately.*

I should have kept my mouth shut, he thought, *but I never could see why the Kramers needed a three-bedroom apartment—the other two bedrooms are never used.*

Every so often, when Howard stopped by the Kramers', he asked for permission to use the bathroom. That gave him a chance to look into the spare bedrooms. Never once in the nearly ten years since he had started working for Derek Olsen had he noticed any change in the placement of the teddy bears on the pillows of the beds. He knew they never used those rooms, but he told himself that what he *should* have realized was that Lil Kramer took a certain lowbrow pride in her big apartment.

And I know all about lowbrow! he thought ruefully. *When I was a* kid and Pop bought his first brand-new car, the cheapest one on the lot, you would have thought he'd won the lottery. We had to show it off to all the relatives just because Pop hoped they'd be drooling with envy.

I should start a blog and write about my own messed-up family, Howard told himself. I can't let the Kramers retire. Maybe Olsen would get over it if I got some good new people in fast. On the other hand, it would be just like him to fire me and give my job to that sicko nephew of his. In thirty days, Olsen would probably be on his knees begging me to come back, but that's a chance I can't take. So what approach do I take with the Kramers?

Howard Altman considered possible solutions over the weekend. Then, satisfied with the plan he had come up with, at quarter of ten on Monday morning he stepped into the West End Avenue building where the Kramers lived.

He had definitely decided that pleading with them to stay, offering them a raise, and assuring them that the large apartment would always be their home was exactly the wrong way to go. If Gus Kramer thought that by quitting he could get me fired, he'd do it even if he doesn't really want to retire now.

When he turned the key in the outside door and went into the lobby, he found Gus Kramer polishing the already gleaming brass mailboxes.

Gus looked up. "I guess I won't be doing this much longer," he said. "Hope the next guy you get is half as good as I've been for nearly twenty years."

"Gus, is Lil around?" Howard said, almost whispering. "I need to speak to both of you. I'm worried about you two."

Seeing the look of outright fear in Kramer's face, he knew he was on the right track.

"She's in the apartment sorting stuff out," Gus said. Without bothering to wipe the final cloud of polish from the mailboxes, he turned and walked across the lobby to his apartment. He unlocked the door, pushed it open, and walked in, leaving Howard to grab it before it slammed in his face.

"I'll get Lil," Gus said abruptly.

It was obvious to Howard that Kramer wanted a chance to talk to his wife and possibly warn her before she saw him. She's in one of the two bedrooms down the hall, he thought. That's where she must be sorting things out. She's finally found a use for that extra space.

It was almost five minutes before the Kramers joined him in the living room. Lil Kramer was visibly agitated. She was rubbing her lips together in a compulsive manner, and when Howard extended his hand to her, she rubbed her own hand on her skirt before she reluctantly responded to the greeting.

As he had expected, her palm was wringing wet.

Do the one-two punch right now, Howard thought. Send them reeling. "I'm going to talk straight from the shoulder," he said. "I wasn't here when the MacKenzie kid disappeared, but I was here the other day when his sister showed up. Lil, you were as nervous then as you are now. It was clear to me as an observer that you were afraid to talk to her. That tells me that you know something about why or how that boy disappeared, or that maybe you had something to do with it."

He watched as Lil Kramer threw a terrified look at her husband and Gus Kramer's cheekbones darkened to an ugly purple-red shade. I'm right, he thought. They're scared to death. Emboldened, he added, "The sister isn't finished with you. Next time she might bring a private investigator or the cops with her. If you think you'll get away from her by rushing to Pennsylvania, you're both crazy. If you're gone when she comes back, she'll ask questions. She'll find out you quit abruptly. Lil, how many people have you told over the years that you don't intend to budge from New York until you're at least ninety?"

Now Lil Kramer was biting back tears.

Howard softened his tone. "Lil, Gus, think about it. If you leave now, Carolyn MacKenzie and the cops will be sure you have something to hide. I don't know what it is, but you're my friends, and I want to help you. Let me tell Mr. Olsen that you've reconsidered and don't want to leave. The next time Carolyn MacKenzie calls to make an appointment, let me know, and I'll be here. I'll tell her in no uncertain terms that the management doesn't welcome her bothering the employees. What's more, I'll remind her that there are stiff penalties for stalking."

He saw the relief on their faces and knew he had convinced them to stay. And I didn't have to give them a raise or promise to leave them in this apartment, he thought exultantly.

But as he accepted Lil's groveling gratitude and Gus's terse expression of thanks, he was burning to find out why they were so afraid, and what, if anything, they knew about the reason for Mack MacKenzie's disappearance ten years ago.

29

Sunday morning I went to the last Mass at St. Francis de Sales. I got there early, slipped into the last pew, and after that tried to study the faces of the arriving congregation. Needless to say, I didn't spot anyone who even vaguely resembled Mack. Uncle Dev always delivers a thoughtful homily, frequently laced with Irish humor. Today, I didn't hear a word of it.

When the Mass was over, I stopped in at the rectory for a quick cup of coffee. Smiling and waving me into his office, Devon said he was meeting friends in Westchester for a round of golf, but they could wait. He poured coffee into two thick white mugs and handed one to me as we sat down.

I hadn't yet told him that I had gone to see the Kramers, and when I did I was surprised to learn that he remembered them clearly. "After we knew that Mack was missing, I went over with your Dad to that apartment on West End," he said. "I remember the wife was all upset at the thought that something might have happened to Mack."

"Do you remember anything about Gus Kramer's reaction?" I asked.

When Uncle Dev gets a thoughtful frown on his face, his resemblance to my father is almost startling. Sometimes that gives me comfort. Other times it hurts. Today, for some reason, was one of the days it hurt.

"You know, Carolyn," he said, "that Kramer is an odd duck. I think he was more upset by the possibility of media attention than he was concerned about Mack."

Ten years later that was exactly my reaction to Kramer, but knowing Devon had to be on his way soon, I didn't take the time to talk that over with him. Instead, I took out the recorder I had found in Mack's suitcase and explained how I had discovered it. Then I played the tape for him. I watched my uncle's sad smile at the sound of Mack's voice speaking to the teacher, then his bewildered frown when Mack began to recite, "When, in disgrace with fortune and men's eyes, I all alone beweep my outcast state, and trouble deaf heaven with my bootless cries."

After I turned off the recorder, my uncle said, his voice husky, "I'm glad your mother wasn't around when you came across that tape, Carolyn. I don't think I'd ever play it for her."

"I don't intend to let her hear it. But, Devon, I'm trying to figure out its significance, if any. Did Mack ever talk to you about taking private lessons with a drama teacher at Columbia?"

"I remember that in an offhand way he did. You know when Mack was about thirteen and his voice was changing, he went through a period where it was really high-pitched. He got unmercifully teased about it at school."

"I don't remember Mack having a high-pitched voice," I protested, then paused to search my memory. When Mack was thirteen I was eight years old.

"Of course, his voice deepened, but Mack was a more sensitive kid than most people realized. He didn't show his feelings when he was hurt, but years later, he admitted to me how miserable he had been during that period." Uncle Dev tapped the side of his mug, remembering. "Maybe some residual of that pain got him involved in the voice lessons. On the other hand, Mack wanted to become a trial lawyer and a good one. He told me that a good trial lawyer must also be a good actor. Maybe that could account for both the lessons and the passage he recited on that tape."

Obviously, we could come to no conclusion. Whether Mack had chosen that dark passage because of his own state of mind, or was simply reciting a prepared text, could only be a guessing game. Nor could we possibly know why he either stopped recording, or erased the rest of the session with the drama teacher.

At 12:30, Uncle Devon gave me a warm hug and went off to his golf game. I went back to Sutton Place and was glad to go there because I no longer felt at home in my West Village apartment. The fact that I lived next door to where Leesey Andrews lived was terribly troubling to me. If it were not for that fact, I thought, I am sure that Detective Barrott would not be trying to connect Mack to her disappearance.

I wanted to talk to Aaron Klein, the son of Mack's drama teacher. It would be easy enough to contact him. Aaron had been working at Wallace and Madison for nearly twenty years and was now Uncle Elliott's chosen successor. I remembered that a year after Mack disappeared, his mother was the victim of a robbery and was murdered, and that Mom and Dad went with Uncle Elliott to visit him when he was sitting shiva.

The problem was I didn't want Uncle Elliott to be involved in our meeting. As far as Elliott was concerned, he believed that Mom and I were planning to accept Mack's request, which, in so many words, was "Leave me alone." If Elliott knew I was contacting Aaron Klein because of Mack, as sure as day follows night he would feel it his duty to discuss it with Mom.

That meant I had to make an appointment with Klein outside the office and ask him to keep whatever conversation we had confidential, then trust him not to go blabbing to Elliott.

I went back to Dad's office, flicked on the light, and went over Mack's file again. I knew Lucas Reeves, the private investigator, had interviewed Mack's drama teacher, as well as other members of the Columbia University Faculty. I had read his comments the other day and knew they weren't helpful, but now I was looking specifically for what he had written about Esther Klein.

It was very short. "Ms. Klein expressed her sorrow and shock over Mack's disappearance. She was unaware of any specific problem he may have been having."

An innocuous statement, I thought, remembering the dictionary definition of the word "innocuous": "Pallid; uninspiring; without power to interest or excite."

The few words she and Mack had exchanged on the tape suggested they had had a warm relationship. Had Esther Klein been deliberately evasive when she was talking to Reeves? And if so, why?

It was a question that made me toss and turn in bed that night. Monday morning couldn't come fast enough for me. I took the chance that Aaron Klein was one of those executives who gets to his desk early, and at twenty of nine phoned Wallace and Madison and asked for him.

His secretary had the usual question: "What is this in reference to?" and seemed miffed when I said it was personal, but when she gave Aaron Klein my name, he took my call immediately.

As briefly as I could, I explained to him that I did not want to upset Elliott or my mother by continuing to search for my brother, but that I had come across a tape of Mack and Aaron's mother, and could I possibly meet him outside the office to play it for him?

His response was warm and understanding. "Elliott told me that your brother phoned on Mother's Day last week and left a note saying that you were not to search for him."

"Exactly," I said. "Which is why I want to keep this between us. But the tape that I found may suggest that Mack was having a problem. I don't know how much your mother may have talked to you about him."

"She was very fond of Mack," Klein said swiftly. "I do understand why you don't want to involve Elliott and your mother. I've always been so sorry about your brother. Listen, I'm leaving early today. My boys are in a school play this evening and I don't intend to miss it by being caught in traffic. I have all the tapes my mother made with her private students in a box in the attic. I'm sure any she made with your brother are there. Would you want to drive up to my house at about five o'clock this evening? I'll give them all to you."

Of course I promptly agreed. I called down to the garage and told the attendant I'd be picking up my mother's car. I knew it would be hurtful to hear Mack's voice over and over again, but at least if I could be reasonably sure that the tape I found in the suitcase was one of many in that vein, it would end the gnawing fear that he disappeared because he had a terrible problem he could not share with us.

Satisfied that I had made the connection, I made a fresh pot of coffee and turned on the morning news, then listened with a sinking heart to the latest report on the Leesey Andrews case. Someone had tipped a reporter at the *Post* that she had phoned her father Saturday and had promised to call again on Mother's Day.

ON MOTHER'S DAY!

My cell phone rang. Every instinct told me that it was Detective Barrott. I did not answer, and a moment later when I checked my messages, I heard his voice. "Ms. MacKenzie, I'd like to see you again as soon as possible. My number is . . ."

I disconnected, my heart racing. I had his number, and I had no intention of calling him back until after I saw Aaron Klein.

At five o'clock that evening, when I arrived at the Klein home in Darien, I walked into a firestorm. After I rang the bell, the door was opened by an attractive woman in her late thirties who introduced herself as Aaron's wife, Jenny. The strained expression on her face told me that something was terribly wrong.

She brought me into the den. Aaron Klein was on his knees on the rug, surrounded by overturned boxes. Stacks of tapes had been separated in individual piles. There must have been three hundred of them at least.

Aaron's face was deathly pale. When he saw me, he got up slowly. He looked past me to his wife. "Jenny, they are absolutely not here, not one of them."

"But it doesn't make sense, Aaron," she protested. "Why would—?"

He interrupted her and looked at me, his expression hostile. "I have never been satisfied that my mother was the victim of a random crime," he said flatly. "At the time, it didn't seem as if anything had been taken from her apartment, but that isn't true. There is not a single tape of your brother's lessons with her here, and I know there were at least twenty of them, and I know they were there after he disappeared. The only person who would want them would be your brother."

"I don't understand," I said, sinking into the nearest chair.

"I now believe my mother was killed because someone had to get something from her apartment. The person who killed her took her house key. At the time, I couldn't find anything missing. But there *was* something taken—the box that contained all the tapes she had made of your brother."

"But your mother was attacked nearly a year after Mack disappeared," I said. "Why would he want them? What use would they be to him?" Then, suddenly outraged, I demanded, "What are you insinuating?"

"I'm not insinuating," Aaron Klein snapped at me. "I am telling you that I now believe that your missing brother may have been responsible for my mother's death! There may have been something incriminating in those tapes." He pointed out the window. "There is a girl from Greenwich who has been missing all week. I don't know her, but if the newscast I heard coming up here in the car is accurate, she called her father and promised to call again next Mother's Day. Isn't *that* the day of choice for your brother to call? No wonder he warned you not to try to find him."

I stood up. "My brother is not a killer. He is not a predator. When the truth is known, Mack will not be responsible for whatever happened to your mother and Leesey Andrews."

I walked out, got into the car, and began to drive home. I guess I was in such a state of shock that I was on some kind of mental autopilot, because my next clear memory is of pulling up in front of our building on Sutton Place—and seeing Detective Barrott waiting for me in the lobby.

30

Oh, come on, Poppa. You're not really mad at me. You know I love you." Steve Hockney's tone was wheedling as he sat across the table from his elderly uncle, Derek Olsen. He had collected Olsen at his apartment and taken him by cab to Shun Lee West on Sixty-fifth Street for dinner. "We're having the best Chinese food in New York. So we're celebrating your birthday a few weeks late. Maybe we'll celebrate it all year."

Steve saw that he was getting the reaction he wanted. The anger was disappearing from his uncle's eyes and an unwilling smile was hovering around his lips. I've got to be more careful, Hockney warned himself. Forgetting his birthday was the stupidest thing I've done in a long time.

"You're lucky I don't throw you out of your apartment and make you support yourself for a change," Olsen muttered, but without rancor. It always surprised him, the swift rush of emotion he felt when he was with his dead sister's handsome son. It's because he looks so much like Irma, Olsen reminded himself—the same dark hair and big brown eyes, the same wonderful smile. Flesh of my flesh, he thought, as he took a bite of steamed dumplings Steve had ordered for him. It was delicious. "These are good," he said. "You take me to nice places all the time. I must be giving you too much money."

"No you're not, Poppa. I've been doing a lot of gigs downtown. My big break is just around the corner. You're going to be so proud of me. Think about it. My band is going to be the next Rolling Stones."

"I've been hearing that since you were twenty. How old are you now? Forty-two?"

Hockney smiled. "Thirty-six and you know it."

Olsen laughed. "I know I know it. But listen to me: I still think you should take over running the apartments. Howie gets on my nerves sometimes. He irritates people. I would have fired him today, except that the Kramers changed their minds about leaving, thank God."

"The Kramers? They'll never leave New York! Their daughter made them buy that place in Pennsylvania, and I'll tell you why. She doesn't want her parents to be superintendents. Hurts her image with her dreary, stuck-up friends."

"Well, Howie talked them into staying, but you should think about getting a lot more involved in the business."

Oh, please! Steve Hockney thought. Then he suppressed the feeling of irritation. Be careful, he warned himself again, be very careful. I'm his only living relative, but with his moods he could leave everything to charity, or even give a big cut to Howie. This week he's mad at him. Next week he'll be telling me that nobody runs his business like Howie, that he's like a son to him.

He took a couple of bites, then said, "Well, Poppa, I've been thinking that I should be more of a help to you. Look at all you do for me. Maybe the next time you make the rounds of the buildings, I should go along with you and Howie. I'd really like to do that."

"You really would?" Derek Olsen's tone was sharp, his eyes focused on his nephew's face. Then, satisfied with what he saw, he said, "You mean it. I can tell."

"Of course I mean it. Why do I call you 'Poppa'? You took over being my father when I was two years old, after all."

"I warned your mother not to marry that man. He was a no-good. Dishonest, conniving. When you were in your teens, I was afraid you'd end up just like him. Thank God you straightened yourself out. With some help from me."

Steve Hockney smiled appreciatively, then reached into his pocket and took out a small box. He put it on the table and slid it across to his uncle. "Happy Birthday, Poppa."

Ignoring the last steamed dumpling, Olsen quickly untied the ribbon, tore the birthday wrapping paper, and opened the box. It was a Montblanc pen with his initials engraved on the gold clip. A pleased smile brightened his face. "How did you know I lost my good pen?" he asked.

"The last time I saw you, you were using a cheap giveaway. It wasn't that hard to make the deduction."

The waiter arrived with a platter of mandarin duck. For the rest of the dinner, Steve Hockney carefully directed the conversation to reminiscences of his late mother, and how she had always said that her big brother was the smartest, nicest man she'd ever known. "When Mom was sick, she told me that all she ever wanted me to do was to be just like you."

He was rewarded with the sight of sentimental tears filling his uncle's eyes.

When dinner was over, Hockney hailed a cab and deposited his uncle at home, not leaving him until he was inside his apartment. "Double-lock the door," he cautioned, with a final affectionate hug. As soon as the click confirmed that Olsen had followed instructions, he rushed downstairs, and with rapid steps hurried to his own apartment, ten blocks away.

Inside, he ripped off his jacket and slacks and shirt and tie, and changed into dungarees and a sweatshirt. Time to check out SoHo, he told himself. God, I thought I'd go nuts sitting with that old man for so long.

His ground-floor apartment had a private entrance. When he went out, he looked around, and, as he often did, thought of the previous resident, the drama teacher who had been murdered on the street, only a block away.

That other place I had was the pits, he thought. But after the teacher's death, Poppa was glad to let me have this. I convinced him that people are superstitious. He agreed with me that it was better not to rent it while her death was still in the news. That was nine years ago. By now, who remembered?

I'm never going to leave it, he swore to himself. It suits my purposes exactly, and there are no damn security cameras to keep track of me.

31

Detective Barrott had one good reason for tracking me down. He wanted the note that Mack had left in the collection basket. I had left it in Mack's file in my father's office. I invited Barrott to come upstairs with me, and he followed me into the apartment.

I was deliberately rude, leaving him standing in the foyer while I went for the note. It was still wrapped in the plastic sandwich bag. I took it out and studied it. Ten words in block letters. "UNCLE DEVON, TELL CAROLYN SHE MUST NOT LOOK FOR ME."

How could I be sure that Mack had printed those words?

The paper appeared to be unevenly cut from a larger sheet. When I offered it to Barrott last Monday, he hadn't been interested. He'd said that it had probably been handled by at least one usher, my uncle, my mother, and myself. I don't remember if I told him I had shown it to Elliott as well. Was there any chance that Mack's fingerprints were still on it?

I put it back in the plastic and brought it out to Barrott. He was speaking on his cell phone. When he saw me coming down the hall, he ended the conversation. I had hoped that he would simply take the note and leave, but instead he said, "Ms. MacKenzie, I need to talk with you."

Let me stay calm, I prayed, as I led him into the living room. My knees suddenly felt weak, and I sat in the big Queen Anne wing chair that had been Dad's favorite spot in this room. I glanced up at the portrait of him my mother had had painted, still hanging over the mantelpiece. The wing chair faced the fireplace, and Dad used to joke that when he sat in it, he did nothing but admire himself. "My God, Liv, cast your eyes on that grand-looking devil," he would say. "How much extra did you pay the painter to make me look that good?"

Sitting in Dad's chair somehow gave me courage. Detective Barrott sat on the edge of the couch and looked at me, without a hint of warmth. "Ms. MacKenzie, I've just been told that Aaron Klein, of Darien, Connecticut, has called our office and told us he believes your brother is the person who murdered his mother nine years ago. He said that he always felt that whoever killed her wanted something in her apartment. He now is convinced it was the tapes with your brother's voice. He said you told him you were bringing up a tape to play for him. Do you have that tape?"

I felt as if he had dashed freezing water in my face. I knew how that tape would sound to him. He and everyone else in the District Attorney's office would decide that Mack had been in big trouble and had confided in Esther Klein. I grasped the arms of the wing chair. "My father was a lawyer as I am," I told Barrott, "and before I say another word or give you anything, I am going to consult a lawyer."

"Ms. MacKenzie, I want to tell you something," Barrott said. "As of Saturday morning, Leesey Andrews was still alive. There is nothing more important than finding her, if it isn't already too late. You must have heard the news reports that she phoned her father two days ago and told him she'd call again next Mother's Day. You must surely agree that it defies belief that it's just a coincidence she is following— or being *forced* to follow—your brother's modus operandi."

"It wasn't a secret that Mack phones on Mother's Day," I protested. "Other people knew about it. A year after Mack disappeared, a reporter wrote an article about him and mentioned it. All that's on the Internet, for anyone who wants to look it up."

"It isn't on the Internet that after your brother's drama teacher was murdered, all the tapes of his voice were stolen from her apartment," Barrott shot back. He gave me a stern look. "Ms. MacKenzie, if there is something on the tape you are holding that might in any way help us to find your brother, your sense of decency ought to compel you to give it to me now."

"I won't give you the tape," I said. "But I *will* swear to you that there is nothing on it that would give you any idea of where Mack might be. I'll go further. The tape is less than a minute long. Mack says a few words to his drama teacher and then starts to recite a passage from Shakespeare. That is it."

I think Barrott believed me. He nodded. "If you do hear from him," he said, "or if something occurs to you that might help us find him, I hope you will keep in mind that Leesey Andrews's life is far more important than trying to protect your brother."

When Barrott left, I did the one thing I knew I had to do immediately—call Aaron Klein's boss, Elliott Wallace, my father's best friend, my surrogate uncle, my mother's suitor, and tell him that by violating our agreement to accept Mack's wishes, I had made my brother a suspect in both a murder and a kidnapping.

32

Nick DeMarco had spent an uneasy weekend. He did not want to admit to himself how unsettling it had been to see Carolyn again. "Pizza and Pasta" had been his code name for himself when he used to have dinner at the MacKenzie home on Sutton Place.

I had zero social graces, he remembered. I was always watching to see what fork they used, how they placed their napkins on their laps. Pop tucked his under his chin. Even hearing Mr. MacKenzie joke about his own working-class background didn't do it for me. I thought he was just being a nice guy trying to help an awkward idiot feel welcome.

And that crush I had on Barbara? When I look back, it was just one more way in which I was jealous of Mack.

It wasn't about her at all.

It was about Carolyn.

I always felt comfortable with her. She was always funny and sharp. I enjoyed being with her the other night.

Mack's family was my snobby ideal. I loved my own mom and dad, but I wished Dad didn't wear suspenders. I wished Mom didn't give a bear hug to all the regular customers. What's that saying? Something like "Our children begin by loving us; as they grow up they judge us; sometimes they forgive us."

It should be the other way around. "Parents start out by loving us, as we grow up they judge us. Sometimes they forgive us." But not often.

I hadn't wanted Pop to have a storefront anymore. I didn't know what I was doing to him when I put him in charge of my new restaurant. He was miserable. Mom missed being in the kitchen, too. Their high-class son wouldn't let them be who they are.

Nick DeMarco, the big success, voted bachelor of the month, the guy the girls chased, he thought, with an edge of bitterness. Nick De-Marco, the big risk-taker. And now maybe it's Nick DeMarco, the fool who took one chance too many.

Leesey Andrews.

Did anyone hear me offer to help her get a start in show business? It wasn't on the camera when I gave her the card with my address, but did anyone happen to see me slide it over to her?

33

On Tuesday morning, Captain Larry Ahearn and Detective Bob Gaylor, both relatively fresh from six hours' sleep, were back in the tech room of the District Attorney's office, reviewing security tapes from the three other nightclubs in which young women had last been seen before they disappeared.

The cases of all three young women, Emily Valley, Rosemarie Cummings, and Virginia Trent, had been reopened. The grainy photos from Emily Valley's case, now ten years old, had been sharpened and brightened by the latest in cutting-edge technology. In the crowd of students who had entered the club, named The Scene, it was possible to identify clearly Mack MacKenzie and Nick DeMarco.

"When we started looking for Emily Valley, all those Columbia kids came forward in a group after we contacted the ones who signed with credit cards," Ahearn commented, thinking aloud. "It was only a month or so after we talked to all of them that the MacKenzie boy disappeared. Looking back, maybe we should have treated that disappearance as suspicious and tied it to the Valley case."

"He doesn't show up in any security videos of the clubs where the other missing girls were hanging out. Of course, it was three years later that the Cummings girl vanished, and the Trent girl was four years ago. In all that time, he could have changed his appearance a lot. He was heavy into dramatics in prep school *and* in college," Gaylor pointed out.

"I'd have sworn that DeMarco is our guy, but the missing tapes from the drama teacher's apartment and the reference to Mother's Day throw it back into Mack MacKenzie's court," Ahearn said, frustration in his tone and on his face. "How has he managed to hide for ten years? What is he living on? How can he be moving between Brooklyn and Manhattan carrying her cell phone without somebody spotting him? Every cop in New York has an age-enhanced picture of him. And where did he keep Leesey from the time she disappeared till the time she made that call Saturday? And if she's still alive, where is he keeping her now?"

"And what is he *doing* to her?" Roy Barrott asked bitterly.

Neither of his associates had heard him come into the tech room. They both looked up, startled.

"You're supposed to be home getting some sleep," Ahearn said.

Barrott shook his head. "I did. I got as much as I need anyway. Listen, I just stopped at the tech room. They finished enhancing the two pictures that Leesey's roommate, Kate, took of her, including the one we used on the poster. She took these two pictures less than a minute after she snapped pictures of Angelina Jolie and Brad Pitt and their kids. We can now see the faces of the people in the background."

"And what did you find?" Ahearn asked.

"Look at *this* picture. See if you recognize the guy on the left."

"It's DeMarco!" Ahearn said, then repeated it as if he could not believe what he was seeing. "DeMarco!"

"Exactly," Barrott confirmed. "DeMarco never told us he had been in Greenwich Village a week before Leesey disappeared and was across the street when Kate took her picture. He also told us that when he isn't using his SUV, he drives a Mercedes convertible. There wasn't any mention of his chauffeur-driven Mercedes sedan."

Ahearn stood up. "I think it's time we invite this guy back for some more questioning and squeeze him real hard," he said. "It would have been easy for him to have his chauffeur get Leesey out of his loft apartment in the middle of the night and hide her somewhere. Our guys keep coming up with new stuff on him. DeMarco's bought a lot of property, with not much money down. He's on thin ice, financially. If he loses the liquor license from that fancy new Woodshed place, he could end up back in Queens running a pasta joint." Ahearn looked at Bob Gaylor. "Bring him in."

"Ten to one he'll have a lawyer with him," Barrott snapped. "I'm surprised he took a chance on coming in alone last week."

34

Mother was scheduled to fly home from Greece on Wednesday, and my anxiety was mounting. Elliott had come over after my frantic phone call to him on Monday evening to calm me down. There was something intensely comforting to me about the way he took everything that I had to tell him, including the fact that Aaron Klein, his designated successor at Wallace and Madison, now believed that Mack was responsible for his mother's death.

"That's absolute nonsense," Elliott said emphatically. "Aaron forgets he told me at the time nothing had been taken from her apartment. I remember his words clearly—'Why would someone have killed my mother, stolen her key, and not bothered to rob the apartment?' I told him that whoever killed her was probably a drug addict who panicked when he realized she was dead. Aaron has been fixated on trying to find someone to blame for his mother's death for ages, but I'll be damned if he's going to try to pin it on Mack."

There was nothing formal or reserved about Elliott's heated response. Dad himself could not have been more vehement. I think that was the moment when any hesitation I felt about the growing closeness between Mom and Elliott disappeared for good. It was also the moment when I decided to drop "Uncle" and call him Elliott.

We agreed that it was inevitable I would be called in for questioning about Mack and that we had to hire a defense lawyer. "I will not allow Mack to be tried and convicted in the newspapers," Elliott swore. "I'll search around and get the best person I can find."

We also agreed that we had to let Mom know what was going on. "It won't be long before an enterprising reporter links Mack's disappearance with that of the missing girl, because of the reference to Mother's Day," Elliott decided. "Worse yet, I wouldn't put it past the detectives to leak it to the media deliberately. Your mother must *not* look as if she's hiding from them."

Elliott made the call and suggested gently that she head home early. By the time Mom got home on Wednesday evening, everything Elliott had predicted had come to pass. The media, like bloodhounds on a fresh scent, had effectively reopened the cases of the other three young women who had disappeared from nightclubs, and reported the fact that Mack and his college friends had been present at the Scene the night the first girl, Emily Valley, vanished. The Mother's Day connection between Mack's routine phone calls and Leesey Andrews's message to her father was also headline news, of course.

Mom, Elliott's arm around her firmly, had to fight her way past the cameras and microphones when she and Elliott arrived at Sutton Place. Her greeting to me was exactly what I expected but hoped wouldn't happen. Circles under eyes that were swollen with weeping, for the first time looking every day of her sixty-two years, my mother said, "Carolyn, we agreed to let Mack live his own life. Now because of your meddling, my son is being hunted down like a criminal. Elliott has very kindly offered me the hospitality of his home. My bags are still in his car, and I intend to go there. In the meantime, you can contend with the mess out on the streets and make your apologies to our neighbors for destroying *their* privacy. Before I go I want to hear that tape."

Quietly I retrieved the tape, then sat with her in the kitchen and played it for her. Mack's voice, joking with his drama teacher, "Do I sound like Laurence Olivier or Tom Hanks?"—then—the dramatic change in his tone when he began to recite the Shakespeare quote.

When I turned it off, Mom's face was pale with grief. "There was something wrong," she whispered. "Why didn't he come to me? Nothing could have been so bad that I wouldn't have helped him." Then she reached out her hand to me. "Give me the tape, Carolyn," she said.

"Mom, I can't," I said. "I wouldn't be surprised if we get a subpoena for it. You think it means Mack was in trouble. Another explanation is that he was simply reading a drama assignment. Elliott and I are meeting tomorrow morning with a criminal defense lawyer. I need to have it with me to play for him."

Without another word, my mother turned from me. Elliott whispered, "I'll call you later," before he rushed down the hall after her. When they were gone, I turned on the tape again. ". . . I all alone beweep my outcast state, and trouble deaf heaven with my bootless cries—"

Mack may have been acting, or he might have been talking about himself, but with a combination of pain and bitterness, I thought that now those words were fully applicable to me. A couple of minutes later, the apartment phone rang. As I picked it up and said, "Hello," whoever was on the other end hung up.

35

He couldn't get enough of the new media stories about the other three girls, Emily, Rosemarie, and Virginia. He remembered them all so clearly. Emily had been the first. The newspapers hadn't made too much of her disappearance at the beginning. She had been a runaway, so when she once again didn't come home to Trenton, New Jersey, even her parents conceded it was possible she had simply chosen to disappear.

But when Rosemarie went missing three years later, they began to think it was possible Emily had been abducted. Then, when Virginia vanished four years ago, the media had a field day connecting the three of them.

Of course, it didn't last. Every so often some would-be Pulitzer Prize winner would write a feature story linking the three young women, but with nothing new to report, the public's interest dropped to zero.

Leesey had changed all that. "Mack, where are you now?" was the question on everyone's lips.

Dressed in a hooded running suit and wearing dark glasses, he was jogging on Sutton Place. As he expected, it was crowded with media vans. Wonderful, he thought, wonderful. He removed the small metal box from his pocket, unsnapped it, and took out Leesey's cell phone. Now when he dialed, they'd be able to pinpoint his location as being around here. But that's what I want, isn't it? he asked himself with a smile, as he dialed the phone number of the apartment, waited to hear Carolyn answer the call, then disconnected. Then, quickening his pace, he disappeared into the brisk pedestrian traffic on Fifty-seventh Street.

36

Bruce Galbraith and his wife, Dr. Barbara Hanover Galbraith, had, so far as possible, avoided talking about Mack MacKenzie. But finally, on Wednesday evening, after the children were in bed and they had finished watching the ten o'clock news, Bruce knew he had to raise the subject.

They were in the library of their spacious Park Avenue apartment. Whenever Bruce was away on a business trip, the realization of how happy he was in his home and with his family hit him afresh. Barbara had changed to light green pajamas and unpinned her ash blond hair so that it fell loose on her shoulders. He had long since passed the days when he felt clumsy and awkward in her presence, but even so, the sense that he might one day wake up and find he'd been dreaming, that life as he knew it was an illusion, always lingered in his subconscious.

He had witnessed the growing tension in Barbara for the past few days since the media began linking Mack to the disappearance of Leesey Andrews, the girl from Connecticut, and then to the murder of the drama teacher.

During the broadcast, with the jealousy he had never overcome, Bruce had watched his wife's face when pictures of Mack were flashed on the screen. After he pushed the power button on the remote and watched the screen turn dark, he knew it was time to discuss what needed to be done.

"Barb," he said, "I was in the nightclub the night that first girl disappeared."

"I know, but so were twenty other guys from Columbia, including Nick and Mack," Barbara said, avoiding his eyes.

"Carolyn MacKenzie called me, but I haven't returned her call. I'll bet anything that she follows up on it. As the police investigation widens, it's inevitable they'll look me up. Nick and I were Mack's roommates, after all."

He watched as his wife tried to force back tears. "What are you driving at?" she asked, her voice unsteady.

"I think you and the kids should visit your father in Martha's Vineyard. He's had three heart attacks. No one would question it if you tell people he's in bad shape again."

"What about school?"

"For what we're paying, we can arrange to get lesson plans and a private tutor. The school year is over in a few weeks' time anyhow."

He saw the uncertainty on his wife's face. "Barbara, you joined a practice with two other pediatric surgeons so you'd have a measure of control over your personal life. I would say this is a time to assert that control."

He got up, walked over to her, bent down, and kissed the top of her head. "I could kill Mack for what he did to you," he said quietly.

"I'm over it, Bruce. I really am."

No you're not, he thought. But I've learned to live with that, and there's no way on God's earth I'll let Mack hurt you again.

37

On Wednesday evening, shortly after Mom and Elliott left, Detective Barrott phoned. I had thought that things couldn't get much worse, but I was wrong. Barrott quietly asked if I knew that the call I had just received, that I had thought was a wrong number, had been made from Leesey Andrews's cell phone. I was so shocked that I think it was a full minute before I said something like, "But that's impossible." I paused to digest the fact. "That's absolutely impossible."

Barrott curtly assured me that it was true and did I think it was my brother trying to reach me?

"When I answered it, someone hung up. I thought it had to be a wrong number. Can't you *tell* that I didn't speak to anyone?" I asked him angrily.

"We know that. We also know that this is an unlisted phone in your home, Ms. MacKenzie. Make no mistake. If your brother is the one who has Leesey's phone, and if he tries again to contact you and you do *not* help us find him, you could become an accessory to a very serious crime."

I didn't answer him. I simply broke off the connection.

Sometime between four and seven A.M. on Thursday morning, I decided to phone Lucas Reeves and ask to meet with him as soon as possible. I needed help from someone I could trust to be thorough and impartial. I had already seen, from studying his file on Mack, that he had done a good job interviewing seemingly every possible person who had been close to my brother. The opinion he had given Dad was very clear. "There is nothing in your son's background that would suggest he was experiencing a problem that would cause him to flee. I would not rule out the possibility of a mental illness that he had successfully concealed from everyone."

Elliott and I were meeting at noon at the office of Thurston Carver, the criminal defense lawyer whom Elliott had found to represent us. At nine A.M., I phoned Reeves. He was not in yet, but his secretary promised he would call me back as soon as he arrived. It was obvious that she recognized my name. A half hour later, he returned the call. As briefly as possible, I explained what had happened. "Is there any chance you could see me this morning?" I asked, hearing the desperation in my voice.

His voice was deep and resonant as he answered. "I'll rearrange my schedule. Where is your meeting with the lawyer?"

"On Park and Forty-fifth" I said, "the MetLife Building."

"My phone number is the same, but I moved my office two years ago. I'm on Park Avenue and Thirty-ninth Street, just a few blocks down from MetLife. Can you be here at ten thirty?"

Yes, I could. I was already showered and dressed. The unpredictable weather had served up another blustery day. Looking out the window at people wearing jackets and keeping their hands in their pockets, I changed from the light suit I had planned to wear to a velour running suit, which made me look less like a lawyer and more like somebody's sister. I won't say that it flattered me. It was dark gray, and when I looked in the mirror I could see that it brought out the circles under my eyes and the unusual paleness of my skin. I don't usually bother with much makeup during the day, but I took the time to use foundation, a touch of eye shadow, blush, mascara, and lip gloss. All tarted up in defense of my brother, I thought, then hated the bitterness in my thinking.

If only I had not gone to see Detective Barrott. If only I had not found the tape in Mack's suitcase. Useless thoughts.

I could feel the beginning of a headache, and even though I wasn't hungry, I went down to the kitchen, made a pot of coffee, and toasted an English muffin. I carried it to the breakfast alcove and sat at the table, gazing at the spectacular view of the East River. Thanks to the strong breeze, the current was visibly swift, and I found myself identifying with it. I was being carried by a current I could not fight, and I had to let it take me along until it either overwhelmed or re-leased me.

I had been glad that Mom was in Greece for those few days and I had the apartment to myself. But that was when she was supposed to be somewhere else. It was incredible to me that she was in New York and not staying in her own home, but when I left the apartment, I understood why. The media trucks were there in full force, and reporters rushed to me looking for a statement. This is what happened to her last night, I thought.

I had phoned down to the doorman to hail a cab for me, and he had one waiting. Ignoring the microphones, I jumped into it and said, "Start driving." I didn't want anyone to overhear my destination. Twenty minutes later, I was in the reception room of Lucas Reeves's office. Promptly at ten thirty, he escorted a tense-looking couple, whom I guessed to be other clients, to the outer door, looked around, and came over to me. "Ms. MacKenzie, come right in."

I only remember meeting him once, when he came to Sutton Place ten years ago, so either he remembered my face or, since I was the only one in the waiting room, he assumed I was Carolyn MacKenzie.

Lucas Reeves was even shorter than I remembered. I don't think he was more than five feet four with shoes on. He had a thick head of wiry salt-and-pepper hair that had clearly been dyed to give the illusion of natural graying. His face was creased with small lines around the mouth which suggested to me that he almost certainly had been a serious smoker. His deep, pleasant voice was incongruous coming from such a small man, but it matched the warmth in his eyes and his hearty handshake.

I followed him into his private office. Instead of going to his desk, he led me to a seating area with two chairs, a couch, and a coffee table. "I don't know about you, Ms. MacKenzie," he began, as he waved me to one of the chairs, "but for me it's time for midmorning coffee. How about you? Or, like my British friends, would you prefer a cup of tea?"

"Black coffee would be perfect," I said.

"That's two of us."

The receptionist opened the door and poked her head in. "What'll it be, Mr. Reeves?"

"Two black. Thanks, Marge." Turning to me, he said, "In this day and age of political correctness, I started to make the coffee myself in our little kitchen. My assistant, my secretary, my receptionist, and my accountant bodily threw me out. They said my coffee would peel the paint from a wall."

I was so grateful for his attempt to put me at ease that I felt quick tears rush to my eyes. He pretended not to notice. I had offered to bring Mack's file with me, but he had said he had a duplicate of it. His was on the coffee table. He pointed to it. "Bring me up to date, Carolyn." His eyes never left my face as I explained how, because of me, Mack had become a suspect in both the Leesey Andrews and Esther Klein cases.

"And now they think Mack has Leesey's cell phone. Sure, we have a private number, but it's been the same one since I was a child. Hundreds of people know it." I bit my lip. It was quivering so much I could not go on. The thought flashed through my mind that the reason Mom wanted to stay in the apartment all these years was to be sure she'd never miss a call from Mack.

Listening to me, Reeves's expression had become increasingly troubled. "I am afraid your brother is a very convenient suspect, Carolyn. I will be honest. I could see no reason why a twenty-one-year-old man with his background would choose to disappear. Quite frankly, in the last few days, with all the media attention on him, I have been studying his file and doing some follow-up, purely for my own satisfaction. Your father paid me generously, and I could give him absolutely no help in solving your brother's disappearance."

He looked past me. "Ah, here is the coffee I did not prepare." He waited until the cups were on the table and we were alone again before he continued. "Now I am looking at it from the viewpoint of the police. The night the first girl disappeared, your brother was at that club, The Scene. But so were his two roommates, other Columbia students, and about fifteen more patrons. It was a small club, but there were also, of course, a bartender, some waiters, and a small musical group. That list, as complete as I could make it, is there in your brother's file. Since the police now believe your brother may be involved in that first disappearance, let us think like them. With technology, it is increasingly easy to follow people's lives. I am proud to say that this agency has a technical system second to none. We will begin to update our knowledge of everyone we know to have been in that club ten years ago when all of this started."

He took a sip of his coffee. "Excellent. Strength without bitterness. Admirable qualities, don't you agree?"

I wondered if that was an admonition. Had he sensed my growing bitterness toward Mack, and even, I admitted to myself, to my mother?

He didn't wait for an answer. "You said you felt that the superintendents, the Kramers, might have something to hide?"

"I don't know whether they have something to hide," I said. "I do know that they seemed terribly nervous, almost as if they were being accused of knowing something about Mack's disappearance."

"I interviewed them ten years ago. I'll have my staff check to see if there was anything out of the ordinary in their lives that might be of use for us to know. Now tell me about Nicholas DeMarco. Trust me with any slight nuance that you may have received from him, either positive or negative."

I wanted to be objective. "Nick is obviously ten years older now." I said. "He's more mature, of course. At age sixteen, I had a crush on him, so I don't know that I could possibly have judged him honestly. He was handsome, he was fun, looking back I think he was flirting with me, and I was young enough to think that I was special to him. Mack warned me away from Nick, and after that, the few times he came to dinner I made it a point to be out with my friends."

"Mack warned you away?" Reeves raised an eyebrow.

"Big-brother stuff. I guess I was wearing my heart on my sleeve and Mack said that all the girls fell for Nick. Other than that, I would say that when I saw him last, I had the feeling that Nick seemed like someone with a lot on his mind."

"Did you talk with him about the other roommate in that apartment, Bruce Galbraith?"

"Yes. Nick is out of touch with him. Frankly, I don't think he liked Bruce very much. He even called him 'the Lone Stranger.' I told you I left a message asking to meet with Bruce, but so far he hasn't responded."

"Call him again. I doubt that with all the media attention your brother is getting, Bruce Galbraith would ignore your request to see him. In the meantime, I'll get started immediately on updating our files on the others. Because of the reference to Mother's Day, the police were already trying to tie Mack to the disappearance of Leesey Andrews, and by extension to the disappearance of all those young women. Now that call to your home from Leesey's cell phone will make them certain of his guilt. Every clue leads conveniently back to

Mack. I am beginning to wonder if everything that has happened began that night in The Scene, weeks before Mack disappeared."

I pounced on that. "Mr. Reeves, are you saying that someone else may be deliberately trying to tie Mack to the disappearance of those four women?"

"I think it's possible. As you yourself said, there was a feature article some years ago that made public the fact that your brother only calls on Mother's Day. Who knows if someone did not tuck that piece of information in his mind and is now using it to deflect suspicion from himself? There are all kinds of identity theft. Following the known pattern of someone who has vanished and chooses not to defend himself may be one of them. Leesey's abductor has her cell phone. He may also have your unlisted number."

It was a possibility that made sense. When I left Reeves's office, I felt that this time I had come to the right person, somebody who would search for the truth without the preconceived notion that Mack had become a killer.

38

Accompanied by his lawyer, Paul Murphy, Nick DeMarco returned to the Detective Squad section of the District Attorney's office on Thursday afternoon. This time, the atmosphere in Captain Ahearn's office was openly hostile. There were no handshakes, no brief expression of thanks that he had promptly responded to the phone call requesting his presence as soon as possible.

But Nick had other problems on his mind. Early Tuesday morning, after a frantic call from his mother that his father was being rushed to the hospital with chest pains, Nick had flown to Florida. By the time he got there, the tests had so far been negative, but his father had been kept in the hospital to guard against the possibility that he was building up to a heart attack. When Nick entered the hospital room, his mother had rushed into his arms and hugged him fiercely. "Oh, Nick, I thought we had lost him," she cried.

His father, an older image of himself, propped up on pillows, his face pale, an oxygen tube in his nostrils and an IV drip in his hand, was clearly unhappy. "Nick, I hate hospitals," was his greeting, "but maybe it isn't such a bad thing this happened after all. In the ambulance, I was thinking about things I wish I'd said to you, only your mother wouldn't let me say them. Now you're going to hear them. I'm sixty-eight years old. I've been working since I was fourteen. For the first time in my life, I feel useless, and I don't like it."

"Dad, I bought a restaurant for you to run," Nick protested. "*You're* the one who decided to retire."

"Sure, you bought a restaurant here, but you should have known it wasn't right for me. I was a round peg in a square hole in that place. It made me sick to see you bleeding money with your fancy overhead and pricey food. I've seen these places come and go. Do yourself a favor and sell that one, or else put some staples on the menu that people can count on when they don't want fois gras and caviar."

"Dominick, don't excite yourself," his mother pleaded.

"I *have* to excite myself. I've got to get this off my chest before I *do* have a heart attack. Bachelor of the Month! It was disgusting to watch how pleased you were. You'd think you got the Congressional Medal of Honor. While I'm still around to tell you, cut it out."

"Dad, I hear you. And believe it or not, I'm listening this time. Tell me, what do you want? What can I do to make you happy?"

"I don't want to play golf and I don't want to sit in a pricey condominium where I might get beaned by a golf ball because we're next to the sixteenth hole."

"Dad, all that's easy to take care of. What else?"

Nick had not yet gotten over the look of scorn in his father's eyes. "You're thirty-two years old. Get real. Be the son we were so proud of. Stop running around with the women you meet in clubs. In fact, get out of the club business! You'll get in trouble. Find yourself a nice girl. Your mother and I are pushing seventy. We were married fifteen years before God sent us a son. Don't make us wait fifteen years from now to have a grandchild."

All this was going through Nick's mind as he and his attorney settled themselves in hard, uncomfortable chairs in front of Captain Ahearn's desk. Detectives Barrott and Gaylor were seated on either side of the captain.

It's a firing squad, Nick thought. A glance at his attorney showed him that Murphy was having the same reaction.

"Mr. DeMarco," Ahearn began, "you didn't tell us you have a Mercedes 550 sedan which you only use when you are being driven by your chauffeur."

Nick frowned. "Wait a minute. If I'm right you asked about cars I drove. I never drive the sedan. It's either the convertible or the SUV when I'm on my own."

"You didn't mention your chauffeur, either."

"I wouldn't have thought there was a reason to mention him."

"We don't agree, Mr. DeMarco," Ahearn told him. "Particularly since your chauffeur, Benny Seppini, has an extensive criminal record."

Without looking at him, Nick knew what Paul Murphy was thinking. Why didn't my client tell me that?

"Benny is fifty-eight years old," Nick told Ahearn. "As a kid, he had no home life and became involved in a street gang while he was in his teens. When he was seventeen, he got sentenced as an adult to prison for burglary and served five years. When he got out, he started working for my father. That was thirty-five years ago. When my father retired five years ago, he began working for me. He is a decent, good man."

"Didn't his ex-wife get a restraining order on him ten years ago?" Ahearn snapped.

"Benny's first wife died young. His second was trying to get him to sign over their condo to her. That was a phony, trumped-up charge and she dropped it the minute she got the condo."

"Uh-huh. Mr. DeMarco, do you do much walking around Greenwich Village in the daytime?"

"Of course I don't. I'm a businessman."

"Did you ever see Leesey Andrews before Monday night a week ago?"

"To the best of my knowledge, absolutely not."

"Let me show you a picture we have of you, Mr. DeMarco." Ahearn nodded to Barrott, who shoved copies of the enhanced photographs Leesey's roommate had taken of her across the desk to Nick and Murphy.

"Recognize the fellow in the background of the second one, Mr. DeMarco?" Barrott asked.

"Of course that's me in the background," Nick snapped. "I remember that day. I was meeting a real estate agent for lunch. I'm interested in buying property in the area near where the old railroad tracks are being developed. Once that development starts, the surrounding property will go sky-high. I saw all the paparazzi in action and looked over to see what was going on. Brad Pitt and Angelina Jolie were there."

"Where were you having lunch?"

"At Casa Florenza, right around the corner from where the picture was taken."

"Then you claim you didn't see Leesey Andrews being photographed by her friend?"

"I not only claim, I *didn't* see her," Nick replied heatedly.

"Do you have the bill for that luncheon?" Gaylor asked in a tone that suggested he would be surprised to see one.

"No, I do not. The real estate broker is trying to sell me property, so he paid. If he succeeds, his commission will keep putting gas in his car for a long time."

"How long will you be able to continue putting gas in all *your* cars, Mr. DeMarco?" Ahearn asked. "You're stretched pretty thin financially, aren't you?"

"What do Mr. DeMarco's business affairs have to do with our presence here?" Paul Murphy demanded.

"Maybe nothing at all," Ahearn replied. "And maybe a great deal. If the state decides to cancel the liquor license of the Woodshed, I don't think your client will make a living selling Popsicles there. And trust me, we *will* find a reason to have it canceled if we even suspect that Mr. DeMarco is not being totally candid with us."

Ahearn turned to Nick. "Do you have the unlisted phone number of the MacKenzie home on Sutton Place?"

"Unless it's been changed, I'm sure I have it somewhere. I remember phoning Mrs. MacKenzie after her husband died on 9/11."

"Do you think Leesey Andrews is dead?"

"I certainly hope not. That would be a tragedy."

"Do you know if she's still alive?"

"What kind of unbelievable question is that?"

"We're out of here, Nick." Murphy was on his feet.

Ahearn ignored him. "Mr. DeMarco, do you own a cell phone that is not registered to you, one that uses a prepaid card, the kind gamblers and wiseguys use?"

"That's it! We're not going to listen to any more of your cheap insinuations," Murphy shouted.

It was as though Larry Ahearn had not heard him. "And does your troubled chauffeur have a similar phone, Mr. DeMarco? And if he does, did he respond to your frantic call to get Leesey out of your loft apartment? And if she wasn't already dead, did he decide to keep her around for his own amusement? And if that was the case, has he kept you informed as to her welfare?"

Nick, his fists clenched, was almost at the door when he heard Ahearn's final question. "Or are you protecting your college roommate Mack MacKenzie, or perhaps helping his pretty sister to protect him? You had a little tête-a-tête with her last Friday night, didn't you?"

39

After I left Lucas Reeves, I met Elliott at Thurston Carver's office in the MetLife Building. Instantly, I realized that I had seen Carver around court while I was clerking for Judge Huot. He was a big man with a mane of hair that I guessed to be prematurely white—I doubted that he was more than fifty-five years old.

I felt somewhat fortified by my meeting with Reeves, and told Carver the theory he had suggested to me. Mack was missing. That he called every year on Mother's Day was public knowledge, and whoever had kidnapped Leesey Andrews was trying to throw suspicion on Mack by the phone calls he was making.

Elliott, who looked tired and deeply concerned, seized on that possibility. He told me that last night my mother was so upset when they reached his apartment she broke down, crying and sobbing, to the extent that he was desperately worried about her now. "I realized last night that Olivia has always been sure that something must have snapped in Mack's mind to make him disappear like that," he explained to Carver. "Now she believes that if he *is* guilty of these disappearances, he may be completely insane and might end up being shot when the police find him."

"And she blames me," I said.

"Carolyn, she has to blame *someone*. That won't last. You know it won't."

You've been my rod and staff through all this. That's what Mom had said to me last week, after Mack's call on the morning of Mother's Day. I still had every faith that at some point she would understand why I had tried to bring Mack's situation to some kind of closure. In the meantime, she had Elliott to help her, and I realized how deeply grateful I was to him for being there for her now. No matter how this turned out, at that moment, sitting in the elegantly paneled office of Thurston Carver, I surrendered any jealousy I felt at the probability that Elliott would replace my father in my mother's life.

Later that day I called Bruce Galbraith. After I had waited for what seemed an eternity, he got on the phone and grudgingly agreed to meet me in his office on Friday afternoon. "I must tell you, Carolyn," he said, "I have neither seen nor heard from Mack since the day he disappeared. I can't imagine what you hope to learn from me."

I was chilled by the venom in his voice but did not give him the answer that was on the tip of my tongue. *I want to know why you hate Mack so much.*

On Friday afternoon I was ushered into Galbraith's office. It was on the sixty-third floor of his building on the Avenue of the Americas and offered sweeping views of the city. The only comparable view I can think of is from the Rainbow Room in Rockefeller Center.

My memory of Bruce was blurry. Dad and Mom had kept me away from the search for Mack when they were going back and forth to his apartment after he disappeared. I had a vague memory that Bruce had sandy hair and rimless glasses.

His greeting was cordial enough, and he chose to sit, not in what I think would be his usual chair, but in one of the two matching leather chairs on either side of his desk. He began by offering sympathy for the way the tabloids were tying Mack to the disappearance of Leesey Andrews. "I can only imagine what that is doing to your mother," he said. Then he added, after a pause, "And of course to you."

"Bruce," I said, "you can understand how desperate I am not only to find Mack, but whether I find him or not, to clear his name of any connection with the women who disappeared."

"I absolutely understand that," he said. "But the point is that Mack, Nick, and I merely shared an apartment. Mack and Nick were tight. They hung out together, they dated together. Nick was at your house for dinner a fair amount. He's a much better person to ask about Mack than I am. You might as well be talking to the rest of the graduating class at Columbia, for all I can tell you."

"What about Barbara?" I asked. "She came to dinner once. I thought she was Nick's girlfriend, but he told me she had a crush on Mack, then she married you after Mack disappeared. Have you ever talked with her about Mack? Would she have any idea what was in his mind before he vanished?"

"Barbara and I have of course talked about Mack with all this recent publicity. She is as bewildered as I am at the idea that he could be involved in any crime. She said that certainly isn't the person she knew."

His voice was calm, but I saw a deep flush creep up from his neck to his cheeks. He *does* hate Mack, I thought. Is it jealousy? And how far would that jealousy have carried him? He was so buttoned up, so contained, an ordinary-looking man, who, judging from his success, was an extraordinarily gifted real estate tycoon. An image of Mack, with his stunning good looks, his wonderful sense of humor, his ever-present charm flooded my mind.

I remembered having heard that Mack beat Galbraith out by a fraction to be in the top ten of the graduating class. That must have been a massive blow to Galbraith's ego, I thought. And after Mack disappeared, Barbara, the girl Nick said had been crazy about Mack, married Galbraith, maybe as her ticket to medical school. . . .

"I met Barbara at my house years ago," I said. "I'd appreciate a chance to talk with her."

"I'm afraid that isn't possible," Galbraith said flatly. "Her father is very ill. He lives on Martha's Vineyard. She flew up there with the children to be with him in his final weeks." He stood up, and I got the message the meeting was over. He walked me to the reception room, and I reached out to shake his hand. I didn't miss the way he rubbed his palm on his trouser leg before he reluctantly accepted mine. His was still sweaty and damp. A plain man in an expensive suit, his eyes shuttered.

I remembered that Nick had called him "the Lone Stranger."

40

If there was one person Lil Kramer disliked more than Howard Altman, it was Steve Hockney, Derek Olsen's nephew. That was why when he arrived unannounced on Friday morning, Lil felt thoroughly rattled. Howie's advice to her and Gus—that it would be unwise to rush to Pennsylvania as if they had something to hide—they had originally welcomed with gratitude. But she was totally aware of Olsen's shifting alliances between his nephew Steve and his assistant, Howie, and seeing Steve alone terrified her.

Howie is on the outs with Olsen, she thought, and Steve is going to take over. She was glad Gus had gone upstairs to change the filters in some of the air conditioners. He was in a foul mood after cleaning the staircase between the second and third floors. One of the college kids had spilled beer there during the night.

"They must have been dragging up a keg," he had grumbled minutes before Hockney arrived. "Spilled beer all over the whole flight. Wouldn't have killed them to have mopped it up themselves."

It's a good thing Gus noticed it before Hockney got here, she thought. He'll probably make a big show of checking out the halls and the staircases trying to find something wrong. A sudden feeling of fatigue overcame her. Maybe, after all, it would be nice *not* to be busy all the time. Trying to sound civil, she invited Hockney in and asked if he'd like a cup of tea. He flashed her a broad smile as he strode past her.

He certainly is good-looking, she thought, and he *knows* it. He always was full of himself, and when he was around twenty, Olsen had to bail him out of a few problems. He almost went to jail. Now there was a certain insolent glitter in his eyes. He declined the tea but settled on the couch, his arm over the back, his legs crossed.

"Lil," he began. "My uncle turned eighty-three last month."

"I know it," she said. "We sent him a card."

"You're better than I am." Steve smiled again. "But I feel it's time that I took over a lot of the management of his affairs. You know him. He won't show that he's feeling his age, but I can see that he is. I also know that Howie Altman is getting on his nerves a lot lately."

"We get along with him," Lil said carefully.

"He's been bullying you about giving up this apartment, hasn't he?"

"I think that's over."

"He's a bully. I know my uncle would listen to you if you made him aware just how nasty Howie has been and can be to you both."

"Why would I cause trouble when it's none of my business what Mr. Olsen thinks of Howie?"

"It's because I want your help, Lil. You seem to forget that I was here in the building when Mack MacKenzie all but accused you of stealing his watch. That was only a few days before he disappeared."

White-lipped, Lil stammered, "He found that watch. He apologized."

"Did anyone *hear* him apologize?"

"I don't know. I mean, no, I don't think so."

Hockney unfolded himself from the couch. "Lil, you're lying about the apology. I can tell. But don't worry. I never told anyone about Mack's watch and I never will. We don't like Howie, do we Lil? By the way, I'll tell Uncle Derek that this building is the jewel in his crown, thanks to the way you and Gus keep it."

41

Derek Olsen was far from being only the irascible, petulant old man that his nephew Steve and his buildings manager, Howie, thought him to be. He was in fact a shrewd investor who had watched his real estate holdings in strategically chosen apartment buildings turn into a personal fortune worth many millions of dollars. Now he had come to the conclusion that the time was right to begin liquidating his assets.

On Friday morning he called Wallace and Madison and brusquely demanded to be put through to Elliott Wallace. Elliott's secretary, long used to Olsen's behavior, did not bother to tell him that Mr. Wallace was on his way to an urgent meeting. Instead, she asked him to hold, and rushed down the corridor to catch Elliot at the elevator. "It's Olsen," she said.

With an exasperated sigh, Elliott retraced his steps to his office and picked up the phone. "Derek, how are you?" he asked, his tone hearty.

"I'm all right. Your so-called nephew's in a lot of trouble, "I see."

"As you well know, Mack has been missing for ten years. It is absurd that the police are trying to connect him to any crime. What can I do for you?"

"He caused *me* a lot of trouble by disappearing when he was living in one of my apartments. Anyhow, that's not why I called. My birthday was last month. I'm eighty-three years old. It's time to sell every-thing."

"I've been suggesting that for the past five years."

"If I had sold five years ago, I wouldn't get the price I'll get now. I'm coming in to talk to you. Monday morning, ten o'clock, okay for you?"

"Monday at ten would be fine," Elliott said, cordially. When he was sure Olsen had hung up, he slammed the phone down into the cradle. "I'll have to reschedule the entire day," he snapped to his sec-retary as he hurried back to the elevator.

She watched him go with sympathetic eyes. The meeting that had been scheduled was to decide who would assume Aaron Klein's re-sponsibilities in the firm. After staying home for four days, Klein had phoned in his resignation, saying that it was impossible for him to work side by side with someone who was the champion of his mother's killer.

42

Gregg Andrews had set out a pattern for himself, and he stuck to it. After he left the hospital, he went straight home, grabbed something to eat, and went straight to bed. His alarm was set for one A.M. By two A.M., he was nursing a beer at the bar of the Woodshed and stayed there until closing time. Then, sitting in his car down the street, he watched to see the pattern of how the waiters, bartenders, and band members exited the building, checking to see that they all left within a few minutes of one another, and that no one came out alone, as they'd all claimed about the night Leesey disappeared.

For the last three nights, he had then walked the mile distance between the club and Leesey's apartment, stopping to talk to anyone he saw on the street and asking if by any chance they had been around at the time Leesey vanished and perhaps had seen her. The answer was always negative. The fourth and fifth nights, he drove back and forth covering other streets, just in case she might not have taken the most direct route.

On Saturday morning, at 3:30, after watching the employees lock the door of the Woodshed, he was about to start driving around the neighborhood when there was a rap at the window. A man with streaks of dirt on his face and unkempt hair was staring in at him. Sure it was a request for money, Gregg rolled the car window down only a few inches.

"You're the brother," the man said, his voice hoarse, his alcohol-laden breath sour. Instinctively, Gregg pulled his head back. "Yes, I am."

"I saw her. Will you promise I get the reward?"

"If you can help me find my sister, yes."

"Take my name down."

Gregg reached into the glove compartment and pulled out a pad.

"It's Zach Winters. I live at the shelter on Mott Street."

"You think you saw my sister?"

"I saw her the night she disappeared."

"Why didn't you come forward at once?"

"Nobody believes people like me. I tell them I saw her, next thing they'll be saying I did something to her. That's what happens." Winters put a grimy hand on the car to steady himself.

"If whatever you tell me helps us find my sister, I will personally hand the reward to you. What do you know?"

"She was the last customer out. She started to walk that way." He pointed. "Then a big SUV pulled up and stopped."

Gregg felt his insides twist. "Was she forced into it?"

"No way. I heard the driver call, 'Hey, Leesey,' and she jumped right in the SUV herself."

"Could you tell what kind it was?"

"Sure. It was a black Mercedes."

43

On Saturday morning he was overcome with one of his periodic episodes of remorse. He felt terrible about what he had done. I didn't think I'd ever kill anyone again, he thought. I was scared. After the first one, I tried to be good. But then it happened again twice. I still tried to stop. But I couldn't. But then *he* made me do it again—and again. And after that I couldn't stop.

Sometimes I feel like telling him. But that would be crazy, and I'm not crazy.

I have an idea that I'm thinking about. It would be dangerous, but then, it's always been dangerous. I know someday I'll be caught. But I won't let them send me to prison. I'll go my own way and take whoever's around with me.

I haven't touched the phone since Wednesday night. I'll make the next phone call on Sunday.

It's such a good idea.

And after that, I'll find someone else.

It isn't time to stop yet.

44

Early Saturday morning, Gregg Andrews called Larry Ahearn's cell phone, the words tumbling from his mouth, to report that someone had seen Leesey get into a black Mercedes SUV the night she disappeared. "And she knew the driver," Gregg insisted, his voice hoarse with fatigue and strain. "He called out her name, and she jumped right in."

In the eleven or twelve days since Leesey had been reported missing, Ahearn had not slept more than four hours a night. When his phone rang, he was at home in a heavy sleep from exhaustion. Now, fighting to awaken, he looked at the clock. "Gregg, it's 4:30 in the morning. Where *are* you?"

"I'm on my way to my apartment. I have Zach Winters, a street person, with me. He's drunk. I'll let him sleep it off at my apartment, then I'll bring him in to talk to you. I'm convinced he doesn't know any more than what I told you, but it's our first solid lead. How about that nightclub owner, the one who invited Leesey to sit at his table? What does he drive?"

Nick DeMarco was driving an SUV that night, Ahearn thought. He told us he used that vehicle because he was carrying his golf clubs. I'm not sure if he said what color it is. Now, fully awake, he sat up, slid out of bed, and walked out into the hall, closing the bedroom door behind him. "DeMarco has at least three different sets of wheels," he said carefully. "Let's find out if his SUV is a black Mercedes. I think I remember that it is. Gregg, we'll also have to check on this witness. You said his name was Zach Winters?"

"That's right."

"We'll look him up, too. If you're bringing him to your apartment, be careful. He sounds like a wino."

"He is. But I don't care. Maybe he'll remember something more about Leesey when he wakes up. *Oh, God!*"

"Gregg, what is it?"

"Larry, I'm falling asleep. I almost hit a cab that cut in front of me. I'll see you around ten o'clock in your office."

A click told Ahearn that Gregg Andrews had disconnected his cell phone.

The door from the bedroom opened. Larry's wife, Sheila, still tying the sash on her robe, said matter-of-factly, "I'll make coffee while you shower."

An hour later, Larry was in his office with Barrott and Gaylor. "It sounds fishy to me," Barrott said flatly.

Gaylor nodded. "My guess is that if this guy, what's-his-name, Zach Winters, was on the Woodshed block that night, he was probably too drunk to see, never mind hear what was said. I'll bet anything he's just trying to get the reward."

"That's the way I read it," Ahearn agreed. "But let's start checking him out. Gregg said he'd bring him in here around ten o'clock."

Gaylor was consulting his notes. "When DeMarco was here the first time, he talked about having his SUV in the loft garage because he was going to transport his golf clubs to the plane the next morning." He looked at Barrott and Ahearn. "His SUV *is* a black Mercedes," he said crisply.

"So maybe after he left the club, he went to his loft, picked it up, and decided to go back and try to connect with Leesey." Ahearn's lips were a tight, narrow line. "I think it's about time we put the heat on DeMarco and let the media know that he's a 'person of interest' in Leesey's disappearance."

Barrott was opening the MacKenzie file. "Listen to this, Larry. The first time the father came here after the son had been reported missing, the guys took notes of what he said. 'No reason for Mack to take off. He's on top of the world. Graduated in the top ten of his class. Duke Law School. Bought him a Mercedes SUV as graduation present. You never saw a kid so thrilled. Only a couple of hundred miles on it when he disappeared.' "

"So what?" Ahearn snapped.

"He left it in the garage when he disappeared."

"Did you ask what color it was?"

"It was black. I'm just wondering if it's *still* Mack's favorite vehicle."

"What happened to the one the father bought him?"

"I don't know. Maybe the sister can tell us."

"Give her a call," Ahearn commanded.

"It's not even six o'clock," Gaylor pointed out.

"We're up, aren't we?" Barrott said.

"Hold on." Ahearn held up his hand. "Roy, did you ask Carolyn MacKenzie to give you the note her brother left in the collection basket?"

"She handed it to me the day she came to see me two weeks ago," Barrott said somewhat defensively. "I gave it back to her. It was a scrap of paper in block printing with ten words on it. I thought it was useless to try to do anything with it. We don't have her brother's fingerprints on file. Her uncle the priest, at least one usher at the church, MacKenzie herself, and her mother had handled it."

"It probably is useless, but I want a subpoena issued for it, and for that tape she didn't give you the other night as well. Now call Carolyn and ask what happened to her brother's car. My guess is that after a year or two, they sold it."

Barrott admitted to himself that there was some satisfaction at waking Carolyn so early. Her refusal to play the tape or give it to him on Monday evening had convinced him that beyond any doubt she was protecting her brother. He was pleased when she answered on the first ring, suggesting to him that she had not been sleeping well. Neither have the rest of us, he thought. He spoke to her briefly. From the startled look on his face, Ahearn and Gaylor knew he had stumbled onto an interesting development.

When he disconnected, Barrott said, "She'll check with her lawyer. If he agrees, she will turn over the tape and the note. You may have heard me assure her that he will agree."

"What about her brother's SUV?

"You're not going to believe this. It was stolen out of the Sutton Place garage in the family's apartment building about eight months after Mack took off."

"Stolen!" Gaylor exclaimed.

"Were other vehicles taken?" Ahearn asked quickly.

"No. That was the only one. It's not a large facility. One kid was on duty, asleep in the booth after midnight. Next thing he knew, he had a bag over his head, tape over his mouth, and was handcuffed to the chair. By the time he was found, that SUV was gone."

The three men looked at one another. "If Mack stole his own wheels, it's entirely possible he's still driving it," Gaylor suggested. "My father-in-law has had his Mercedes for twenty years."

"And if he's still driving it, and if the wino's story checks out, there's an equally good chance that Leesey may have driven off with MacKenzie, not DeMarco," Larry Ahearn said somberly. "All right, let's get those subpoenas. Maybe that tape MacKenzie made with the drama teacher will give us something to work with."

45

Howard Altman was well aware of his boss's shifting loyalties, but his first hint that something was seriously wrong occurred when Mr. Olsen did not go out to brunch with him on Saturday morning. He had noticed Olsen using the new Montblanc pen and correctly guessed that it was probably a present from Steve Hockney, Olsen's nephew.

Steve is schmoozing the old man, Howard thought bitterly. It would be just like Olsen to leave everything to him. The first thing Steve would do is fire me. Then he'd sell all the apartment houses and pocket the cash.

The building he lived in on Ninety-fourth Street was one of the smallest Olsen owned. It was four stories high, with only two apartments on each floor. Most of the tenants had been there for years. His apartment was the only one on the lobby floor. Sparsely furnished and immaculately neat, the living room was dominated by his sixty-inch television set. Most of Howard's evenings were split evenly by his two favorite activities, watching movies on television and visiting on the Internet with buddies from all over the world. He found them infinitely more interesting than the people he met in his daily life.

An excellent chef, he always cooked himself a good dinner, watched a movie while he had a couple of glasses of wine and ate from a tray table, then turned off the television set and went directly to his bedroom computer.

Howard loved this apartment, which came with his job. He loved his job, especially now that he was in charge of all Olsen's buildings. I earned it, he told himself, defensively. I got it because I proved myself. I can fix anything that's broken. I can put up a wall to make two rooms out of one. I can replace old wiring and build cabinets. I can paint and wallpaper and scrape floors. That's why Olsen kept promoting me. But what happens if he leaves everything to Steve?

The question persisted in his mind. For once, he could not focus on the movie in his DVD player. How could he get Olsen to sour on his nephew?

And then the answer came to him. He had a master key to all the apartments in the building where Steve Hockney lived. He'd put a security camera in Steve's apartment. I've seen him when he's high, and I've always suspected that he deals in drugs, Howard thought. If I can prove it, that would finish him with his uncle.

Blood is thicker than water. Maybe.

Pleased at finding a possible solution to the impending problem, he turned off the television and went down the hall to his bedroom. He smiled at the familiar whooshing sound he heard as he turned on his computer.

He realized how much he was looking forward to connecting with his friend Singh in Mumbai tonight.

46

I had barely slept Friday night, and the six A.M. call Saturday morning from Detective Barrott finished any hope I had of drifting off again for at least a few more hours.

Why is Barrott so interested in what happened to Mack's SUV? I asked myself, as I replaced the receiver and got out of bed. As usual, I had left the windows of my bedroom open, and padded across the room to close them. The sun had already risen over the East River and it held the promise of a beautiful day. The breeze was cool, but I could see that this time the weather forecasters were right—it would be sunny and pleasant, about seventy degrees by noon. In short, a perfect morning in late May, which meant that right now there was undoubtedly an exodus from the city by people who hadn't already left for their summer place last night. The residents of Sutton Place who didn't have a second home in the Hamptons almost inevitably had one on the Cape, or Nantucket, or Martha's Vineyard, or *somewhere*.

Dad had never wanted to be anchored to one vacation home, but before Mack disappeared we always went away in August. My favorite was the year I was fifteen, when Dad rented a villa in Tuscany, about half an hour from Florence. It was a magical month, all the more so because it was the last time we were all together.

My mind snapped back to the present. Why did Barrott call me about Mack's SUV?

Our garage is relatively small. It only accommodates the automobiles of the residents of the building, with about ten extra spaces for visitors. Dad had just bought the SUV for Mack a week before he disappeared. Mack had parked it in a garage on the West Side, near his apartment. When he'd been missing two weeks, Dad took the spare key and brought the SUV back here. I remember Mack had obviously driven it in bad weather, because it had some mud splatters on the side and on the driver's mat. Dad paid a guy in our garage to clean it, and he did a great job—so great that nothing was recovered when the cops decided to check the car for prints.

When it was stolen, Dad had been sure that one of the garage attendants had spotted it and planned to steal it. He always thought that the guy who had been tied up was in on the scheme, but there was no proof, and he quit soon after that.

Why did Barrott call me about Mack's SUV?

It was a question that kept repeating itself in my mind as I made coffee and scrambled an egg. The newspapers were at the door, and I glanced through them as I ate. The tabloids were still milking the Leesey Andrews disappearance and speculating about Mack's involvement. Aaron Klein's accusation that Mack had killed his mother to recover his tapes was still a hot story. Now, on page three, there was Mack's yearbook picture, but it had been enhanced to show how he might look today. Trying not to cry, I studied it. Mack's face was a little fuller, his hairline slightly higher, his smile ambiguous. I wondered if Elliott had these same newspapers delivered, and if so, had Mom seen them?

Knowing her, she would have insisted on seeing them. I thought of what Elliott had told me at Thurston Carver's office—that Mom had always been convinced some kind of mental breakdown had caused Mack to disappear. Now I wondered if she could be right, and if so, was it possible that Mack had stolen his own automobile? The prospect was so incredible to me that I realized I was shaking my head. "No, no, no," I said aloud.

But I spoke to him two weeks ago, I admitted to myself. He left that message for Uncle Dev. The only rational explanation for Mack's behavior may be that he is irrational. Mother is afraid that if he is responsible for Leesey Andrews's disappearance and is tracked down by the cops, he may be shot if he resists arrest. Is that reasonable, or possible? I wondered.

Neither Mom nor Dad nor I saw any hint of a change in Mack's behavior before he disappeared, but maybe someone else did. How about Mrs. Kramer? I asked myself. Between cleaning and doing the laundry, she was in his apartment regularly. She acted so nervous when I met her. Did she perceive me as a threat? Maybe if I could get her alone, without her husband around, I could get her to open up to me, I thought.

Bruce Galbraith hates Mack. What happened between them to cause that? Nick suggested that Barbara was crazy about Mack. Is Bruce simply jealous, or did something happen that still makes him angry after ten years?

That train of thought made me speculate on Dr. Barbara Hanover Galbraith's trip to Martha's Vineyard to see her ailing father. I wondered how long she planned to stay there. I remembered that Bruce had responded heatedly when I told him I'd like to talk to her. The thought occurred to me that he might have gotten her out of town to prevent my seeing her or the police from looking her up. Her name is in Mack's file as a close friend, I reminded myself.

I put my few dishes in the dishwasher, went into Dad's office, and turned on the computer to see if I could get her father's address and phone number on Martha's Vineyard. There were several Hanover couples, "Judy and Syd," "Frank and Natalie," and one Richard

Hanover listed in the Vineyard. I knew Barbara's mother had died just around the time she graduated, so taking a chance, I dialed Richard Hanover's number.

A man answered on the first ring. It was an older voice but certainly cheerful enough. I had planned what I would say. "This is Cluny Flowers in New York. I want to verify the address of Richard Hanover. Is it eleven Maiden Path?"

"That's right, but who's sending me flowers? I'm not sick, dead, or having a birthday." He sounded fit and healthy.

"Oh, I'm afraid I've made a mistake," I said quickly. "The arrangement is for a Mrs. Judy Hanover."

"No problem. Next time they might be for me. Have a good day."

When I disconnected, my first reaction was to be ashamed of myself. I had turned into an outright liar. My second thought was that Dr. Barbara Hanover Galbraith had left New York not because her father had suffered a heart attack, but because she did not want to be around to be questioned about Mack.

I knew what I was going to do. I showered, dressed, and began to throw a few things in a bag. I had to confront Barbara face-to-face. If Mom was right, and Mack had snapped ten years ago, had she witnessed behavior that might have suggested mental illness? I realized that I was becoming frantic to frame a defense for Mack if he was really out there, alive, unstable, and committing crimes.

I called Elliott's cell phone. The fact that he did not say my name and in a low voice promised he'd call me back told me that Mom was within earshot.

When he did call back half an hour later, I could not believe what he told me. "Your Detective Barrott came here looking to talk to your mother. I told him we would have our lawyer present, but then Olivia screamed at him something like, 'Don't you realize my son had a breakdown? Don't you understand he's not responsible for any of this? He's sick. He doesn't know what he's doing.' "

My mouth was so dry I could only whisper, though there was no need to. "What did Barrott say?"

"He verified what your mother said, that she believed Mack may be mentally ill."

"Where is Mom now?"

"Carolyn, she was so hysterical, I called a doctor. He gave her a shot, but he feels she should be under observation for a few days. I'm driving her up to a wonderful sanitarium in Connecticut where she'll be able to get some rest—and, ah, counseling."

"What place?" I asked. "I'll meet you there."

"It's Sedgwick Manor, in Darien. Carolyn, don't come. Olivia doesn't want to see you, and it will only upset her more if you insist on visiting her. In her mind, you've betrayed Mack. I promise I'll take care of her and I'll call you back as soon as she is settled in there."

I could do nothing but agree. Nothing could be worse for Mack than having Mom telling the police again that she's sure he's insane. When I clicked off, I went into my bedroom and got out Mack's tape and played it while I studied the scrap of paper on which he had printed the ten words he had written to Uncle Devon. "UNCLE DEVON, TELL CAROLYN SHE MUST NOT LOOK FOR ME." I listened to his voice: "When, in disgrace with fortune and men's eyes, I all alone beweep my outcast state, and trouble deaf heaven with my bootless cries."

I could only imagine Barrott's reaction if he was able to get his hands on that note and tape after hearing Mother's outburst. I had barely finished that thought when the concierge phoned to say that Detective Gaylor was on his way up. "I'm sorry, Miss Carolyn, he wouldn't let me announce him. He showed me a subpoena he has to deliver to you."

Before the bell rang, I frantically called Thurston Carver, our criminal defense lawyer, on his cell phone. He told me, as he had when we met at his office, that I could not refuse to turn over what was ordered in the subpoena.

When I opened the door for Detective Gaylor, he handed me the subpoena, his manner professional and impersonal. It was for the note Mack had left in the collection basket and the tape I had found in his suitcase. Shaking with fury, I almost threw them at him. I took some comfort in knowing that I had made a copy of each.

After he left, I slumped into the nearest chair and again heard myself repeating over and over in my head Mack's taped quotation, "I all alone beweep my outcast state . . ." Finally, I got up, walked to my bedroom, and emptied the bag I had started to pack. It was obvious that any plans I had been making to drive up to Martha's Vineyard would have to be postponed. I was so deep into concentrating on what my next logical move would be that I didn't realize my cell phone was ringing. I rushed to pick it up. It was Nick, about to leave a message. "I'm here," I said.

"Good. This would have been a convoluted message. Carolyn," he said, tersely, "I think you should know that I've just been named a person of interest in the disappearance of Leesey Andrews. I see from the papers that the cops' other theory is that Mack has been running around killing people. I might as well tell you that when I was down at the DA's Office on Thursday, they even suggested you and I might be cooperating to protect Mack."

He didn't give me a chance to reply before he said, "I'm flying to Florida this morning for the second time this week. My father's been in the hospital. He had a mild heart attack yesterday. I expect to be back tomorrow. Barring any reason I have to stay in Florida, can we have dinner tomorrow night?" Then he added, "It was so good to see you, Carolyn. I'm beginning to understand why I looked forward to being invited to dinner with your family and why it wasn't the same when Mack's kid sister wasn't around."

I told him that I hoped his father would recover quickly, and that yes, tomorrow night was fine. I held my cell phone to my ear for a few moments after Nick clicked off. My mind was a mess of conflicting emotions. The first one was that I acknowledged to myself I'd never gotten over my crush on him, that all week I'd been hearing his voice, remembering the warmth I'd felt sitting across the table from him the other night.

The second reaction was to wonder if Nick was playing some kind of cat and mouse game with me. The D.A.'s office had named him a "person of interest" in Leesey Andrews's disappearance. I knew that was very, very serious, practically an accusation of guilt. But the police also believed he might be helping me to protect Mack. Nick had not contacted me all week, even though Mack's name had been in the headlines. When we had dinner, he had not been even remotely sympathetic to my fear that Mack might need help.

Had Nick really been named a person of interest? Or was it just a device suggested to him by the police to disarm me? And was Nick, close friend of his former roommate-turned-criminal, now hoping to use his influence to persuade me to turn Mack in if he contacted me again?

I shook my head, as if to clear it of all these questions, but they didn't go away.

Worse still, they didn't lead me anywhere.

47

Dr. David Andrews had not left his home in Greenwich since the phone call from Leesey came in. Sleepless, and now a gaunt shadow of the man he had been before his daughter's disappearance, he kept a vigil by the phone, grabbing it at the first ring every time it rang. He always carried the portable receiver from room to room with him. When he went to bed at night, he placed it on the pillow next to his head.

When he *did* get a call, he immediately cut the conversation to a few words, explaining that he wanted to leave the line open in case Leesey called again.

His housekeeper of twenty years, who usually left after lunch, began staying into the evening, trying to get Dr. Andrews to eat something, even if it was only a cup of soup or coffee and a sandwich. He had made it clear to his friends that he did not want anyone to tie up the line, and refused to allow them to stop by and see him. "I'm better off if I don't feel obliged to keep up a conversation," he told them.

On Saturday morning, Gregg took Zach Winters down to Larry Ahearn's office, but as he sat in while Ahearn interrogated Zach, he saw his story about seeing Leesey get into the black Mercedes SUV begin to unravel. Zach had said that he hung around on that block for about half an hour, but the employees of the Woodshed, who left only a few minutes after Leesey, all swore they hadn't seen him on the street. He admitted that he was a chronic drunk who had once been thrown out of the Woodshed when he came in and tried to panhandle the customers. He admitted that he was angry at Nick DeMarco, the owner, for having him thrown out, and that he knew Nick owned a black Mercedes SUV.

After the lengthy interrogation, Gregg drove Zach back to where he had found him. Exhausted, Gregg went straight to his apartment and fell asleep until nine o'clock Sunday morning. Then, feeling clearheaded and focused again, he showered, dressed, and drove to Greenwich.

The change in his father in the one week since he had last seen him was shocking. His father's housekeeper, Annie Potters, who never came in on Sunday, was there. "He won't eat," she whispered to Gregg. "It's eleven o'clock and he hasn't touched a morsel since yesterday."

"Would you fix some breakfast for both of us, Annie?" Gregg asked. "I'll see what I can do."

After greeting him, his father had immediately returned to his recliner in the living room, the portable phone within reach. Gregg went back into the living room and sat on the chair nearest the recliner. "Dad, I've been walking the streets at night looking for Leesey. I can't do it anymore, and you can't do *this* anymore! We're not helping Leesey, and we're destroying ourselves. I've been down to the District Attorney's office. There is absolutely nothing Larry Ahearn and his people aren't already doing to find Leesey. I want you to come in and eat something, then we're going out for a walk. It's a beautiful day." He got up, and bent down to hug his father. "You know I'm right."

Dr. David Andrews nodded, then his face crumbled. Gregg embraced him. "Dad, I know. I know. Now, come on, and leave the phone here. If it rings, we'll answer it."

He was cheered to see his father eat half the serving of scrambled eggs and bacon Annie put before him. Gregg was nibbling on a slice of toast and drinking his second cup of coffee when the phone rang. His father bolted up and raced from the table, but he didn't reach the phone before the message began.

It was Leesey, unmistakably. "Daddy, Daddy," she wailed, "help me. Please, Daddy, he says he's going to kill me."

The message ended as Leesey began to sob.

Dr. David Andrews lunged for the phone and grabbed it, but by then he heard only a dial tone. His knees buckled, and Gregg was in time to ease him into his recliner before he collapsed.

Gregg was checking his father's pulse when the phone rang again. It was Larry Ahearn.

"Gregg, that *was* Leesey, wasn't it?"

Gregg pressed the speaker button so that his father could hear. "Absolutely, Larry. You know that."

"Gregg, she's still alive, and we're going to find her. I swear that to you."

Dr. David Andrews grabbed the receiver. His voice hoarse, he shouted, "You've got to find her, Larry. You *heard* her! Whoever has her is going to kill her! For God's sake, find her for me before it's too late!"

48

Exhaustion was forgotten as Larry Ahearn played the tape of Leesey's cry for help to the squad. "The call came in at eleven thirty, exactly one hour ago," he said. "It was made from mid-Manhattan. Of course, there is always a possibility that the abductor made a tape of her voice and played it in a different location."

"And if that's the case, he may already have killed her," Barrott said, quietly.

"We're going to go forward under the assumption that she's still alive," Ahearn snapped. "There's no question that whoever has her is on a short leash. He wants attention. I've talked to our profiler, Dr. Lowe. He thinks that this guy is loving the headlines and the way the story is being covered by Greta Van Susteren and Nancy Grace. He's probably also anticipating the uproar when we release the fact that Leesey called her father again and left that message."

Too restless to sit any longer, he stood and tapped his fingers on his desk. "I don't want to even think this, but it has to be considered. In another five days, maybe seven, the fact that Leesey phoned will stay big news, but without new information, it won't be the headline anymore."

Every detective from the squad room was crowded tightly into Ahearn's office for the briefing. The expressions on their faces became increasingly grave as they followed the thought Ahearn was voicing. "Leesey went to that club on Monday night and disappeared. Her message promising to call again on Mother's Day came the following Sunday, six days later. After a one-week interval, this new call has come in. It's Dr. Lowe's opinion that our guy may not wait another week to give us a new headline."

"MacKenzie's the one doing this," Roy Barrott said emphatically. "You should have seen his mother yesterday when I went to her boyfriend's apartment."

"Her boyfriend?" Ahearn exclaimed.

"Elliott Wallace, the big investment banker. Aaron Klein, the drama teacher's son, worked for him for fourteen years. Klein told me they became really close when his mother was murdered. Wallace was still so distraught about MacKenzie's disappearance the year before that it gave them a common bond. Mack MacKenzie's father was in Vietnam with Wallace, and they became lifelong friends. It's Klein's opinion that Wallace has always been in love with Olivia MacKenzie."

"Is she living with him?" Ahearn asked.

"I wouldn't call it that. With all the media around Sutton Place, she went home with him. Having said that, Klein wouldn't be surprised if she married Wallace eventually. He sure was quick to stash her away in a private psychiatric residence so she can't keep telling us her son is crazy."

"Is there any possibility she's in touch with her son?"

Barrott shrugged. "I'd say if Mack has contact with anyone in his family, it's more likely with the sister."

"All right." Ahearn turned to address the group. "I still say that De-Marco may be the one behind all this. I want a tail on him 24/7. I want one on Carolyn MacKenzie, too. We'll apply for a wiretap for any and all phones that aren't already tapped: MacKenzie in her Thompson Street apartment, in Sutton Place, and on her cell phone; DeMarco, wherever he works or hangs his hat."

"Larry, I'd like to make another suggestion," Bob Gaylor said.

"Zach Winters may be a wino, but I think he saw something that night. He curls up in doorways. The fact that the band members and waiters from the Woodshed didn't see him on the street doesn't prove anything, and I'd swear he was holding back on us when he was here."

"Go talk to him again," Ahearn said. "He lives in that shelter on Mott Street, doesn't he?"

"Sometimes, but when the weather's good, he puts his stuff in a laundry cart and sleeps outside."

Ahearn nodded. "All right. We're cooperating with the FBI, but I want all of you to keep something in mind. I've known Leesey since she was six years old. I want her back, and I want *us* to be the ones who find her!"

49

On Sunday morning, using the service entrance to duck the media, I went for a long, long walk along the river. I felt whiplashed after Elliott's phone call about Mom, and sick with my doubts about Nick—and, let's face it, about Mack.

The day had fulfilled its promise—warm with a light breeze. The current of the East River, often so strong, seemed as mellow as the sunshine. The boaters were out, not too many of them, adding to the scenery. I love New York. God help me, I even love that blaring, intrusive Pepsi-Cola sign on the Long Island City side of the river.

By the end of a three-hour walk, I was physically and mentally exhausted. When I got back to Sutton Place, I stripped, showered, and got into bed. I slept all afternoon, and woke up at six o'clock feeling at least somewhat clearheaded and a bit more able to cope. I dressed casually, in a blue and white pinstriped shirt and white jeans. I didn't care if Nick showed up in a jacket and tie. I wanted no suggestion of little Carolyn dressing up for a date.

Nick arrived promptly at seven o'clock. He was wearing a sport shirt and chinos. I had intended to steer him straight out the door, but his first words were, "Carolyn, I really need to talk with you, and it might be better if we do it here."

I followed him into the library. "Library" sounds impressive. It really isn't that pretentious. It's just a room with bookshelves and comfortable armchairs and a paneled area that opens to disclose a built-in bar. Nick went straight to it, poured himself a scotch on the rocks, and, without asking, a glass of white wine with a couple of ice cubes for me.

"This is what you had last week. I read somewhere that the Duchess of Windsor put ice in her champagne," he said, as he handed me the glass.

"And I read that the Duke of Windsor liked his whiskey neat," I told him.

"Married to her, I shouldn't wonder." He gave a brief smile. "Joking, of course. I have no idea what she was like."

I sat on the edge of the couch. He chose one of the armchairs and swiveled it around. "I remember loving these chairs," he said. "I promised myself that if I ever got rich I'd have at least one of them."

"And?" I asked.

"Never had time to think about it. When I started to make money and bought an apartment, I got an interior decorator. She was into the Western look. When I saw it all finished, I felt like Roy Rogers."

I had been studying him, and I realized that the gray around his temples was even more pronounced than I had thought. There were fresh pouches under his eyes, and the concerned expression I had observed last week had now become one of deep worry. He had flown to Florida yesterday because his father had a heart attack. I asked Nick how he was doing.

"Pretty good. It really was a mild attack. They are releasing him in a couple of days."

Then Nick looked straight at me. "Carolyn, do you think Mack is alive? And if you do, is he capable of what the cops think he's doing?"

It was on the tip of my tongue to be honest, to say that at this point, I simply didn't know, but I caught myself in time. "What on earth makes you ask that? Of course not." I hoped that I sounded as indignant as I wanted to sound.

"Carolyn, don't look at me like that. Can't you understand that Mack was my best friend? I never could figure out why he chose to disappear. Now I wonder if something was going on in his head that nobody realized at the time."

"Are you worried about Mack or about yourself, Nick?" I asked.

"I won't answer that. Carolyn, the one thing I beg of you, *plead* with you, is that if he is in contact with you, or if he *does* call you, don't think you're doing him a favor by shielding him. Did you hear the message Leesey Andrews left for her father this morning?" He looked at me expectantly.

For a moment I was too shaken to speak, then managed to say that I hadn't turned on the radio or television all day. But when Nick told me, all I could think of was Barrott's theory that Mack stole his own car. It's crazy, but it reminded me of the day I was five or six years old and Mack suddenly had a terrible nosebleed. Daddy was home, and he grabbed one of the monogrammed towels from a rack in the bathroom to stem the flow. We had an elderly housekeeper at that time who adored Mack. She was so upset that she tried to yank the towel out of Dad's hand. "That one's for show," she shrieked, "it's for show!"

Daddy always got a kick out of telling that story, but he always added, "Poor Mrs. Anderson was so worried about Mack, but to her the fancy towels just weren't disposable. I told her the towels have our name on them, and Mack can ruin them if he likes!"

I could imagine Mack stealing his own car, but not Mack holding Leesey hostage and torturing her father. I looked at Nick. "I don't know what to think about Mack," I said. "I swear to you and to anyone who will listen that other than those Mother's Day calls, I have not heard from Mack or seen him in ten years."

Nick nodded, and my guess is that he believed me. Then he asked, "Do you think that *I* am responsible for Leesey's disappearance? That I have her hidden somewhere?"

I examined my heart and my soul before I answered. "No, I don't," I said. "But both of you have been dragged into this, Mack because I went to the police, you because she disappeared from your club. If it's neither one of you, then who *is* responsible?"

"Carolyn, I don't know where to begin to look for the answer to that."

We talked for more than an hour. I told him I was going to try to see Lil Kramer alone, because she was afraid to say anything in front of her husband. We went round and round about the fact that, just before he vanished, Mack had been upset with Mrs. Kramer but hadn't told Nick why. I told Nick how Bruce Galbraith had been so hostile about Mack when I saw him last week, and that I thought Barbara had rushed to visit her father in Martha's Vineyard just to avoid being questioned.

"I'm going to drive up there tomorrow or Tuesday," I said. "Mother doesn't want to see me, and Elliott will take care of her."

Nick asked me if I thought that Mom would marry Elliott.

"I think so," I said. "Quite honestly, I hope so. They're very good together. Mom certainly loved Dad, but he delighted in being a bit of a rebel. Elliott is actually more of a soul mate, which of course is a little hard for me to swallow. They're both perfectionists, and I think they'll be very happy together." Then I added words I'd never thought I'd say. "That's why Mack was always her favorite. He did everything right. I'm too impulsive for Mom's taste. Witness going to the police and opening up this whole mess."

I was appalled that I had confided that to Nick. I think he was about to come over to me, maybe put his arms around me, but he must have known that wasn't what I wanted. Instead, he said, his tone light, "See if you can guess this one: 'She sprang full-fledged from her father's brow.' "

"The goddess Minerva," I said. "Sister Catherine, sixth grade. Man, how she loved teaching mythology." I stood up. "You did ask me to have dinner, you know. How about Neary's? I want a sliced-steak sandwich and french fries."

Nick hesitated. "Carolyn, I have to warn you. There are cameras outside. My car's near the door. We can make a run for it. I don't think they'll follow us."

That was the way it turned out. The camera lights flashed the moment we exited the building. Someone tried to shove a microphone in my face. "Ms. MacKenzie, do you think your brother . . ." Nick grabbed my hand, and we ran for his car. He drove up York Avenue until Seventy-second Street, then turned and doubled back. "I think we should be okay now," he said.

I didn't agree or disagree. My one consolation was that Mom was in a safe place where the media couldn't get at her.

Neary's is an Irish pub on Fifty-seventh Street, a block away from Sutton Place. It's like a second home for many of us in the neighborhood. The atmosphere is warm, the food is good, and the odds are that on any given night, you'll know half the diners.

If I needed moral support, and God knows I did, Jimmy Neary provided it. When he saw me he crossed the room instantly. "Carolyn, it's a disgrace what they're insinuating about Mack," he told me, putting a warm hand on my shoulder. "That boy was a saint. You wait and see, the truth will come out."

He turned, and recognized Nick. "Hey, kid. Remember when you and Mack came in, you bet me that your father's pasta was a match for my corned beef?"

"We never put it to the test," Nick said. "And now my Dad is in Florida, retired."

"Retired? How does he like it?" Jimmy asked.

"He hates it."

"So would I. Tell him to come back, and we'll finally get the answer."

Jimmy ushered us to one of the corner tables in the back. That was where Nick told me more about the visit to Florida. "I begged my mother to keep the New York papers away from Pop," he said. "I don't know what it will do to him if he finds out I've been designated a 'person of interest' in Leesey's disappearance."

Over sliced-steak sandwiches, by unspoken mutual consent, we drifted into neutral territory. Nick talked about opening his first restaurant and how well it did. He hinted that these last five years, he'd moved too fast. "I think I read Donald Trump's success story once too often," he admitted. "I got the idea that skating on thin ice was fun. I've banked an awful lot on the Woodshed. It's the right spot at the right time. But if the State Liquor Authority wants to shut it down, they'll find a way. And if that happens, I'm in big trouble."

We talked cautiously about Barbara Hanover. "I remember thinking how beautiful she was," I told him.

"She is and was, but Carolyn, there's something else about Barbara, a kind of calculated 'What's best for Barbara?' agenda. It's hard to explain. But after we all graduated and I went for my MBA, Mack was gone, and as for Bruce, I didn't care if I ever saw him again."

We both had a cappuccino, then Nick drove me back to Sutton Place. There was just one television van halfway down the block. He rushed me into the building and to the elevator. As the operator held the door open, Nick said, "Carolyn, I didn't do it and neither did Mack. Hang on to that thought."

He skipped the social kiss and was gone. I went upstairs. The message light was blinking. It was Detective Barrott. "Ms. MacKenzie. At eight forty P.M. tonight, you received another call from Leesey Andrews's cell phone. Your brother didn't leave a message."

50

Lucas Reeves had not taken the weekend off. He had spent it in his office, working with his technicians. Charles MacKenzie Sr. had hired him nearly ten years ago to find his missing son, and the fact that he had never been able to uncover even the slightest hint of what happened to Mack had given Reeves a sense of failure that was never far from his consciousness.

Now he considered it even more urgent that he find the answer, not only to learn what had happened to Mack, but to find the real killer and perhaps save Leesey Andrews's life.

On Monday morning, Lucas was back in his office on Park Avenue South at eight o'clock. His three permanent investigators had been told to get in early. By eight thirty they were seated around his desk. "I have a hunch, and some of my hunches have worked in the past," he began, "so I'm going to act on it. I am going to assume that Mack is innocent of these crimes, and I am going to assume that someone who knew him at least reasonably well *is* responsible. By that, I mean knew him well enough to hear about the Mother's Day calls, and to have his family's unlisted phone number."

Reeves looked from one investigator to the other. "We are going to start by concentrating on the people around Mack. By that I mean his two roommates, Nick DeMarco and Bruce Galbraith. We are going to dig up everything we can learn about the superintendent couple, Lil and Gus Kramer. From there we will concentrate on Mack's other friends from Columbia who were with him in the night-club the evening that first girl disappeared. Over the weekend, our techs have gathered all the newspaper accounts and media clips that were headlines when each of those other three girls vanished. We have enhanced the faces of everyone caught in those pictures, whether he or she was identifiable or not. Study those faces. *Memorize* them."

Lucas had come in so early that he had made his own coffee. He took a sip, grimaced, and continued. "The media is camped outside Sutton Place. One of you must be in the vicinity at all times. Have your cell phone out, and be using it as a camera. Somebody also has to be on the street when the Woodshed opens tonight, taking pictures not only of guests entering and leaving, but of people hanging around in the streets. There are a couple of other clubs opening in SoHo this week. Be there with the paparazzi."

"Lucas, that's impossible," Jack Rodgers, his most senior aide, protested. "The three of us can't cover all that ground."

"No one asked you to," Reeves snapped, his normally deep voice several octaves higher. "Get out the list of the guys we use when we need extra help. We must have thirty retired cops available."

Rodgers nodded. "Okay."

Reeves lowered his voice. "My hunch is that the perpetrator loves attention. He may want to be on-site when there's a media rush. The faces that show in every picture you snap will be enhanced in our lab. I don't care how many there are, and I assume there will be hundreds. Maybe, just maybe, one of them will be a match for someone who was around during the media frenzy that followed those other disappearances. I repeat, for the present we are going to assume that Mack MacKenzie is innocent."

He looked at Rodgers. "Why don't you say it, Jack?"

"All right, Lucas, I'll say it. If you're right, we may find a picture of a guy who shows up all over the place. He may be fat, he may be thin, he may be bald, he may have a ponytail. He'll be someone his own mother wouldn't recognize, and he'll be Charles MacKenzie Jr."

51

Detective Bob Gaylor began searching for Zach Winters on Sunday after the squad meeting. He was not at the Mott Street shelter that was his off-and-on home. He had not been seen on the streets since early Saturday morning, when he had been hanging around the Woodshed, and then had gone to Gregg Andrews's apartment. He had been interrogated on Saturday afternoon, then presumably had gone back to his usual haunts. But he had not gone back to the shelter.

"Zach usually shows up at least every other day" Joan Coleman, an attractive thirty-year-old volunteer kitchen worker on Mott Street, confided to Gaylor. "Of course, it depends on the weather. He loves the club area in SoHo. He brags that he gets better handouts there."

"Did he ever talk about being near the Woodshed the night Leesey Andrews disappeared?"

"Not to me. But he's got a couple of what he calls his 'real good buddies.' Let me talk to them." She brightened at the idea of doing detective work.

"I'll go with you," Gaylor volunteered.

She shook her head. "Not if you want to get any information, you won't. I don't usually come in for dinner, but I'm subbing for a friend tonight. Give me your phone number. I'll call you."

Bob Gaylor had to be content with that. He spent the better part of the day wandering through SoHo and Greenwich Village to no avail.

Zach Winters might have disappeared from the face of the earth.

52

 True to his word, Derek Olsen arrived at Elliott Wallace's office promptly at ten A.M. His gait stiff, his suit cleaned and pressed, but shiny with age, his remaining tufts of white hair plastered down on his skull, there was a certain buoyancy about him. Elliott Wallace observed him and correctly interpreted that Olsen, if he followed his plan to liquidate all his holdings, was looking forward to telling his nephew Steve, his buildings manager, Howie, and anyone else he could think of, to go jump in a lake.

A cordial smile on his face, Wallace urged Olsen to take a chair. "I know you won't refuse a cup of tea, Derek."

"Last time, it tasted like dishwater. Tell your secretary I want four lumps of sugar and heavy cream, Elliott."

"Of course."

Olsen barely waited for Elliott to instruct his secretary before he said with a satisfied smile, "You and your advice. Remember you said I should get rid of those three broken-down town houses that have been closed for years?"

Elliott Wallace knew what was coming. "Derek, you've been paying taxes and insurance on those dumps for years. Of course real estate has gone up, but if you wish I will show you that if you had sold them and bought the stocks I recommended, you'd be ahead."

"No, I wouldn't! I knew that someday they'd tear down those

buildings on the corner of 104th Street and developers would want my place."

"The developers seem to have managed without it. They already broke ground for those condominium apartments."

"The same firm came back to me. I close on the sale this afternoon."

"Congratulations," Wallace said sincerely. "But I do hope you remember that I've made you quite a lot of money investing on your behalf."

"Except for that hedge fund."

"Except for the hedge fund, I agree, but that was quite a while ago."

Olsen's tea and Elliott's coffee arrived. "This is good," Olsen said, after taking a wary sip. "The way I like it. Now let's talk. I want to sell everything. I want to establish a trust fund. You can run it. I want it to be used for parks in New York, parks with lots of trees. This city has too many big buildings."

"That's very generous of you. Are you planning to leave anything to your nephew or anyone else?"

"I'll leave Steve fifty thousand dollars. Let him get a new set of drums or a guitar. He can't look at me over a dinner plate without trying to figure how much longer I'll last. I heard from a couple of my building supers that he announced he'll be taking over Howie's job as my overall manager. He buys me a fountain pen and takes me to dinner, and because I show good feelings to him, he thinks he can take over my business. Him and his gigs. Every time he stops getting jobs at those club dumps, he invents a new name for himself and his loser band, finds the latest kind of weird outfit, and hires a broken-down PR agent. If it wasn't for his mother, my sister, God rest her, I'd have given him the bum's rush years ago."

"I know he's been a disappointment to you, Derek." Elliott tried to maintain his compassionate expression.

"Disappointment! Hah! By the way, I want to leave Howie Altman fifty thousand dollars, too."

"I'm sure he'll appreciate it. Does he know your plans?"

"No. He's been getting pushy, too. I can tell he has the nerve to think he's entitled to a big inheritance from me. Don't misunderstand. He's done a good job, and I thank you for recommending him when that other guy didn't work out."

Elliott nodded, acknowledging the thanks. "One of my other clients was selling a building and mentioned his availability."

"Well, he'll soon be available again. But he's not blood, and he doesn't understand that when you have good workers like the Kramers, you don't squeeze them out of an extra bedroom or two."

"George Rodenburg is still your lawyer, isn't he?"

"Of course. Why would I change?"

"What I meant was that I'll talk to him about setting up the foundation. You say you're closing on the 104th Street property this afternoon. Do you want me there?"

"Rodenburg will handle it. The offer's been on the table for years. It's only the dollars that are different."

Olsen got up to go. "I was born on Tremont Avenue in the Bronx. It was a nice neighborhood then. I have pictures of my sister and me sitting on the steps of one of those little apartment buildings, the kind I own now. I drove up there last week. It's pretty bad. There's a corner lot near where we lived. It's a mess, weeds and beer cans and garbage. While I'm still alive, I want to see it become a park." A beatific smile crossed his face as he turned to the door. "Good-bye, Elliott."

Elliott Wallace walked his client through the reception room, down the corridor to the elevator, returned to his private office, and for the first time in his adult life, went to the bar refrigerator and, at eleven A.M., poured himself a straight scotch.

53

Late on Monday morning, I drove up to Mack's old apartment building. I pushed the Kramers' button on the intercom, and was rewarded after a moment by a hesitant greeting. I knew I had to talk fast, "Mrs. Kramer, this is Carolyn MacKenzie. I need to talk to you."

"Oh, no. My husband is out this morning."

"I want to talk to *you*, not to him, Mrs. Kramer. Please let me come in for just a few minutes."

"Gus won't like it. I can't . . ."

"Mrs. Kramer, you must be reading the newspapers. Surely you know that the police think my brother may be responsible for that girl's disappearance. I need to talk with you."

For a moment I thought she had hung up, but then I heard a click as the door to the lobby unlocked. I went in, crossed the lobby, and rang her bell. She opened it a crack as though to reassure herself that I didn't have an army of people ready to storm the apartment, then opened it just wide enough for me to enter.

The room that had so reminded me of my paternal grandmother's living room in Jackson Heights was in the process of being stripped and dismantled. There were large cartons stacked in the corner. The curtains and draperies had been taken down from the windows. There were no pictures on the wall, and the side tables were bare of the lamps and bric-a-brac I'd seen on my last visit.

"We're moving to our cottage in Pennsylvania," Lil Kramer said. "Gus and I are more than ready to retire."

She's running away, I thought, as I studied her. Even though the room was cool, she had tiny beads of sweat on her forehead. Her gray hair was pulled away from her face and anchored firmly behind her ears. Her complexion was the same dull gray as her hair. I am sure she was unaware that her hands were massaging each other in a fretful, nervous pattern.

Uninvited, I sat on the nearest chair. I realized there was absolutely no use in not coming directly to the point. "Mrs. Kramer, you knew my brother. Do *you* think he's a killer?"

She rubbed her lips together. "I don't know what he is." Then she burst out. "He told lies about me. I was so nice to him. I really liked him. I took such good care of his clothes and his room. And then he accused me."

"Accused you of what?"

"Never mind. It wasn't true, but I couldn't believe my ears."

"When did that happen?"

"A few days before he disappeared. And then he ridiculed me."

Neither one of us had heard the outside door open. "Shut your mouth, Lil," Gus Kramer ordered as he strode across the room. He turned to face me. "And you get out of here. Your brother had the nerve to treat my wife the way he did, and now look at what he's done to those young girls."

Furious, I stood up. "Mr. Kramer, I don't know what you're talking about. I can't believe Mack mistreated your wife in any way, shape, or form, and I would stake my own life that he is not responsible for any crime."

"Keep on believing that, and let me tell you what I'm talking about. My wife is going to have a nervous breakdown worrying that when they catch your killer brother, he'll turn on her and accuse her with his dirty lies."

"Don't call him a killer," I said. "Don't you *dare* call him a killer."

Gus's face flooded with rage. "I'll call him what I want to call him, but I'll give you this. He's a killer who goes to church. Lil saw him the day he left the note in the collection basket, didn't you, Lil?"

"I didn't have my glasses with me, but I'm still sure." Lil Kramer began to cry. "I recognized him. He saw me looking at him. I mean, he had on a raincoat and dark glasses, but it was Mack in that church."

"Just for your information, the cops were here an hour ago, and we told them that," Gus Kramer shouted at me. "Now get out of here and leave my wife alone."

54

On Saturday evening, after he was sure Steve had left for one of his gigs, Howard Altman had let himself into Steve's apartment. Carefully and skillfully, he had placed hidden cameras in the living room and bedroom. The video would be beamed directly into his computer.

Why didn't I think of this sooner? he asked himself, as he set up the surveillance. Thanks, Steve, for making it so easy for me. Steve had left lights on in both rooms, as well as in the bathroom. Derek pays the gas and electric bill for him, Howard thought resentfully. He charges me for mine!

And Steve was a slob. His bed wasn't made. A couple of those stupid costumes he wore to some of his gigs were piled on a chair. The hairpieces and wigs he used when he was acting out some of his characters were tossed in a cardboard box on the floor. Howard tried on one of them, a wig with long dark-brown hair. He stared at himself in the mirror, then ripped it off. He looked like a woman in it, and that made him think of that teacher who had once lived in this apartment and had been murdered.

I don't know how Steve Hockney can live in a place that belonged to someone who was murdered, he thought. I have to get out of here.

On Monday morning, Howard went to pick up Mr. Olsen for one of their scheduled visits to the properties, but he wasn't there. The super in that building told him that Olsen had already been picked up by a car service.

Deeply uneasy, Howard went to their usual first stop, the building where the Kramers were the supers. He was about to unlock the lobby door when it was flung open and a pretty young woman, tears streaming down her cheeks, ran past him.

Carolyn MacKenzie! he thought. What's *she* doing here? He turned and raced after her, catching her a half block away as, remote in hand, she opened the lock on her car door. "Ms. MacKenzie, I'm Howard Altman. We met a couple of weeks ago when you were talking to the Kramers." He spoke in a hurry, slightly out of breath.

He watched as she impatiently brushed away the tears that were still spilling from her eyes. "I'm afraid I really can't talk right now," she said.

"Look, I've been seeing your picture in the papers and reading all that stuff about your brother. That was before I worked for Mr. Olsen, but I wish I could help you somehow."

"Thank you. I wish you could, too."

"If the Kramers have upset you in any way, I'll take care of them," he promised.

She did not answer, but gave his arm a push to oblige him to get out of the way of the driver's door. Howard stepped back, and with a quick movement, she had opened the door, closed it, and started the car. She did not look at him again as she backed up a few feet, turned the wheel, pulled out of the parking space, and was gone.

His face grim, Howard Altman headed straight for the Kramers' apartment. They did not answer the insistent ringing of their doorbell. He tried to open the door with his key, but the security lock was on. "Gus and Lil, I have to talk to you," he shouted.

"Go to hell," Gus Kramer shouted from the other side of the door. "We're out of here today. You can have this job and this apartment and everything that goes with it. And just so you know, Howie, you'd better watch your back. If Steve has anything to do with it, you'll be looking for a place to live yourself. Now get lost."

Standing there in the hallway, there was nothing Howard could do except leave. Was Steve making the rounds with Olsen? he wondered. Why else would Olsen have ordered a car service this morning?

There was one way he could find out for sure if Steve was around. Howard went back to his apartment and turned on his computer. Scanning the videocam footage, he noted Steve had been in and out of his apartment all day yesterday, but he was always alone. Now there was no one in his living room. So maybe he *was* out with Olsen, Howard thought, but then the bedroom camera showed Steve sitting in his underwear on the edge of the bed, trying on one after another of his wigs. The last one he selected was the one with the long brown hair. The camera caught him smiling at his image and blowing a kiss at the mirror. Then Steve turned and looked straight into the lens.

"Howie, I have my own security cameras installed here," he said. "I need them. Some of my friends aren't exactly trustworthy customers. If you're watching this, or when you *do* watch it, have a nice day."

With trembling fingers, Howard turned off his computer.

55

At noon on Monday, Detective Bob Gaylor received a phone call from the young kitchen worker he'd met at the Mott Street shelter. "Hi, it's Joan Coleman," she said, sounding excited. "I promised to find out what I could about Zach."

The squad room was noisy, but Gaylor blocked out everything but Joan Coleman's voice. "Okay." he said. "What can you tell me?"

"He's on the streets for good. No more shelters, now that it's warm. He showed up with his stuff near the Brooklyn Bridge last night, totally drunk. He was telling his friends that he might get a reward in the Leesey Andrews case."

"He's tried that. I don't think it's going to work."

"My informant, Pete, is a young guy who just might make it. He's an addict, but he keeps trying. He's pretty clean right now, so I trust what he's telling me." She lowered her voice. "He says that Winters claims he has some kind of proof, but can't show it because they'll blame everything on him."

"Okay. So, Winters was in the Brooklyn Bridge area last night?"

"Yes, near some kind of construction site, and he's probably still around there. From what Pete told me, he has a lot to sleep off."

"Joan, if you ever want a job in this department," Gaylor said fervently, "you've got it!"

"No, thanks. I've got enough on my plate trying to do what I can for these poor guys."

"Thanks again, Joan."

Gaylor got up, went into Larry Ahearn's office, and briefed him.

Ahearn listened quietly. "You thought Winters was holding back on us," he said. "Looks as if you could be right. Find him and shake it out of him. Maybe he'll still be drunk enough to spill his guts to you."

"Have you heard any more from Leesey's family?"

Ahearn leaned back in his chair with a sigh. "I spoke to Gregg this morning. He's keeping his father pretty sedated. He won't leave him until this is resolved one way or the other." He shrugged. "Having said that, you and I both understand that we may never know what happened, or what *will* happen to Leesey."

"I don't believe that," Gaylor said. "You were right yesterday when you felt this guy wants attention."

"I'm also beginning to believe he wants to be caught, but in a way that will be a spectacular blowup." Ahearn's hands curled into fists. "Gregg told me an hour ago that he feels so damn helpless. Well, so do I."

As Gaylor turned to go, the phone rang again. Ahearn picked up the receiver, listened for a moment, and said, "Put him through." Waving Gaylor back, he said, "It's Gregg Andrews."

Gaylor listened as Larry Ahearn said, "Of course if your father wants an appeal printed in the media, we'll pass it on to them." He sat down and picked up a pen. "It's from the Bible. Okay." He wrote as he held the phone to his ear, stopping Gregg Andrews once, to repeat something, then said, "I have it. I'll take care of it."

With a deep sigh, he put the receiver down. "This is what Dr. Andrews would like to have read on the television stations and printed in the newspapers so that Leesey's abductor understands just how desperately he needs to have her returned to him safe and sound. It's from the prophet Hosea:

" 'When you were a child I loved you . . .
It was I who taught you to walk, took you in my arms . . .
I was to you like those who lift infants to their cheeks.
I bent down and fed you . . .
How could I give you up?' "

Both men's eyes glistened with tears as Detective Bob Gaylor left to search for Zach Winters.

Visions of dollar bills, stacks and stacks of them, were dancing in Zach Winters's brain as he opened his eyes to see some guy standing over him. He had been curled up in one of his favorite spots, a construction site near the Brooklyn Bridge, where the former parking garage had been pulled down, but the new building hadn't been started yet. The board fence had been ripped open, and now that it was warm, he and many of his friends used the site as their home base. Every ten days or two weeks the cops chased them out, but after a day or so they all came back with their gear. Like Zach, they all understood that when construction actually started, they'd be on their way again, but until then, it was a great spot to camp.

Zach had been dreaming about the fifty-thousand-dollar reward he would collect as soon as he figured out a way to collect it without getting himself into trouble, when he felt someone shaking his shoulder.

"Come on, Zach, wake up," a man's voice was demanding.

Zach opened his eyes slowly. A sense of familiarity seeped its way into his brain. I know this guy. He's police. He was in that room when the brother took me to talk about seeing Leesey. Be careful, Zach warned himself. He's the one who was so nasty that day.

Zach rolled over and slowly propped himself up on his elbows. He had covered himself with his winter jacket and now he pushed it aside. He blinked at the strong afternoon sun, then looked around quickly to make sure that his grocery cart was still there. He had slept with it flat on the ground next to him, his legs straddling the handle so that no one could reach into it without moving him first. It was safe enough, though some of the newspapers he had tucked in at the top were slipping out.

He blinked again. "Whadaya want?" he asked.

"I want to talk to you. Get up."

"All right. All right. Take it easy." Zach groped for the wine bottle that had been next to him when he fell asleep.

"It's empty," Gaylor snapped. He grabbed Zach's arm, and yanked him up sharply. "You've been telling your friends that you know something about Leesey's disappearance, something you didn't tell us the other day. What is it?"

"I don't know what you're talking about."

"Yes, you do." Gaylor bent down, grabbed the handle of the cart, and pulled it upright. "You've been telling your friends you have something that might earn you the reward that's been offered for Leesey Andrews. What is it?"

Zach made a gesture of brushing soil from his jacket. "I know my rights. Get away from me." He reached for the handle of his cart. Gaylor refused to let go of it, and blocked his way.

The detective's tone was angry. "Zach, why don't you cooperate with me? I want you to unload that cart and show me everything in it. We know you couldn't have had anything to do with Leesey's disappearance. You're too much of a drunk to have managed it. If you've got something in your stuff that helps us to find her, you'll get your reward. I promise."

"Yeah, sure you do." Zach reached out and tried to grab the handle from Gaylor. The cart swayed and some of the newspapers fell out. Beneath them, a filthy man's shirt was partially wrapped around what Gaylor instantly recognized as an expensive cosmetic case.

"Where'd you get that?" he snapped.

"None of your business." Zach righted the cart quickly and pushed the papers back into place. "I'm out of here." He began pushing the cart briskly toward the nearest sidewalk.

Staying in step with him, Gaylor grabbed his cell phone and dialed Ahearn. "I need a search warrant to seize the contents of Zach Winters's cart," he said. "He's got an expensive silver and black cosmetic bag that I'll bet belongs to Leesey Andrews. I'll stick with him until you get back to me. And find out from Leesey's roommate if she knows what kind of cosmetic bag Leesey was carrying that night."

Forty minutes later, backed up by two squad cars, the warrant in his pocket, Gaylor was opening Leesey Andrews's cosmetic case.

"I was scared you'd think I stole it," Zach Winters was whining. "When she was getting in the SUV, she dropped her pocketbook. Some stuff spilled out. She picked most of it up, but when they drove off, I went over there to see if maybe a few dollars had fallen out of her bag. You know what I mean. And I saw this and I took it, and I'll be honest with you, she had a fifty-dollar bill in it and maybe I gave myself a little reward and—"

"And why don't you shut up?" Bob Gaylor interrupted. "If you'd given this to us, even on Saturday, it might have made a difference."

Besides the usual cosmetics typical of a young woman's accessories, he had taken out a personal card. It belonged to Nick De-Marco, and gave the address and phone number of his loft. On the back of the card he had written, "Leesey, I can open some doors for you in show business and I'd be glad to do it. Call me, Nick."

56

With a satisfied smile, Derek Olsen signed the last of the mountain of papers that transferred the dilapidated town house he owned on 104th Street and Riverside Drive to Twining Enterprises, the multimillion-dollar real estate firm that was building an upscale luxury condominium next door. He had insisted that Douglas Twining Sr., the chairman and CEO of the company, personally attend the sale.

"I knew you'd pay what I wanted, Doug," Olsen said. "It was a lot of baloney that you didn't need my building."

"I didn't need it. I wanted it," Twining said quietly. "I could have done without it."

"And not have the corner? Not have the view? Maybe have me sell it to someone who put up one of those dumb sliver buildings so your fancy people look west at a brick wall? Come on."

Twining looked at his lawyer. "Are we finished here?"

"I believe so, sir."

Twining stood up. "Well, Derek, I suppose I should congratulate you."

"Why not? Twelve million dollars for a fifty-by-one-hundred-foot lot with a broken-down house that I paid fifteen thousand for forty years ago? That's inflation for you." Olsen's gleeful smile disappeared. "If it makes you feel any better, I'm putting this money to good use. A lot of kids in the Bronx, kids who won't grow up in your fancy-schmancy condos and won't go to the Hamptons for the summer, will now have some parks to play in—Derek Olsen parks. So when are you going to tear down the house?"

"The wrecking ball will be there Thursday morning. I think I'll handle it myself. I haven't forgotten how to do it."

"I'll come watch. Good-bye, Doug." Olsen turned to his lawyer, George Rodenburg. "Okay, let's get out of here," he said. "You can buy me an early dinner. I was too excited to eat lunch. And while we're eating, I'll phone my nephew and Howie and let them know that it's coming down on Thursday morning. I'll tell them I just got twelve million bucks for it and it's all going for my parks. I only wish I could see their faces. They'll both have heart attacks."

57

After I left the Kramers', I drove straight into the garage at Sutton Place, passed the flashing cameras, went upstairs, and threw some things in a bag. Wearing the biggest dark glasses I could find, to cover my face, I went back down in the elevator to the garage, this time taking my mother's car to fool them. Then, hoping to God I wouldn't cause an accident, I barreled out onto the street and made a quick turn onto Fifty-seventh Street. I drove up First Avenue as far as Ninety-sixth Street, trying to make sure that I wasn't being followed. I didn't want anyone to have any idea of where I might be going.

Of course, I couldn't be sure, but certainly there was no media van in sight when I turned right on Ninety-sixth and got on the FDR Drive north. The Drive, of course, was named to honor President Franklin Delano Roosevelt. That made me think of Elliott. The chilling thought came to me that if Mack was guilty of all these crimes and was caught, there would be months of publicity and a trial or trials. Elliott had lots of gold-plated clients. I know he's in love with Mom, but would he want to be associated with that kind of publicity? If he were married to Mom, would he want to see her picture in the tabloids during a trial?

Right now, he was her protector, but would that last? If Dad were alive now and Mack ended up in that scenario, I know Dad would be there for him, rock solid and moving heaven and earth to build an insanity defense for him. I thought of Elliott's too often repeated anecdote about FDR—that he chose a Republican to be his hostess when Eleanor was away because there was no Democrat in Hyde Park who was his social equal. I wonder what FDR, or Elliott, would think about having the mother of a convicted serial killer around? The way things were going, I could almost hear Elliott giving a "let's just be friends" speech to Mom.

As I reached the ever miserable Cross Bronx traffic, I tried to stop thinking and concentrate on my driving. With traffic slowing to a crawl, I called ahead and managed to get a reservation on the last ferry to the Vineyard from Falmouth. Then I made a reservation at the Vineyard Hotel in Chappaquiddick. And then I turned off my cell phone. I didn't want to speak to or hear from anyone.

It was nearly nine thirty when I arrived on the island and checked into the hotel. Exhausted but still restless, I went down to the bar and had a hamburger and two glasses of red wine. Then, against all sound medical advice, I took one of the sleeping pills I had found in Mom's night table and went to bed.

I slept for twelve hours straight.

58

At 4:30 P.M. Nick DeMarco was in his midtown office when his phone rang. It was Captain Larry Ahearn with a crisp request that he come to his office immediately. Swallowing over the absolute dryness in his mouth and throat, Nick agreed. As soon as he hung up, he dialed his attorney, Paul Murphy.

"I'll start right down," Murphy told him. "I'll meet you in the lobby there."

"I can do better than that," Nick said. "I was planning to leave in fifteen minutes anyway, which means Benny is probably outside right now circling the block. I'll call you when I'm in the car. We'll swing by and get you."

At five past five, Benny at the wheel, they were driving south on Park Avenue. "The way I see it, it's their way of rattling you," Murphy told him. "The only, and I repeat *only*, circumstantial evidence they can lay at your door are two facts: One, you invited Leesey over to talk with you in the club, and two, you have a black Mercedes SUV, which makes you one of thousands of owners of a black Mercedes SUV."

He shot a look at DeMarco. "Of course, you could have saved me from being surprised last time we were there."

Murphy had dropped his voice almost to a whisper, but Nick still nudged him with his elbow. He knew Murphy was referring to the fact that Benny's second wife had taken out a restraining order against him. He also knew that Benny had superb hearing and missed nothing.

The traffic was so unbearably slow that Murphy decided to phone Ahearn's office. "Just to let you know that we're in the usual five o'clock rush and can't do a thing about it."

Ahearn's response was simple. "Just get here. We're not going anywhere. Is DeMarco's chauffeur, Benny Seppini, driving the car you're in?"

"Yes, he is."

"Bring him up, too."

It was ten minutes of six when Nick DeMarco, Paul Murphy, and Benny Seppini walked through the squad room to Larry Ahearn's private office. They all noticed the frigid stares from the detectives in the squad room as they hurried through it.

Inside Ahearn's office, the atmosphere was even colder. Ahearn was again flanked by Detectives Barrott and Gaylor. There were three chairs in front of the desk. "Sit down," Ahearn said curtly.

Benny Seppini looked at DeMarco. "Mr. DeMarco, I don't think it's my place . . ."

"Cut the servant routine. You know you call him Nick," Ahearn interrupted. "And sit down now."

Seppini waited until DeMarco and Murphy had taken their places, then lowered himself into his chair. "I've known Mr. De-Marco for many years," he said. "He's an important man, and when I'm not alone with him, I call him Mr. DeMarco."

"That's touching," Ahearn said sarcastically. "Now let's all listen to this." He pressed the play button on a recorder, and Leesey Andrews's voice pleading to her father for help filled the room.

There was a moment of intense silence following the recording, then Paul Murphy asked, "What was the point of playing that recording for us?"

"I'm happy to tell you," Ahearn assured him. "I thought it might remind your client of the fact that as of yesterday, Leesey Andrews was probably still alive. We thought it might stir his better self to tell us where we can find her."

DeMarco sprang up from the chair. "I have no more idea than you do of where that poor girl is, and I'd give anything I have to save her life if I could."

"I'm sure you would," Barrott replied, his voice dripping with sarcasm. "You thought she was pretty cute, didn't you? In fact, you slipped her your personal card with the address of your cozy loft apartment."

He held up the card, cleared his throat, and read, " 'Leesey, I can open some doors for you in show business and I'd be glad to do it. Call me. —Nick.' "

He slapped the card down on the table. "You gave it to her that night, didn't you?"

"You don't have to answer that, Nick," Murphy warned.

Nick shook his head. "There's no reason not to answer it. Those few minutes she was at my table, I told her she was a beautiful dancer, which she certainly was. She confided that she'd love to take a year off after college, just to see if she could make it on the stage. I do know a lot of celebrities. So I gave her the card. So what?" He met Ahearn's suspicious gaze.

"You seem to have forgotten to mention it to us," Ahearn stated, scorn in every syllable he uttered.

"I've been here three times," Nick said, clearly agitated now. "Every time you come at me as if I had something to do with her disappearance. I know you can find some way to have my liquor license suspended at the Woodshed, even if you have to *create* a violation—"

"Stop it, Nick," Murphy ordered.

"I won't stop it. I had nothing to do with her disappearance. The last time I was here, you suggested I'm way overextended. You're absolutely right. If you shut down the Woodshed, I'll be thrown into bankruptcy. I've made some lousy decisions, I don't deny that, but hurting or abducting a kid like Leesey Andrews isn't one of them."

"You gave her your card," Bob Gaylor said.

"Yes, I did."

"When did you expect her to phone you at your loft?"

"My loft?"

"You gave her a card with the address of your loft and the phone number of the landline there."

"That's ridiculous. I gave her the card with my business address, 400 Park Avenue."

Barrott tossed the card at him. "Read it."

Perspiration on his forehead, Nick DeMarco read the print on the card several times before he spoke. "That was two weeks ago today," he said, more to himself than to the others. "I had some cards made, with just the loft address. They came in that day from the printer. I must have put one of them in my wallet. I thought I was giving my office card to Leesey."

"Why would you need an address card for the loft and the telephone number there unless you wanted to slip it to beautiful girls like Leesey?" Barrott asked.

"Nick, we can get up and walk out of here right now," Murphy said.

"That's not necessary. I've got my Fifth Avenue apartment up for sale. I plan to live in the loft. I have too many friends I haven't seen in a long time because I've been too busy trying to be a hotshot restaurant and club owner. Having those cards made was a gesture toward the future." He placed the card back on the desk.

"Is one of the people you want to see in the loft Mack MacKenzie's sister, Carolyn?" Barrott asked. "Cute picture of the two of you, hand in hand, rushing for your car last night. It brought tears to my eyes."

Ahearn turned to Benny Seppini. "Benny, let's talk to you now. The night Leesey disappeared, you had taken Nick's, excuse me, I mean Mr. DeMarco's black Mercedes SUV home with you to Astoria, isn't that right?"

"I drove his *sedan* home." Benny's scarred, rough features began to turn a dull red.

"Don't you have a car? Surely you must get paid enough to have your own wheels."

"I can answer that," Nick interrupted, before Benny could speak. "Last year when Benny told me he was trading his car in, I told him it was stupid for him to be paying insurance and upkeep on a car when I was paying to house three vehicles in a Manhattan garage, at Midtown prices no less. I suggested that he drive the SUV between his home and Manhattan and then switch to the sedan at the garage when he drove me to appointments."

Ahearn ignored him. "So, Benny, you drove the black Mercedes SUV, which your kindly employer offered you to use as your own vehicle, to your apartment in Astoria two weeks ago tonight, the night Leesey disappeared."

"No. Mr. DeMarco had the SUV in the garage at the loft because he was going to drive to the airport in the morning with his golf clubs. I dropped him off at the Woodshed at about ten o'clock in the sedan, then drove home to my place that night."

"You then went into your apartment, and to bed."

"Uh-huh. That was about eleven o'clock."

"Benny, the parking problem is pretty lousy in your neighborhood, isn't it?"

"Parking's lousy everywhere in New York City."

"But you lucked out. You got a spot for your employer's vehicle right in front of your apartment building. Isn't that right?"

"Yeah, that's where I parked it. I got home and got into bed and turned on Jay Leno. He was really funny. He was talking about . . ."

"I don't care what he was talking about. I care about the fact that the black Mercedes vehicle owned by Nick DeMarco wasn't there the whole night. Your neighbor in apartment 6D saw you pulling into a space in front of the building at about 5:15, when he was leaving for work. Tell us, Benny, where had you been? Did you get an emergency call from Mr. DeMarco? Had there been some kind of problem?"

Benny Seppini's expression became angry and mulish. "None of your business," he barked.

"Benny, do you have a cell phone with a prepaid card?" Ahearn demanded.

"You don't have to answer that, Benny," Paul Murphy shouted.

"Why not? Sure I do. I place a few bets. A hundred bucks here and there. So arrest me."

"Didn't you buy one of those cell phones and prepaid cards as a joke birthday present for Nick, I mean Mr. DeMarco?"

"Keep quiet, Benny!" Paul Murphy shouted.

Benny stood up. "Why should I? I'll tell you what happened that night. I got a call around midnight from a very nice lady who is separated from a drunken bum husband. She was scared. The husband knows she and I like each other. He left a crazy message on her cell phone, threatening her. I couldn't get back to sleep, so I got dressed and drove over there. Her place is about a mile away from mine. I sat outside her building in the car to make sure he didn't show up after the bars closed. I stayed till five o'clock. Then I went home."

"You're a real Sir Galahad, Benny," Ahearn said. "Who is this woman? Who's the guy threatening her?"

"He's a cop," Benny said flatly. "One of New York's finest. She has grown kids who think he's the world's best guy and just has a small problem with booze. She don't want trouble. *I* don't want trouble. So I'm not going to say nothing more."

Paul Murphy stood up. "We've had enough," he told Ahearn, Barrott, and Gaylor. "I'm sure you'll be able to confirm Benny's story, and I know my client would do anything to help the young girl who is missing." He threw them all a scornful look. "Why don't you stop barking up the wrong tree, and go find the abductor of Leesey Andrews and those other young women? And why don't you stop wasting your time trying to put round pegs in square holes while there may still be a chance to save her life?"

The three detectives watched the men depart. When the door closed behind them, Ahearn said, "That story is full of holes. Sure, Benny could have covered himself by being outside his girlfriend's building for a while, but he still had plenty of time to respond to an emergency call from Nick and get Leesey out of that loft."

They looked at one another in an agony of frustration, each man hearing in his head, once again, Leesey Andrews's desperate cry for help.

59

And the walls came tumbling down . . ." Was that an old gospel folk hymn? Something about Joshua and the walls of Jericho? He wasn't sure. The only thing that *was* sure was that time was running out, fast.

I really, *really* didn't want to end up like this, he thought. It was forced on me. I really did try to stop after the first one. That wasn't counting the *real* first one, of course, the one nobody knew about. But then I wasn't allowed to stop.

Not fair. Not fair.

The end is coming, he thought, feeling his pulse quicken. I can't stop it. It's all over. I'll be found out, but I'm not going to be arrested. I'm going to die, but I'm going to take someone new with me. What's the best way—the most *exciting* way—to do it?

I'll figure it out, he told himself.

After all, he always had.

60

Martha's Vineyard is about three hundred miles northeast of Manhattan, and slower to warm up. On Tuesday morning when I woke up, I looked out the window at the bright cold day. Feeling physically and emotionally stronger, I got out of bed and considered what to wear when I confronted Barbara Hanover Galbraith. It was cool enough for the running suit I had thrown in my bag, but that was not necessarily the outfit I would choose for our meeting.

I didn't want to seem either overdressed or too casual. I wanted no sense of being Mack's little sister when I saw Barbara. She was a pediatric surgeon. I was a *juris doctoris*, an attorney-at-law, and had just completed a clerkship with a civil court judge. My alternative was a dark-green cashmere jacket, white fitted camisole, and white jeans I had taken from the closet at the last minute. Now I was glad that I had the option of wearing them.

Although it was nearly lunchtime, I called room service to order a continental breakfast, and drank black coffee and nibbled on a cinnamon bun while I dressed. I realized I was so nervous that my fingers were clumsy, fumbling as they unpinned the cleaner's tags from the clothes.

I was perfectly aware that I might be on a fool's errand. Barbara and her children might be back in Manhattan by now. But I didn't think that would be the case. I believed that she was hiding out up here to avoid being questioned about Mack, in which case she'd have stayed put.

I was sure that if I called first she would put me off. But if I simply showed up, there was almost no civil way she could close the door in my face, since she had once been a guest for dinner at Sutton Place.

At least I hoped not.

Checking my watch, I realized I needed to get moving if I wanted to catch Barbara at home. In the car, I set the navigation system. The street where Richard Hanover lived was about six miles away. My plan was to drive to the house and ring the bell. If no one was there, I'd go into the center of town and walk around for a while, then make periodic trips back to the house until she was in.

It seemed like a good plan, but of course the day's events didn't unfold that way. I reached the house at about 12:30. There was no one there. I came back every hour until 5:30. By then, I had decided it was a totally wasted trip, and was as thoroughly disheartened as any human being could possibly be. Then, just as I was making a U-turn, a Jeep with New York plates passed me and turned into the driveway. I caught a glimpse of a woman at the wheel, with a man beside her and some kids in the back.

I drove around for ten minutes or so, then went back to the house and rang the bell. A man in his early seventies answered the door. He obviously had no idea who I was but his smile was cordial. I introduced myself, and said that Bruce had told me his family was visiting. "Come in," he said. "You must be a friend of Barbara's."

"Mr. Hanover," I said, stepping across the threshold, "I'm Mack MacKenzie's sister. I need to talk to her about him."

His expression changed. "I don't think that's a very good idea," he said.

"It's not a matter of its being a good idea," I said. "I'm afraid it's necessary." Not giving him a chance to reply, I walked past him into the living room.

The house was one of those early Cape Cods that had been expanded over the years. The living room wasn't large, but it was charming, with Early American furniture and a hooked rug. Overhead, I could hear the sound of running feet and shrieks of laughter. The children sounded young. I thought I remembered hearing that Barbara and Bruce Galbraith had a boy and twin girls.

Richard Hanover had disappeared, presumably to tell his daughter I was here. While I waited, three little girls came pounding down the stairs, followed by a girl of about eleven. The little ones rushed over to me. Two of them were obviously twins. The girls crowded around me, pleased to be greeting a guest.

"What's your name?" I pointed to one of the twins.

"Samantha Jean Galbraith," she said proudly. "Everybody calls me Sammy, and we took the ferry to Cape Cod today."

They'd been on an all-day excursion to the Cape, I thought. I pointed to the other twin. "What's your name?"

"Margaret Hanover Galbraith. I'm named after my grandmother who is in heaven, and everybody calls me Maggie." Both girls have their mother's blond hair, I thought to myself.

"And is this your cousin or your friend?" I asked, indicating the other little girl.

"This is Ava Grace Gregory, our very best friend," Samantha explained. Ava Grace took a step closer to me and beamed. Samantha turned and tugged at the older girl's hand. "And this is Victoria Somers. She visits us here and sometimes we visit her at her ranch in Colorado."

"I go with them sometimes," Ava Grace told me earnestly. "And my daddy took all of us to the White House."

"I've never been there myself," I told her. "That's wonderful." I love kids, I thought to myself. Someday I'm going to have at least four of my own, I hope.

"Okay, you guys. Go upstairs and get cleaned up before it's time to go out for dinner." The tone was light and the children were facing me, so they could not see the expression on Barbara Hanover Galbraith's face. She looked at me with such intense dislike that the only emotion I could feel was astonishment.

I had met her once at dinner when I was sixteen years old. I had been heartbroken, because it had looked as if Nick had a crush on her, but now he claims that it was she who had a crush on Mack. Suddenly I wondered if I was reading her expression correctly. Was it scorn that I was seeing in her narrowed eyes and tense body language, or something else?

With a chorus of good-byes, the girls were on their way upstairs. Barbara said, "I'd rather talk in the den."

I followed her down the narrow hall. There was a large country kitchen at the end that spilled into a family room. The den was to the left before the kitchen. If I were to guess, I would say that this was where Richard Hanover spent his evenings when he was alone. It had cheery wallpaper, a patterned carpet, a medium-sized desk and chair, and a recliner that faced a wall-mounted television. There was a reading lamp to the left behind the recliner, and a basket of books and magazines within easy reach.

I could visualize my father in that room.

Barbara closed the door and sat behind the desk, leaving me only the reclining chair, which seemed too big and too deep for me. I knew she was Mack's age, thirty-one, but she was one of those women whose early beauty doesn't last. Her face, which I remembered as being flawless, was too thin now, her lips too narrow. The cascade of blond hair that I had once both admired and envied was now drawn tight in a chignon. But she was still compelling in a slender, autocratic way. I imagined that her commanding presence must be a comfort to the parents of her pediatric patients.

"Why did you come here, Carolyn?" she demanded.

I looked at her, trying to reflect the same hostility that was emanating from her. "Barbara," I said, "from what I understand you and Mack were dating ten years ago when he disappeared. Frankly, I've been told that you were pretty crazy about him. If, as the police believe, and as you surely have read in the newspapers, Mack is committing crimes, there can only be one reason for it, and that is that he's had a complete mental breakdown. I need to know if you saw any sign of it."

She said nothing.

I stared back at her. "I'm telling you right now that when I met your husband at his office, he showed such hostility about Mack that I was floored. What did Mack ever do to Bruce, and did it have anything to do with his disappearance? What reason do you have for rushing up here to avoid questioning? If you think you can hide out up here, you're wrong. The media is camped outside our home on Sutton Place. Every time I go in or out, they try to shove a microphone in my face. Unless I can get some honest answers from you, and I am satisfied that you know nothing about the reason for Mack's disappearance, then the next time I'm hounded by the media I'm going to tell them you and your husband are holding back information that may be helpful in finding Leesey Andrews."

I watched as the color drained from her face. "You wouldn't *dare* to do that!"

"Oh, yes, I would," I assured her. "I will do *anything* to find Mack and stop him, if he is committing these crimes, or clear his name if he is innocent. For all I know, he's a victim of amnesia and may be living three thousand miles away."

"I don't know where he is, but I *do* know why he walked away." Barbara Galbraith's chin began to tremble. "If I tell you, will you swear to leave us alone? Bruce had nothing to do with his disappearance. Bruce loved me and saved my life. It's because of what Mack did to me that he hates him."

"What did he do to you?" I could almost not form the words. I had been wrong. I hadn't been seeing only hatred from Dr. Barbara Hanover Galbraith. I had been witnessing pain that she had been trying not to unleash.

"I was crazy about Mack. We were going out together. To him, it was casual, I know that. But then I got pregnant. I was frantic. My mother was dying. The health insurance was pitiful, and all the money that had been put aside for medical school had been spent. I had been accepted at Columbia Presbyterian, and I knew I couldn't go. I told Mack."

She gulped to avoid sobbing. "He said he would take care of me. He said we'd get married, and I could defer school for one year, then start."

That sounds like Mack, I thought.

"I believed him. I knew he didn't love me, but I was also sure I could *get* him to love me. Then he disappeared. Just like that. I didn't know what to do."

"Why didn't you go to my parents?" I demanded. "They would have taken care of you."

"Maybe give me a handout to support their son's child? No, thank you." Barbara bit her lip. "I am a pediatric surgeon. I thrill to touch a tiny baby and save its life. I have saved babies so small that they fit in the palm of my hand. I have the gift of healing. But there is one baby I didn't save. My own. I had an abortion because I was desperate." She averted her eyes, and continued. "You know something, Carolyn? Sometimes in the pediatric nursery, when a little one is crying, I go over and pick it up and comfort it, and when I do, I think of the baby I had scraped out of my own womb."

She stood up. "Your brother wasn't that sure about being a lawyer. He told me that he'd get the degree to please his father, but that he'd really have liked to try his hand at acting. I don't think he's crazy—I think he's out there somewhere and maybe even has the grace to be ashamed of himself by now. Do I think he's committing these crimes?

Absolutely not. I loathe him for what he did to me, but he is not a serial killer. I'm surprised you'd even give that possibility a second thought."

"I'm going to go, and I promise I will never mention you in any way to anyone, nor bother you again," I said quietly as I stood up, "but I have one more question. Why does Bruce hate Mack so?"

"There is a very simple answer. Bruce loves me. All through Columbia, from the time we were freshmen, I knew that. After I had the abortion, I went to a hotel room and swallowed sleeping pills. And then I decided I wanted to live. I called Bruce. He came rushing to me. He saved my life. He'll always be there for me, and I love him for that, and I've learned over time to love him for himself. Now, do me a favor and get out of this house."

The downstairs of the rest of the house was quiet as I walked along the hall to the front door. From upstairs I could hear the voices of the children, and my guess was that Richard Hanover had kept them there so that they could not hear what we were saying.

If I could describe my emotions, I would say I felt as though I were in a whirlwind, being slammed back and forth against opposite walls. At last I had the answer to why my brother disappeared. Mack had been unutterably selfish, but he didn't want to go to law school, and didn't love Barbara, and her pregnancy was what galvanized him into running away. Even the quote on the tape made sense. "When, in disgrace with fortune and men's eyes . . . I all alone beweep my outcast state, and trouble deaf heaven with my bootless cries."

In his defense, he must have counted on Barbara going to my parents for support for his baby.

Barbara's flat statement that Mack was not responsible for these crimes, her shock that I would even consider the possibility, was both a reproach and a relief to me. In my mind, I had been trying to form an insanity defense for him. Now whatever fears I had that he was abducting and killing women were over. I knew I would stake my immortal soul on the fact that he was innocent.

Then who was doing this? Who? I asked myself as I got into the car. Of course, I had no answer.

I drove back to the hotel, keeping my fingers crossed that I could extend my stay. The place was really more of an inn than a hotel, and only had eight or ten bedrooms. I had planned to leave at six P.M., and was being billed for a late checkout.

Thank God, my room was available. I didn't think there was any way I could have waited at the ferry and then driven home in my present frame of mind. Driven home to what? I asked myself bitterly. The media at my heels. Barrott's insinuating calls. An absent mother who wanted no part of me. A "friend," Nick, who was probably using me to help clear his own name.

I went upstairs. The room was cold. I had left a window open that the housekeeper hadn't closed. I closed it now and turned up the thermostat, then I looked in the mirror. I looked gaunt and weary. My hair, which I'd left loose, seemed limp on my shoulders.

I grabbed the courtesy bathrobe from the closet, went into the bathroom, and began to run the tub. Three minutes later, I was feeling the warmth of the bathwater begin to permeate the chill in my body. When I dressed, I put on the running suit that, thankfully, I had brought with me. It felt good to be wearing it, zipped high at the neck, only my face and head showing. I twisted my hair back and pinned it, then applied a little makeup to hide the stress I saw in my eyes and expression.

Celebrities in dark glasses at night have always amused me. I often wondered how they managed to read the menu in a restaurant. This evening, I put on the glasses I had worn while I was driving up yesterday. They covered half my face and made me feel shielded.

I picked up my shoulder bag and went downstairs to the restaurant, then was dismayed to see that except for a large middle table with a reservation sign on it, there didn't seem to be anything available. But the maitre d' took pity on me. "There is a small table in a corner, near the kitchen door," he said. "I don't like to assign it, but if you don't mind . . ."

"It will be fine," I told him.

I had been settled there long enough to order a glass of wine and review the menu when they came into the dining room. Dr. Barbara Hanover Galbraith, her father, the four girls. And one other person. A boy about nine or ten years old, a boy with sandy hair, whose face I recognized as clearly as I would my own if I looked in the mirror.

I stared at him. The wide-set eyes, the high forehead, the cowlick, the straight nose. He was smiling. Mack's smile. I was looking at Mack's face. My God, I was looking at Mack's *son!*

I suddenly felt light-headed as the realization hit me. Barbara had lied. She *didn't* have the abortion. She never went into any pediatric nursery and longed for the child she had destroyed. She had borne that child, and was raising him as Bruce Galbraith's son.

How much of the rest of her story was true? I asked myself.

I had to get out of there. I stood up and walked through the kitchen, ignoring the stares of the workers. I crossed into the lobby, stumbled upstairs, packed my bag, checked out, and caught the last ferry from the Vineyard. At two A.M. I got back to Sutton Place.

For once, there was no media truck on the block.

But Detective Barrott was standing in the garage. Obviously, he must have known that I was on the way home, and I realized I must have been followed. I was dizzy with exhaustion. "What do you want?" I almost screamed.

"Carolyn, Dr. Andrews received another message from Leesey an hour ago. Her exact words were, 'Daddy, Mack said that he's going to kill me now. He doesn't want to take care of me anymore. Good-bye, Daddy. I love you, Daddy.' "

Barrott's voice echoed through the garage as he shouted, "And then she screamed, 'No, *please don't* . . . ' He was strangling her. He was *strangling* her, Carolyn. We couldn't save her. Where is your brother, Carolyn? I know you know. Where is that stinking killer? You've got to tell us. Where is he now?"

61

At three o'clock on Wednesday morning, as he was driving around SoHo looking for a vulnerable target, his cell phone rang.

"Where are you?" a tense voice asked.

"Cruising in SoHo. Nothing special." This was his favorite neighborhood. Lots of drunken young women stumbling home at this hour.

"Those streets are alive with cops. You wouldn't try to pull anything stupid, would you?"

"Stupid, no. Exciting, yes," he said, his eyes still scanning. "I need one more. I can't help it."

"Get home and go to bed. I have someone else for you, and she'll make the biggest headlines of all."

"Do I know her?"

"You know her."

"Who is she?"

He listened as he heard the name. "Oh, that's really good," he exclaimed. "Did I ever tell you that you're my favorite uncle?"

62

The horror of the recording of Leesey's final good-bye to her father had shaken even the hardened detective squad to the core. Catching the serial killer before he could strike again had become a burning need for each of them. Over and over, the full squad reviewed every fact that had come to light during the investigation.

On Wednesday morning, they were crowded into Ahearn's office again.

Gaylor was reporting his findings. Benny Seppini's story had checked out. He was seeing Anna Ryan, the separated wife of Walter Ryan, a police sergeant who was known for his heavy drinking and volatile temper. Anna Ryan confirmed that she had been speaking to Benny Monday night two weeks ago and expressed to him her fear of her husband. When told that Benny claimed he had been parked in his car outside her apartment building, she had smiled and said, "That's just what Benny *would* do."

"That doesn't mean Benny didn't get an emergency phone call from DeMarco that night," Ahearn pointed out. "But we'll never prove that."

Ahearn began reading from his notes. In the several days since he had been followed by plainclothes detectives, Nick DeMarco had done nothing unusual. His wiretapped phone conversations had been mostly business-oriented. Several from a real estate agent confirmed that his Park Avenue apartment was for sale. In fact, an offer had been made that he said he would consider. He had tried to phone Carolyn MacKenzie half a dozen times, but she had obviously turned off her cell phone. "We know she was on her way to Martha's Vineyard," Ahearn said. "DeMarco didn't know, and he was getting pretty worried about her."

Ahearn looked up to make sure he still had everyone's attention. "Carolyn went to see her brother's ex-girlfriend, Dr. Barbara Hanover Galbraith, but she didn't stay long. The husband wasn't up there. Then, when the family came into the hotel where Carolyn was staying, she bolted and drove home. Carolyn didn't get any calls in the hotel. She hasn't used her cell phone from the time she left town Monday, after she saw the Kramers, till now."

"She was crying when she left the Kramers' Monday morning. We have a picture of her leaving the building. Then a guy followed her to her car. This is a shot of him with her." Ahearn put down his notes and handed photos to Barrott. "We checked him out. His name is Howard Altman. He works for Derek Olsen, who owns a bunch of small apartment buildings, including the one Mack lived in. Altman didn't start the job until a couple of months after MacKenzie disappeared."

The pictures were passed around and put back on Ahearn's desk. "Our guys went back to see the Kramers Monday afternoon." Ahearn's voice was increasingly weary. In his head, he could not stop hearing Leesey's cry, "No, *please don't . . .*" He cleared his throat. "Gus Kramer said he told Carolyn that his wife saw Mack at that Mass when he left the note in the collection basket and that he was a killer and she should leave them alone. Carolyn started crying and ran out."

"The first time we saw her," Gaylor said, "Mrs. Kramer didn't tell us that she saw Mack in church the morning he left the note, because she didn't have her distance eyeglasses with her so she couldn't be

sure it was him. Then Monday afternoon she said that now she's convinced it *was* Mack. Do we believe her?"

"I don't believe anything the Kramers tell us," Ahearn said flatly,
"but I don't think Gus Kramer is a serial killer." He looked at Barrott.
"Brief them on what Carolyn MacKenzie told you when you met her
in the garage this morning."

The dark circles under Roy Barrott's eyes had given way to deep
pouches. "We had it out in the garage. She swore that her brother is
innocent, that just because Leesey used his name doesn't mean she
wasn't made to say it. She said she's going to comb every statement we
make or have made and read every word that's been published, and if
she finds anything that says her brother is a killer, she will sue until
the cows come home." He paused, rubbing his forehead. "She told
me she was a lawyer and a damn good one, and she was out to prove
it to me. She said that if her brother was guilty, she'd be the first to
turn him in before he ends up in a shootout, and then she'd work like
hell to create an insanity defense for him."

"Do you believe her?" Chip Dailey, one of the newest detectives,
asked.

Barrott shrugged. "I believe she believes he's innocent, yeah. I
also now believe she's not in touch with the brother. If he's the one
who called her mother's apartment using Leesey's cell phone, it's just
another one of his games."

Ahearn's phone rang. When he answered, his expression
changed, then he said, "Be sure there's no possibility of a mistake."
When he broke the connection, he said, "Lil Kramer spent two years
in prison when she was twenty-four years old. She was working for
an elderly woman. When the woman died, a lot of her jewelry was
missing. Lil was convicted of stealing it."

"Did she admit it?" Barrott asked.

"Never. Doesn't matter. She was convicted at trial. I want her and

Gus Kramer brought down here now." He looked around the room. "All right. You all know your assignments." His eye fell on Barrott, who was almost asleep on his feet. "Roy, go home and sleep. You're truly convinced that Carolyn isn't in touch with her brother?"

"Yes."

"Then forget tailing her. We know we don't have enough to detain the Kramers, but once they leave here I want both of them followed."

As the squad turned to file out, Ahearn said something that he had not been sure he was going to share. "I've listened to that recording at least one hundred times. This may sound crazy, but we're dealing with a lunatic. You hear Leesey scream and then a gasping, gurgling sound, but then he disconnected her cell phone. We didn't actually hear her die."

"You seriously think she's still alive?" Gaylor asked incredulously.

"I think the guy we're dealing with would not be above that kind of game, yes."

63

After my shouting match with Detective Barrott, I went upstairs to find concerned messages from both Nick and Elliott on the machine. "Where are you, Carolyn? Please give me a call. I'm worried about you." That was from Nick. His final message had been left at midnight. "Carolyn, your cell phone isn't turned on. When you get home, please call me, no matter what time it is."

Elliott had left three messages, the latest at 11:30 P.M. "Carolyn, your cell phone is off. Please call me. I'm so concerned about you. I saw your mother this evening, and I feel that she is much stronger emotionally, but I feel as if in my concern for her, I may have been failing you. You *know* how dear you are to me. Call me as soon as you get this message."

Listening to all the messages, the concern in both their voices, felt like stumbling into a warm room after an ice storm. I loved them both, but I was hardly going to call either one of them at 3:30 in the morning. I had rushed out of the restaurant in Martha's Vineyard without having dinner, and now I realized I was starving. I went into the kitchen and had a glass of milk and half a peanut butter sandwich. I hadn't eaten peanut butter in ages, but somehow at that moment I craved it. Then I got undressed and fell into bed. I was so wired that I didn't think I would sleep, but the minute I closed my eyes I was gone.

Gone into a maze of mournful dreams and weeping shadows and something else. What was it? What face was I trying to see that was eluding me, taunting me? It wasn't Mack. When I dreamt about him, I saw a boy of ten, with a cowlick and sandy hair and wide-set eyes. *Mack's son. My nephew.* I woke up around eight o'clock, put on a robe, and, still half groggy, went down to the kitchen.

In the morning light, the kitchen seemed reassuringly familiar. Whenever Mom went on a trip, she let our longtime housekeeper have a mini-vacation; Sue would come in only once a week to keep the apartment fresh. All the little signs showed me that she had been in yesterday while I was at the Vineyard. There was fresh milk in the fridge, and the mail that I had dumped on a counter in the kitchen was neatly stacked. I was just grateful that she'd been here the one day I was away. I couldn't have endured having her commiserate with me about Mack.

I didn't have the faintest desire for anything to eat. But my head was clear, and I had some decisions to make. I tried to think them through over three cups of coffee.

Detective Barrott. I honestly thought I convinced him that I was not protecting Mack, but on the other hand, I had not told him about something that might have had everything to do with Mack's disappearance . . .

Barbara had told me that Bruce's anger at Mack was because of Mack's treatment of her. But maybe there was a lot more to it than that. Bruce had always been desperately in love with Barbara. He obviously married her on her terms—"Be my baby's father and send me to medical school." Did he have anything to do with forcing Mack to run away? Did he threaten him? And if so, with what?

That simply didn't make sense to me.

Mack's child. I had to protect him. Barbara didn't know I had seen him. He was growing up as the son of a pediatric surgeon and a wealthy real estate entrepreneur. He had two little sisters. I could never shatter his world, and if I tried to cast suspicion on Bruce, and Barrott began digging into the relationship between Barbara and Mack before Mack disappeared, that could happen.

I needed someone to talk to, someone whom I could trust implicitly. Nick? No. The lawyer we'd hired, Thurston Carver? No. And then the answer came, and it was so simple I couldn't believe I hadn't thought of it sooner: Lucas Reeves! He had been in on the investigation since the beginning. He had interviewed Nick and Barbara and Bruce and the Kramers. I called his office. It was only 8:30, but he was already there. He told me to come over as soon as I could make it. He said that he and his staff were working on nothing but finding Leesey's abductor.

"Even if it's Mack?" I said.

"Of course, even if it's Mack, but I absolutely do not believe the answer lies with him."

I showered, then turned on the television and watched as I dressed. The police had released to the media the fact that another call had been received from Leesey. "The contents have not been revealed, but a police source confirmed that there is a high probability that she is now dead," the CNN anchor said.

As I pulled on jeans and a long-sleeve cotton sweater, I thought that at least, by not releasing the exact contents of the conversation, Mack's name had been kept out of it.

I like jewelry, and I always wear earrings and something around my neck. Today I chose a thin gold chain with a pearl that Daddy had given to me, and then I fished in the drawer for the earrings that Mack had presented to me on my sixteenth birthday. They were a gold sunburst design with a tiny diamond in the center. I felt close to both Daddy and Mack as I fastened them.

It was about a mile from Sutton Place to Reeves's office, but I decided to walk. After so much time in the car in the last few days, I needed the exercise. The question was how I could avoid the media.

I did it by going down to the garage and waiting for a few minutes until a resident of the building came along. Then I begged a ride. He was a distinguished-looking older man. I had never met him. "Could I just hide on the floor of your backseat until we're a couple of blocks away?" I pleaded.

He looked at me sympathetically. "Ms. MacKenzie, I certainly understand why you want to get away without the media, but I'm afraid I'm not the one who should help you. I'm a federal judge."

I almost laughed in disbelief. But then the judge signaled to someone who had just gotten off the elevator. "Hi, David," he said. "This young lady needs help, and I know you'll provide it." Feeling my cheeks burn with embarrassment, I thanked them both.

David whoever-he-was dropped me off at Park and Fifty-seventh. I walked the rest of the way, my thoughts as scattered as the scraps of paper that the breeze was picking up and depositing near the curb. The month of May was almost over. *O Mary, we crown thee with blossoms today, Queen of the Angels, Queen of the May.* We used to sing that every May at the Academy of the Sacred Heart, and one year, when I was about seven, I got to crown the statue of the Virgin.

Fast-forward to the scene today—me kneeling on the floor of the car to avoid microphones and cameras!

When I got to Lucas Reeves's office, the sight of that small, strong-featured man with the resonant voice helped me to focus again. He pumped my hand vigorously, as if he understood I needed human contact. "Come inside, Carolyn," he said. "I've got quite a setup in here." He led me into a large conference room. The walls were covered with pictures in which faces had been enlarged. Some of them were inside shots, others had obviously been taken outside. "These start when the first young woman disappeared ten years ago," Reeves explained. "We've culled them from newspaper pictures, television clips, security cameras. They were taken in and around the clubs where the four young women disappeared. I have invited the detective squad of the District Attorney's office to come here and inspect them to see if, just maybe, one face will trigger a connection that has been missed so far. Why don't you look at them?"

I walked around the room, stopping when I saw the faces of Mack and Nick and some of their friends at that first club. They looked so young, I thought. Then I walked around all four walls, from one collage to the next, and then to the next, my eyes searching and searching. At one point, I stopped. That looks like—, I thought, then almost laughed out loud. How stupid. I couldn't even see the man's face, just his eyes and forehead.

"Anything?" Lucas asked.

"No. Just the obvious ones of Mack and Nick in that first club."

"All right. Let's go into my office."

We settled in there. The ritual coffee was delivered, and then I told Lucas Reeves what I had learned in Martha's Vineyard. He listened, his expression becoming increasingly grave. "So it now seems that Mack had a very good reason for disappearing. A woman he did not love was bearing his child. He did not want to marry her. He did not want to go to law school. So rather than risk the certain disappointment your parents, especially your father, would have felt, he ran away. The root cause of a vast majority of crimes is one of two factors, love or money. In Mack's case, the primary motive for his disappearance would be his lack of love for Barbara."

Reeves leaned back in his chair. "People have run away for less. If—and I repeat, if—Mack was involved in the death of that first young woman, that also might explain the theft of the tapes from his former teacher. When she was interviewed, she could give no explanation for his disappearance, except to say that he would have made an exceptionally fine actor. But perhaps he confided too much to her, and felt he had to retrieve his tapes somehow. I have studied the records. Her death was caused not so much by the blow to her head that rendered her unconscious, but by the fall itself onto the sidewalk. That was what caused the bleeding in the brain that took her life."

He stood up and walked to the window. "Carolyn, there are questions here that we have not yet answered. Even if your brother *is* part of it, I don't think he is *all* of it." He paused, then added: "When I called Captain Ahearn, he did not divulge the full contents of the message Leesey left, but he did say she spoke about Mack."

"Detective Barrott told me what she said." My throat closed as I quoted Leesey's agonizing words, and then I repeated what I had shouted at Barrott.

"And you are correct. She may have been forced to use his name."

"I keep coming back to the fact that Bruce Galbraith hates Mack," I said. "Think how much he must have hated him when Mack was involved with Barbara. Suppose Mack *did* just take off." I started to speculate. "Suppose Bruce is still afraid he'll show up someday, and Barbara will go running to him. She claims she hates Mack, but I wonder if that's true. Mack was such a special human being. He always said that Bruce had zero personality. When I saw Bruce last week, he was openly hostile, so it was obviously not a normal social exchange. But he's a plain-looking guy, and while he may be hugely successful, I bet that on a day-to-day basis, he's still the same dull and boring person. Nick said they called him 'the Lone Stranger,' and he was in the club the night the first girl disappeared." I watched Reeves as he considered all of this.

"I wonder how thoroughly Mr. Galbraith was investigated ten years ago," Reeves said. "I'll look into it."

I got up. "I won't keep you any longer, Lucas," I said. "But I'm glad to have you in my corner." I corrected myself, "In Mack's corner, too."

"Yes, I am." He walked with me through the reception area to the door. "Carolyn, if I may be personal, you are living under a strain that would break the most hardy of men. Is there a place you could get away to, to be by yourself, or with a close friend?" He looked at me with concern.

"I'm thinking about it," I said. "But first I'm going to visit my mother, whether she wants to see me or not. As you know, she's in that private sanitarium in Connecticut, where Elliott brought her."

"I do know." At the door, Reeves took my hand again. "Carolyn, the entire detective squad from the District Attorney's office will be in and out all afternoon. Maybe one of them will spot a face in that sea of faces that will open a door for us."

I walked home. This time I did not try to sneak into the apartment building. The doors of media vans that had been keeping vigil sprang open, and reporters came rushing up to me as I approached our building.

"Carolyn . . . what do you think?"

"Ms. MacKenzie, would you broadcast an appeal to your brother to turn himself in?"

I turned to face the microphones. "I will broadcast an appeal to one and all to presume my brother innocent of any and all crimes. Remember, there is not one *shred* of proof against him. Everything is based on innuendo and supposition. And let me remind all of you that there are libel laws and serious penalties for violating them."

I hurried inside, not giving them a chance to respond. I went up to the apartment and began to return the phone calls I had been ignoring. The first was to Nick. His relief at hearing my voice seemed so spontaneous that I tucked it away in a corner of my mind as something to think about later.

"Carolyn, don't do this to me. I've been a wreck. I even called Captain Ahearn to see if they were holding you there. He said they hadn't heard from you."

"They hadn't heard from me, but they knew where I was," I said. "Evidently I was being followed."

I told Nick that I had seen Barbara in Martha's Vineyard, but it had been a useless trip. I selected carefully the information I would give him. "I agree with you. She probably married Bruce to get a ticket to medical school, but she seems to be keeping her share of the bargain." I also couldn't resist having a chance to slam her. "She let me know what a devoted and loving pediatric surgeon she is, that sometimes when she walks through the pediatric nursery, she goes over to a crying baby and picks it up to comfort it."

"That would be Barbara," Nick agreed. "Carolyn, how are you holding up?"

"Just barely." I could hear the exhaustion in my voice.

"Me, too. The cops have been raking me and Benny over the coals again. One good piece of news?" His tone brightened. "I sold my Park Avenue apartment."

"The one that makes you feel like Roy Rogers?" I smiled.

"Exactly. The agent tells me the buyer is planning to rip it to the studs and redesign it. Good luck to him."

"Where will you go?"

"To the loft. I'm looking forward to it, if there's anything I look forward to at this minute. We caught a nineteen-year-old with a phony driver's license in the club last night. If we'd served her, we could have been shut down. I wouldn't be surprised if she was planted by the cops to put more pressure on me."

"Nothing would surprise me at this point," I said, meaning it.

"Dinner tonight? I want to see you."

"No, I don't think so. I'm going to drive up and try to visit Mom. I need to see for myself how she's doing."

"I'll drive you."

"No, I have to go alone."

"Carolyn, let me ask you something. Years ago, Mack told me that you had a crush on me and that I should be careful not to encourage it by playing up to you." He paused, clearly trying to keep his tone playful. "Is there any way I could revive that crush, or now is it going to stay one-sided on my part?"

I know there was a smile in my voice. "It was mean of him to tell you."

"No, it wasn't." Nick's voice became serious again. "All right, Carolyn. I'll let you go. But hang on to the thought that we're going to make it through this mess."

I started to cry. I didn't want him to hear, and clicked off, but then immediately wondered if Nick hadn't been starting to say, "together," or did I only imagine hearing that word because I wanted so desperately for it to turn out that way?

Then it occurred to me for the first time that it was possible my cell phone and the telephone line in the apartment were being tapped. Of course they must be, I thought. Barrott has been sure I'm in touch with Mack. They wouldn't take a chance on not knowing if he called.

Reflecting on my conversation with Nick, I wondered if their ears were burning at his suggestion that they might deliberately try to entrap him with an underaged drinker in the Woodshed.

I hoped so.

64

Lil and Gus Kramer sat nervously rigid in Captain Larry Ahearn's office. Ahearn eyed them carefully, figuring out his approach to them. It was obvious when Gaylor ushered them in that Lil Kramer was on the verge of a total breakdown. Her hands were trembling. There was a distinct twitch at the side of her mouth. She was on the brink of tears. Start gently, or let her have it? He decided on the rough approach.

"Lil, you didn't let on to us that you spent two years in prison for jewelry theft," he snapped.

It was as if he had punched her in the mouth. She gasped, her eyes widened, and she began to moan. Gus jumped to his feet. "You shut up," he yelled at Ahearn. "Look up that case. She was a young girl from Idaho, without a family, caring for an old lady night and day. She never *touched* that jewelry! The old lady's cousins were the only ones who had the combination of the safe in her house. They framed Lil so that they not only had the jewelry but the insurance, may they rot in hell."

"I never met anyone who went to prison who wasn't framed," Ahearn said brusquely. "Sit down, Mr. Kramer." He turned back to Lil. "Did Mack ever accuse you of stealing anything?"

"Lil, don't say a word. These people are trying to frame you again."

Lil Kramer's shoulders sagged. "I can't help it if they do. No one will believe me. Just before he disappeared, Mack asked about his new watch, if I had seen it. I knew he was hinting that I had taken it. I got so upset, I yelled at him. I said the three of you in that apartment are all so careless, then when you can't find something you blame it on me."

"Who else blamed you?" Ahearn demanded.

"That nasty Bruce Galbraith. He couldn't find his college ring, as if I would have anything to do with taking it. What would I do with it? Then, a week later, he said he had found it in the pocket of his slacks. No apology, of course. No, 'I'm sorry, Mrs. Kramer.' " She was weeping now, tired, hopeless tears.

Ahearn and Gaylor looked at each other, knowing they were thinking the same thing: That would be easy to check.

"Then you don't know if Mack found his watch before he disappeared?"

"No, I don't. And that's why I'm so afraid that when he comes back, he'll accuse me again." Lil Kramer began to wail. "And that's why when I thought I saw him in church that day—"

"You *thought* you saw him in church!" Ahearn interrupted. "You told us you were certain you saw him there."

"I saw someone about his size, then when I heard he had dropped the note, I was sure, but then I wasn't sure, and I guess I'm sure now, but—"

"Why did you suddenly decide to move to Pennsylvania?" Gaylor interrupted.

"Because Mr. Olsen's nephew, Steve Hockney, overheard Mack asking me about the watch, and now Steve is holding that over my head," she screamed. "Because he wants us to complain about Howie to his uncle and get him fired and . . . and . . . I can't . . . take . . . it . . . anymore. I just want to die. I want to die . . ."

Lil Kramer leaned forward and covered her face with her hands.

Her thin shoulders shook as she sobbed. Gus knelt beside her and put his arms around her. "It's all right, Lil," he said, "it's all right. We're going home now."

He looked up, first at Ahearn, and then at Gaylor. "This is what I think of you two," he said, and spat on the carpet.

65

The other phone call after I finished speaking with Nick was to Jackie Reynolds, my psychologist friend, who had been trying to reach me and whom I'd put off calling. Of course Jackie had been reading the newspapers, but we hadn't talked much since our dinner when all of this began. Remembering my suspicion that the phone might be tapped, I gave very general answers to her questions.

I knew she caught on. "Carolyn, I've had a couple of cancellations," she said. "Have you any plans for lunch?"

"No."

"Then why don't you come up here, and we'll send out for sandwiches and coffee?"

That sounded good to me. Jackie's office adjoins the apartment where she lives on East Seventy-fourth Street and Second Avenue. As I hung up, I realized how much I wanted her guidance about my planned visit to Mom. Which reminded me that I had not yet spoken to Elliott.

I dialed his office, and was put straight through to him. "Carolyn, I didn't know what to think when I couldn't reach you."

I heard the reproach in his voice and apologized. I knew I owed him that. I explained that I had gone to Martha's Vineyard and the reason for it. Then, keenly aware of the probable wiretap, I said that it was a wasted visit, and that I was going to drive up later this afternoon to see Mom. "If she refuses to see me, at least I tried. I'll get there between four and five," I told him.

"I think that might be good timing," he said slowly. "I hope to get up there around five myself. I want to talk to you and Olivia together."

With that, we left it. What did he want to talk to the two of us about? I wondered. Surely in Mom's fragile state, he wouldn't withdraw his support from her now. Please, God, not that! She needed him. I thought about the night only a few weeks ago, after Mack left the note and at dinner she announced she had decided to let him live his own life. I thought of the way she and Elliott had looked at each other, and how he had planned to join her in Greece. I thought about the way their shoulders were touching when they walked down the street after we left Le Cirque. Elliott could make Mom happy. Mom is sixty-two. She has every chance of living another twenty or thirty good years—unless, of course, I've ruined it for her by blundering into the Detective Squad room and meeting Barrott.

I changed into a jacket and slacks and, as I did last night in Martha's Vineyard, tried to mask the dark circles under my eyes with foundation and added color to my overall washed-out appearance with mascara and lipstick.

I drove out of the garage, this time in my own car, and—surprise! surprise!—for the present, the media vans were gone. I guess they figured they had about as much out of me as they were going to get for the day.

When I got to Seventy-fourth Street, I left the car in Jackie's garage and went upstairs. When she came to the door, we hugged each other. "Nothing like lots of stress as a daily diet," she commented. "I haven't seen you in two weeks, and I bet you've lost at least five or six pounds."

"At least," I agreed as I followed her into her office. It's a medium-sized, comfortable room with a couple of upholstered armchairs facing her desk. I remembered she collects nineteenth-century English prints of dogs and horses, and admired aloud some really wonderful examples framed on the wall. I imagined new patients remarking on them before revealing the problem that had driven them to seek Jackie's help.

We agreed on ham and Swiss cheese on rye with lettuce and mustard and black coffee. She phoned in the order, then we settled down to talk. I told her about my meeting with Barbara, holding back only the fact that she had given birth to Mack's son. Instead, feeling dishonest, I gave Barbara's version, that she had had an abortion.

"It's a viable reason for Mack to escape," she agreed. "But just suppose he had gone to your father and/or your mother. What would either or both of them have done, do you think?"

"Supported them in their decision to marry and have the baby. Put Mack through law school."

"Put Barbara through medical school?"

"I don't know."

"Knowing your father as I did, he certainly wouldn't have put up with Mack taking a crack at acting."

"Now *that* is a certainty, I agree." Then I told Jackie how worried I was that Elliott might reconsider wanting to marry Mom while the present suspicion of Mack existed, or if he ever was arrested and put on trial.

"I'd worry, too," Jackie agreed frankly. "Appearances mean so much to people like Elliott. I know someone like that. He's about Elliott's age, a widower, one of the nicest people you'd ever want to know, but a snob. I joke with him that he'd be caught dead before he'd date anyone who wasn't a socialite, no matter how accomplished and beautiful she was."

"What did he say when you told him that?" I asked Jackie.

"He laughed, but he didn't deny it."

The desk called to say that the delivery was on the way. We settled down to lunch, and Jackie started to remind me that I was planning to apply for a job in the District Attorney's office. Then I knew she could have bitten her tongue. Can you just imagine the District Attorney of Manhattan hiring the sister of an accused murderer?

66

All afternoon, either alone or in pairs, the members of the Detective Squad visited Lucas Reeves's office and studied the photos he had prepared for their inspection. Sometimes they lingered over one or several pictures. They studied the enhanced shot of Mack MacKenzie as he might look today. Some of them held it up to compare with a headshot on the wall, but in the end they all left shrugging their shoulders in disappointment and defeat.

Roy Barrott was one of the last to arrive, at quarter of five. He had gone home and crashed for three hours. Now, freshly shaved and alert, he went painstakingly through the hundreds of stills while Lucas Reeves waited patiently in his office.

Finally, at seven fifteen, as Lucas came in to check on him, he gave up. "They're all starting to look familiar," he said. "I don't know why, but I feel as if I'm missing something over there." He pointed his hand to the far wall.

Lucas Reeves frowned. "Oddly, Carolyn MacKenzie paused at that area as well. I had the feeling that something interested her, but she must have dismissed the possibility. Otherwise I am sure she would have said something."

Barrott stood in front of it again. "It's not going to happen, at least not tonight."

Reeves reached into his pocket and pulled out a card. "I have written down my cell phone number for you. If anything occurs to you and you want to come back here at any hour, call me and I will instruct the security guard to let you in immediately."

"Good enough, and thanks."

Barrott went back to the squad room to find renewed energy crackling through it. Ahearn, his tie pulled loose, his face haggard and weary, was pacing the floor in his office. "We may be onto something," he said. "Steve Hockney, the nephew of the owner of the apartment building MacKenzie was living in, has a sealed juvenile record. We got a look at it, serious stuff, but nothing violent. Dealing marijuana, burglary, and theft. His uncle was able to hire good lawyers who kept him out of a couple of years in a juvenile center. According to Lil Kramer, Hockney was holding it over her head that MacKenzie was missing his watch. That was only a day or two before Mack disappeared. We're looking for Hockney. His band has regular gigs in the SoHo–Greenwich Village locale, and he uses a lot of costume changes, even wigs and putty to alter his appearance."

"How about the rest of what the Kramers told you?"

"We spoke to Bruce Galbraith. He's one cold fish. He acknowledged that he did ask Lil Kramer about his school ring, but she took it wrong. He wasn't accusing her. He claims he just asked her if she'd seen it when she was cleaning up. She hit the roof and got all upset. Knowing her background, you can understand why she might have been hypersensitive about a question like that."

Bob Gaylor had come in while Ahearn was speaking. "Our guys just reached Hockney's uncle, Derek Olsen, the old man who owns the buildings. He confirmed that there was a rivalry between his assistant, Howard Altman, and his nephew Steve Hockney. He said he's sick of both of them. He's left messages on their phones that he's selling all the property and that the wrecking ball is hitting the 104th Street town house tomorrow morning. We didn't let on that we're hunting for the nephew. We told him we were confirming the Kramers' story."

"What did he say about them?"

"Hardworking, good people. He'd trust them with everything he had."

"Have we got any pictures of Hockney?" Barrott asked. "I want to compare him with a face I saw in Reeves's office just now. I feel as though I've missed something."

"There's one of his publicity pictures with his band on my desk," Ahearn told him. "We've got dozens of them with our guys on the street."

Barrott started rifling through the untidy clutter on Ahearn's desk, then picked up a picture he found there. *"This is the one,"* he said aloud.

Ahearn and Gaylor stared at him. "What are you talking about?" Ahearn demanded.

"I'm talking about *this* guy," he said, pointing. "Where's that *other* picture of Leesey posing for her friend, the one with Nick DeMarco in the background?"

"One of the copies of it is somewhere in that pile."

Barrott rummaged, then, with a satisfied grunt, said, "Here it is." He held up two photos, comparing them. An instant later, he was dialing the cell phone of Lucas Reeves.

67

As I expected, the sanitarium where Mom was staying was about as luxurious inside and out as I would have imagined any place that Elliott would choose for her would be. Thick carpets, soft lights, fine paintings on the walls. I got there around 4:30, and the receptionist had clearly been briefed that I was on my way.

"Your mother is expecting you," she said in one of those professionally melodious voices that seemed to me to fit in with the surroundings. "Her suite is on the fourth floor, with a beautiful view of the grounds." She got up and led me to the elevator, an ornately handsome object with an operator and a velvet seating bench inside.

My escort murmured, "Ms. Olivia's suite, please, Mason," and I remembered hearing that in some of these expensive psychiatric residences last names are not shared. Just as well, I thought. The other guests don't need to know that Mrs. Charles MacKenzie Sr. is in their midst.

At the fourth floor, we got out and walked down the hall to the corner suite. After tapping on the door, my escort opened it. "Ms. Olivia," she called, her voice slightly elevated but still finishing-school modulated.

I walked behind her into an exquisite sitting room. I have seen photos of the suites in the Plaza Athénée in Paris, and I felt as though I was walking into one of them. Then Mom appeared in the doorway from the bedroom. Without another word, the escort was gone and Mom and I looked at each other.

All the conflicting emotions, the roller coaster of emotions that I had been experiencing this last week when Mom took refuge in Elliott's apartment rushed through me as I looked at her. Guilt. Anger. Bitterness. Then they all washed away and the only thing I felt was love. Her beautiful eyes were filled with grief. She was looking at me uncertainly as though she didn't know what to expect of me.

I went over to her and put my arms around her. "I'm so sorry," I said. "I'm so terribly sorry. I guess that no matter how many times I say to myself, 'If only I hadn't tried to find Mack,' I can only tell you I'd give my life to undo that but I can't."

Then her hands began running through my hair the way they did when I was a small child and upset about something. They were loving and comforting, and I knew that she had come to peace with what I had done.

"Carolyn, we'll see it through," she said. "No matter what it turns out to be. If Mack has done everything they say he has done, there is one thing I can be sure of. He is not in his right mind."

"How much have they told you?" I asked her.

"I guess everything. Yesterday I told Dr. Abrams, my psychiatrist, that I didn't want to be protected anymore. I can sign myself out of here anytime, but I'd rather absorb everything that I have to know while I can talk it through with him."

This was the mother I thought I had lost, the one who kept Dad sane when Mack disappeared, the one whose first thought was for me when she knew Dad was lost on 9/11. I had been a junior in Columbia then and had by chance slept home and was still asleep when the first plane hit. Horrified, Mom had watched it by herself. Dad's office was on the 103rd floor of the North Tower, the first one to be hit. She had tried to phone him and actually got through to him. "Liv, the fire's underneath us," he said. "I don't think we'll make it."

The connection had gone dead, and minutes later, she saw the tower collapse. She had let me sleep until I woke up naturally, about forty-five minutes later. I'd opened my eyes to find her sitting in my room, tears streaming from her eyes. Then she'd rocked me in her arms while she told me what had happened.

This was my mother as she was until year after year, the annual Mother's Day call from Mack tore her apart.

"Mom, if you're comfortable here, I wish you'd stay a while longer," I said. "You don't want to be on Sutton Place the way it is now, and once the media got word you were back at Elliott's apartment, they'd be gunning for you there, too."

"I understand that, but Carolyn, what about you? I know you wouldn't come here, but isn't there someplace you can get away from them?"

You can run but you can't hide, I thought. "Mom, I think it's necessary for me to be around and visible," I said. "Because until we have absolute proof to the contrary, I am going to believe and publicly swear that Mack is innocent."

"That's exactly what your father would do." Now Mom smiled, a real smile. "Come on. Let's sit down. I wish we could have a cocktail, but that's not going to happen here." She looked at me, a bit anxiously. "You know that Elliott is coming?"

"Yes. I'm looking forward to seeing him."

"He's been a rock."

I admit I felt a twinge of jealousy and then felt guilty about it. Elliott *was* a rock. Two weeks ago, Mom had said that I was her rod and staff. My guilt faded as I remembered that Elliott might just be about to announce that he needed to separate himself from our problems. Jackie's words played again in my mind. *Appearances mean so much to people like Elliott.*

But when he arrived, everything I feared turned out to be totally wrong. In fact, in his endearing, formal way, he was looking for my blessing to marry Mom. He sat next to her on the couch, and addressed me earnestly.

"Carolyn, I guess you know I've always been in love with your mother," he said. "I always thought she was a shining star beyond my reach. But now I know that I can offer her the protection of a husband at a very difficult time in her life."

I knew I had to warn him. "Elliott, if Mack were ever to go on trial as a serial killer, you have to be aware that the publicity will be awful. Clients of the caliber you have may not be pleased that their financial advisor is in the tabloids on a regular basis."

Elliott looked at my mother, then back at me. With something of a twinkle in his eyes, he said, "Carolyn, word for word, that is the same speech I heard from your mother. I can promise you this: I would rather tell all my distinguished clients to jump in the lake before I give up one day of being at your mother's side."

We had dinner in one of the private dining rooms. It was a low-key celebration. I agreed with their plan that they would be married as soon and as quietly as possible. I drove home that evening feeling so much better about Mom, but also with the strange sensation that Mack was trying to reach me. I could almost feel his presence in the car. Why?

Again there was no sign of the media on Sutton Place. I went to bed and listened to the eleven o'clock news. A clip with part of my statement to the media was shown, and I sounded strident and defensive. By now it had leaked out, or been allowed to leak out, that Leesey had named Mack as her abductor.

I turned off the television. Love or money, I thought as I closed my eyes. That's what Lucas Reeves said were the causes of the majority of crimes. Love or money. Or *lack* of love, in Mack's case.

At three A.M., I heard the buzzing of the intercom. I got out of bed and rushed downstairs to pick it up. It was the concierge. "I'm so sorry, Ms. MacKenzie," he said. "But someone just handed a note to the doorman and said it was a matter of life and death that you have it immediately."

He hesitated, then said, "With all the publicity, this may be someone's terrible idea of a joke, but—"

"Send it up," I interrupted him.

I stood at the door and waited until Manuel came down the hall and handed me a plain white envelope. The note in it was handwritten on plain bond paper.

It read, "Carolyn I am sending this by messenger because your phone may be wiretapped. Mack just called me. He wants to see both of us. He's waiting on the corner of 104th Street and Riverside Drive. Meet us there. Elliott."

68

There he is," Barrott exclaimed, "on the street in front of the Wood-shed the night Leesey disappeared. If you look from the angle the security camera caught him, he could see DeMarco's table. And there he is again, in the same frame as DeMarco, watching Leesey when she was posing for her roommate."

Accompanied by the security guard, who had been given permission to admit them, they were in Lucas Reeves's office. They had studied hundreds of pictures in the wall montages, until they could pinpoint the face they were seeking.

"Here's another one that looks like him, but the hair is shorter," Gaylor said, a note of excitement detectable in his voice.

It was half past ten. Knowing they had a long night ahead, they hurried back to the office to begin to process information on one more potential suspect.

69

Lucas Reeves did not sleep well on Wednesday night. "Love or money" was the phrase that ran through his head in a singsong way. At six A.M., as he was waking up, the question that had been eluding him popped into his head. Who would be interested in having a person who is dead seem to be alive?

Love or money.

Money, of course. It was beginning to fall into place like pieces of a puzzle. So absurdly simple if he was right. Lucas, a notoriously early riser, never minded waking up someone when he needed the answer to a question. This time, fortunately, his advisor, a prominent estate lawyer, was also an early riser.

"Can an inheritance trust be broken, or is it always sacrosanct?" Lucas asked him abruptly.

"They're not easily broken by any means, but if there's a good and valid reason for dipping into it, the executor will usually be amenable."

"That's what I thought. I won't disturb you any further. Thank you, my friend."

"Any time, Lucas. But not before seven next time, okay? I get up early, but my wife likes to sleep."

70

I pulled on slacks, slipped my feet in sandals, grabbed a long raincoat to cover my pajama top, and ran for the elevator, shoving Elliott's note into my shoulder bag as I rushed down the hall. In my hurry to get to Mack before he changed his mind about seeing me, I forgot that the garage closed at three A.M. Manuel reminded me of that when I asked for the garage level.

I did the only thing I could do—got outside, into the street, and looked frantically around to flag down a cab. There was none on Sutton Place, but when I turned up Fifty-seventh Street I saw one of those gypsy town cars coming. I must have seemed a wild sight to him as I waved both arms to catch his eye, but he did stop. I got in, and he made a U-turn to go west.

When we got to the corner of 104th and Riverside Drive, there was no one there, I paid the cabby and climbed out onto the quiet street. Then I noticed a van parked down the block, and even though the lights were off, I had a hunch that Elliott and Mack might be in it. I walked closer to get a better look and made a pretense of reaching for a key, as though I were going to the nearest apartment building. Across the street, I could see a large construction site next to a boarded-up old town house on the corner.

Then a man stepped out of the darkened doorway of the next building. For a moment I thought it was Elliott, but then I could see

that he was a much younger person, someone whose face was familiar. I recognized him as being the representative of the owner of
Mack's apartment building. I had met him that first time I stopped at
the Kramers', and he had spoken to me on Monday after I left their
apartment in tears.

What on earth was he doing here now, I asked myself, and where
was Elliott?

"Ms. MacKenzie," he said hurriedly. "I don't know if you remember me. I'm Howard Altman."

"I remember you. Where is Mr. Wallace?"

"He's with some guy I found camping out in that place. Mr. Olsen
owns it. Every once in a while I check on it, even though it's closed."
He was nodding toward the boarded-up corner building. "The guy I
found gave me fifty bucks to call Mr. Wallace for him, then Mr. Wallace promised me another fifty bucks if I'd write a message for you
and deliver it."

"They're inside that building? What does the other man look
like?"

"He's about thirty, I guess. He started crying when Mr. Wallace
came in. They both did."

Mack was in there, trying to hide in that crumbling ruin. I followed Howard Altman across the street and along the construction
fence to the back door of the house. He opened it and gestured me
to enter, but as I looked into the darkened interior I panicked and
stepped back. I knew something wasn't right. "Ask Mr. Wallace to
come out," I told Howard.

His answer was to grab me and pull me inside the house. I was so
stunned I didn't resist. He yanked the door closed behind him, and
before I could scream or fight to free myself, he shoved me down a
flight of stairs. Somewhere on the way down, I cracked my head and
lost consciousness. I don't know how long it was before I opened my
eyes. It was pitch dark. The air I was breathing was unbearably foul.

My face felt caked with blood. My head was splitting and there was something wrong with my right leg. It was bent under me and throbbing with pain.

Then I felt something move beside me, and a whispery voice moaned, "Water, please, water."

I tried to move but could not. I knew my leg had to be broken. I did the only thing I could think to do. I moistened a finger in my mouth, then groped in the dark until I could find the parched lips of Leesey Andrews.

71

With his ever-increasing arthritis, Derek Olsen often woke up during the night, throbbing pain in his hips and knees. On Wednesday night, when his aching joints woke him up, he could not go back to sleep again. The call from the police about his nephew Steve meant, of course, that he was in some kind of trouble again. *So much for the fifty thousand I was going to leave him,* Olsen thought. *He can go whistle for it!*

The one bright spot was that in a few hours he was going to have the fun of watching the wrecking ball smash that decrepit old town house into smithereens. *Every chip that flies in the air represents money I made on the deal,* he thought with satisfaction. *I wouldn't put it past Doug Twining to operate the rig himself. That's how mad he is at having to pay me so much.*

The pleasurable thought comforted him to the point that sometime before dawn he fell into the deep sleep that normally lasted till eight A.M. But on Thursday morning, his phone rang at six. It was Detective Barrott wanting to know where Howard Altman was. He hadn't returned to his apartment all night.

"Am I his babysitter?" Olsen demanded querulously. "You wake me up to ask me where he is? How do I know? I don't socialize with him. He works for me."

"What kind of car does Howard drive?" Barrott asked.

"When he drives me, he drives my SUV. I don't think he has a car of his own. I don't care."

"Does he ever take your SUV in the evening?"

"Not that I know of. He better not. It's a Mercedes."

"What color is it?"

"Black. At my age do you think I want a red one?"

"Mr. Olsen, we really need to talk about Howard," Barrott said. "What do you know about his personal life?"

"I know nothing. I want to know nothing. He's been working for me nearly ten years. He's done a good enough job."

"Did you check his references when you hired him?"

"He was recommended by an impeccable source, my financial advisor Elliott Wallace."

"Thank you, Mr. Olsen. Have a good day."

"You ruined most of it for me. I'll be tired all day." Derek Olsen slammed down the receiver. But not all of it, he thought as he envisioned the wrecking ball striking a bull's-eye on his piggy bank.

At the other end of the phone, Barrott, unable to conceal his exultation, said, "Elliott Wallace recommended him for the job."

"It ties in with Lucas Reeves's theory," Ahearn agreed. "But we have to go easy. Wallace is a big shot on Wall Street."

"Yes, but he wouldn't be the first executor who dipped into his client's funds, if that's the way it plays," Barrott said. "Any result on the fingerprints?"

"Not yet. We can't be sure the ones we lifted from the outer door of Howard's apartment are absolutely his, but we're running them anyway. I'd swear that guy has a prior record," Gaylor said.

Barrott checked his watch. "The security guard at Wallace's building said he normally gets in at eight thirty. We'll be waiting for him."

72

Once again, Carolyn was not answering her cell phone. Nick phoned her at eight o'clock on Thursday morning with the idea of taking her out for breakfast. He wanted to see her. I *need* to see her, he thought. On the late news, he had watched the clip of her on television, passionately defending Mack.

He wanted to know how she had made out on the visit to her mother. He knew how hurt she had been by her mother's refusal to see her.

At least her cell phone was on. It was ringing. It had been turned off Monday afternoon and all day Tuesday. A gnawing sense that something was wrong made Nick decide to stop at Sutton Place, and make sure that she was home.

The morning concierge had just come on duty. "I don't think she's back yet," he said, when Nick asked for Carolyn. "I understand she had an emergency message at about three A.M. and went rushing out. Whoever handed the note to her doorman said it was a matter of life or death. I hope everything is all right."

Everything *isn't* all right, Nick thought frantically. He began to dial the now familiar number of Detective Barrott.

73

T hank you for seeing us, Mr. Wallace," Barrott said politely.

"That's all right. Is there any news of Mack?" Elliott asked.

"No, I'm afraid there isn't but we do have a few matters you can help us clear up."

"Of course." He gestured for the detectives to take a seat.

"You know Howard Altman?"

"Yes, I do. He is the employee of my client Derek Olsen."

"Didn't you actually recommend Altman to Mr. Olsen ten years ago?"

"I believe I did."

"How did you happen to know Mr. Altman?"

"I'm not really sure. As I recall, a former client had sold some real estate and was looking to place him." Elliott's expression was blank.

"Who was that client?"

"I'm not even sure I can remember. I dealt with him only briefly. But it was one of those coincidences. Olsen had been in and mentioned he was having a terrible time getting good help, and I passed Altman's name along to him."

"I see. We'd certainly appreciate having that client's name, and I'm sure you'd want to find him. Altman may be a suspect in the abduction of Leesey Andrews, which of course would clear the name of Mack MacKenzie."

"Anything that would clear Mack's name would be priceless to me," Elliott told Barrott, his voice shaking with emotion.

Barrott studied him, taking in the beautifully tailored suit, the crisp white shirt, the handsome blue and red tie. He watched as Wallace took off his glasses, polished them, then put them back on. What is it about this guy that I'm seeing, he asked himself. It's the eyes and the forehead. They looked familiar. Then he wondered: *Is it possible? My God, he resembles Altman.* He signaled to Gaylor to take over the questioning.

"Mr. Wallace, isn't it a fact that you are the executor of Mack MacKenzie's estate?"

"I am the executor of all the MacKenzie family trusts."

"The *sole* executor?"

"Yes."

"What are the terms of Mack's trust?"

"It was set up by his grandfather. He was not to receive income from it until he reached the age of forty."

"In the meantime, of course, it continues to grow."

"Certainly. It has been carefully invested."

"What would happen if Mack died?"

"The trust would go to his children, and if he had none, to his sister, Carolyn."

"Could Mack have asked for an advance from his trust for what you as executor deemed to be a responsible reason?"

"It would have to be extremely responsible. His grandfather wanted no playboy heirs."

"How about the fact that he was about to get married; that his future wife was pregnant with his child; that he no longer wanted his parents to pay his way; that he would put himself through college and would want to pay for his wife to go to medical school? Would all that be good and sufficient reason to dip into the trust?"

"It might be, but that situation did not occur." Elliott Wallace stood up. "As you can understand, I have a busy calendar and—"

Barrott's cell phone rang. It was Nick DeMarco. Barrott listened, determined to keep an inscrutable look on his face. Carolyn MacKenzie was missing. The new victim, he thought.

Wallace, holding an arm out, was attempting to usher them out of his office. Lucas Reeves is right, Barrott thought. It all fits into place. He decided to trick Wallace with false information.

"Not so fast, Mr. Wallace," he said. "We're not going anywhere. We have Howard Altman in custody. He's bragging about the abductions. He's bragging about working for you." He paused for a moment. "You didn't tell us you were *related* to him."

Finally, Wallace's unruffled exterior showed signs of strain. "Oh, poor Howie," he sighed. With one hand he leaned on his desk, and with the other he reached into the top drawer. "He's totally delusional, of course."

"No, he isn't," Barrott snapped.

Elliott Wallace sighed again. "My psychopathic nephew promised to die in a breathtaking fashion and take Carolyn and Leesey with him. He couldn't even handle that well."

In a single, quick motion, Elliott Wallace removed a small pistol from his desk drawer and held it to his forehead. "As Cousin Franklin would have put it, 'My fellow Americans, farewell,'" he said, and pulled the trigger.

74

Larry Ahearn was in the squad room when the call came in from Barrott. "Larry, we were right about Wallace. He just blew his brains out. Before he did, he told us that Altman is his nephew. He said that Altman has Carolyn and Leesey and he's going to kill them and then kill himself. But he didn't tell us where they are."

With icy calm, Ahearn absorbed the stunning information. "As of the last few hours, neither trace we have on those phones is giving us anything," he said. "Either the phones are turned off or they're in an area where we can't get reception. What about Altman? He must have a cell phone. I'll call his boss, Olsen, on another line. Hang on."

75

Derek Olsen, camp chair in hand, was about to go out and walk down the block to see the wrecking ball destroy his old town house. Irritated at the second phone call from the detectives, he was even more irritated at the reason for it. "Sure Howie has a cell phone. Who doesn't? Sure I know his number. It's 917-555-6262. But I'm telling you something. That's the one I pay for. I get the bill. I watch it like a hawk. Business only. I guess he has another. How should I know? I'm on my way out for some excitement. Good-bye."

As Barrott waited on the line for Ahearn to check with Olsen, Detective Gaylor moved swiftly to secure the premises. With one hand he locked the door of Wallace's office and with the other dialed 911 on his cell phone.

Then he heard Barrott explode as he reacted to what Ahearn was telling him. "The business cell phone that Olsen gave you for Altman is turned off! But wait a minute. Wallace would never have been stupid enough to call Altman on that line anyway. There must have been another number that he used to reach him. Hold on, Larry."

In two strides Barrott was across the room and kneeling beside Wallace's body, rummaging through his pockets. "Here it is!" He yanked out a small state-of-the-art cell phone, opened it, and scrolled through the directory. This has got to be it, he thought, as he spotted the initials "H.A." He pushed 5 and then the send button and, breathing a prayer, held the phone to his ear.

It rang twice and then was answered. "Uncle Elliott," an edgy, high-pitched voice said, "we did our good-byes last night. I don't want to talk anymore. There's only a few minutes left."

The connection broke. Within seconds, Barrott was back on his own phone, giving Howard Altman's number to Ahearn, who was frantically waiting to pass it on to the phone technicians who would trace it.

76

He came down to the basement three times during that long night. As I lay next to Leesey on that clammy dirt floor, pain vibrating from my leg, my face crusted with dried blood, my fingers entwined in Leesey's, he alternately cried and laughed and moaned and giggled. I dreaded the sound of steps on the stairs, not knowing if this would be the time he would decide to kill us.

"Remember the Zodiac Killer?" he sobbed the first time he came down. "He didn't want to keep going. Neither do I. He wrote a letter to a newspaper that he knew could be traced to him. I wrote one, too, but I tore it up. I am tortured, but I don't want to go to prison. The first girl was when I was sixteen. I had put that behind me. Then it happened again. I was the caretaker on an estate, and the housekeeper's daughter was so pretty. When they found her body, they suspected me. My mother sent me to New York to be with her dear older brother, my uncle, Elliott Wallace . . ."

Elliott Wallace! Uncle Elliott! But that's impossible, I thought, that can't be.

I felt his breath on my cheek. "You don't believe me, do you? You should. My mother told him he had to help me or she'd expose him for the fraud that he was. But even before I met him, it happened again, right after I got to New York, the first girl in the nightclub. I weighed her body down and threw it in the river. Then I met Uncle

Elliott, and I told him about it and said I was sorry, and he had to get me a job or I'd go to the police and turn myself in and tell the newspapers he was a phony."

Altman's voice became sarcastic. "*Of course*, he said he'd find me a job." His lips touched my forehead. "You believe me now, don't you, Carolyn?"

Leesey's breath had become a soft, terrified whimper. I squeezed her hand. "I believe you," I said. "I know you're telling the truth."

"Do you know that I'm sorry?"

"Yes. Yes. I know that."

"That's good."

It was so dark I couldn't see him but sensed that he had moved away from us. Then I heard him going up the stairs again. How long would it be before he came back? I asked myself frantically. I had been so foolish. No one knew where I had gone. It might be hours before someone looked for me. Nick, I thought, Nick, be worried. Know that something's wrong. Look for me. Look for us.

I think a couple of hours passed, and then I screamed. He had been so quiet that I had not heard him come back. His hand covered my mouth.

"It doesn't do any good to scream, Carolyn," he said. "Leesey screamed in the beginning. I'd come down here and tell her about her picture being in the newspapers. She didn't want to record those messages for her father, but I told her that if she did, I might let her go. But I didn't mean it. Now don't scream again. If you do, I will kill you."

He was gone again. My head was pounding. The pain in my leg was unbearable. Would Lucas Reeves or Detective Barrott try to reach me? Would they and Nick realize that something was wrong?

The last time he returned, I had the sense that it was morning. I could see his shadow on the stairs. "I was never going to commit another crime, Carolyn," he said. "I really did like managing those buildings, and I loved the friends I made on the Internet. I still thought I could stop. I really tried. Then Uncle Elliott said that *now* I owed *him* a favor. He needed me to get rid of your brother. Mack went to Elliott. He wanted to tap into his trust fund. His girlfriend was pregnant, and Mack wanted to get married and pay for his own education and hers, too. But Uncle Elliott had cleaned out most of the income from both of your trust funds. He'd invested tons of money in something that fell apart. He tried to put Mack off, but he knew that Mack was suspicious. I had to kill him."

I had to kill him. I had to kill him. Mack is dead, I thought bitterly. They murdered him.

"Elliott had to keep everyone thinking Mack was alive so that the trust funds wouldn't be examined. I made Mack say the words that you heard on the first Mother's Day phone call before I shot him. Then a year later Elliott made me kill the teacher and steal the tapes she had of Mack so he could make new Mother's Day calls. Elliott is a technical genius. For years he mixed what Mack had said on those tapes for the calls. Your brother's buried right here with the other girls. Look, Carolyn."

He directed the thin beam of a flashlight across the basement floor. I raised my head.

"See where the crosses are? Your brother and the other girls are buried there next to each other."

Mack had been dead all these years that we had been hoping and praying for him to come back to us. The reality that Mack was buried here in this miserable, filthy basement filled me with an overwhelming grief. Somehow I had always believed I would find him. Mack. Mack. Mack.

Altman was laughing, a high-pitched giggly sound. "Sure, Elliott was born in England. His mother is from Kansas. She was a maid with an American family that was transferred to England. She got pregnant in London and was sent home after the baby was born. She helped him make up all those stories about being a relative of President Roosevelt. They made them up together. She helped him get that swanky English accent. He's good with voices. The last three years he's even been doing Mack's voice himself. He knows you already had compared Mack's real voice with home movies. Had you fooled, didn't he?"

Altman's voice was becoming more and more shrill. "We only have fifteen minutes before it's all over. They're going to demolish this building. But I want to tell you. I dropped that note in the collection basket. Uncle Elliott was worried that you were going to start looking for Mack. Elliott had me leave it there. Lil Kramer saw me in church. I saw her look at me a couple of times. But then she thought I was Mack because you told her he'd been at that Mass. Good-bye, Carolyn. Good-bye, Leesey."

For the last time, I heard his steps retreating. Fifteen minutes. This building was going to be demolished in fifteen minutes. *I am going to die*, I thought, *and Mom is going to marry Elliott . . .*

Leesey was trembling. I was sure she understood what he had said. I kept holding her hand and moistening her lips, talking to her, begging her to hang on, that everyone was looking for us. But now I did not believe what I was saying. I believed that Leesey and I would be the final victims of this madman and Elliott Wallace. In that moment I thought that at least I would soon be with Mack and Daddy.

77

We've got him. He's on 104th and Riverside Drive," Larry Ahearn yelled.

An alarm went out to all the squad cars in the vicinity. Sirens wailing, they rushed to the scene.

The wrecking ball was in place. A delighted Derek Olsen saw that his business rival Doug Twining was inside the cockpit of the crane.

"One." Derek jumped up and began to count.

"Two." Then his triumphant cheer died on his lips. Someone was pushing open the boarded window on the second floor of the old town house. Someone was swinging his legs over the sill and waving. Altman. It was Howie Altman.

The wrecking ball was swinging toward the house. At the last instant, Twining spotted Altman and swung the controls so that the ball missed the house by inches.

Squad cars, tires screeching, were rounding the corner.

"Come back! Come back!" A screaming Howie Altman was running along the roof of the porch, waving his arms at the crane. As he began to jump up and down, the rotted wood caved in and the house began to crumble, floor by floor toppling into each other. Seeing what was happening, Altman dove back through the window in time to have tons of debris crash down on him.

Police poured out of the squad cars. "The basement," one of them yelled, "the basement. If they're there, it's their only chance."

78

The ceiling was falling around us. I pulled myself up and tried to throw my body over Leesey, who was now barely breathing. I felt a chunk of plaster hit my shoulder and then my head and arm. Too late, too late, I thought. Like Mack and those other girls, Leesey and I were doomed to end our lives here.

Then I heard the sound of the outside basement door being pulled open, and shouting voices approaching me from above. That was when I let myself drift off and escape from the pain. I guess they sedated me pretty heavily, because it was two days before I really woke up. Mother was sitting on a chair by the window of the hospital room, watching over me as she had done on 9/11. As we had that day, we cried together in each other's arms, this time for Mack, the honorable young man, son and brother, who had died because he wanted to accept his responsibilities.

Epilogue

One year later

When the books were checked, we learned that Elliott had robbed us of a fortune. It was clear, as Altman had ranted, that Mack had realized something was wrong with his trust fund, and the realization had cost him his life.

It was a miracle that Leesey was still alive. She had been tied up on that dirt floor for sixteen days and nights, unable to move, Altman alternately threatening to kill her and then taunting her about jumping into the SUV outside the Woodshed when he told her Nick had sent him to drive her home. He had given her only a few sips of water each day. Starving and dehydrated, she was in extremely critical condition when she arrived at the hospital. Just as Mom had kept her vigil at my side, Leesey's father and brother kept theirs in her hospital room, coaxing and begging her back to life.

The Andrews have become our very good friends. Dr. David Andrews, Leesey's Dad, regularly invites Mom and me for dinner at his club in Greenwich. Their friendship has been a great comfort as Mom and I struggle with the pain of Mack's death. I know we have been a help to Leesey as she recovers emotionally from her terrible ordeal. Mother sold the Sutton Place apartment and now lives on

Central Park West. I notice that Dr. David comes down frequently to go to dinner and the theatre with her.

We managed to keep from the media the full story of Mack's reason for becoming suspicious that his trust fund was not in order. Of course, I told Mom about Mack's son. It was not my place to keep it from her. Dr. Barbara Hanover Galbraith came to see us and told us how much she regretted believing that Mack had abandoned her. Even then she was not completely honest. She did not admit that she had borne Mack's child until I confronted her. Then she begged us to wait until he is older to tell him the truth, and we have reluctantly agreed. Mom and I wish with all of our hearts that we could know and be close to Mack's son. We have quietly attended plays and concerts at his school, St. David's, and it is like seeing Mack again. They called him Gary. To Mom and me he will always be Charles MacKenzie the Third.

The Kramers are enjoying life in Pennsylvania. When they learned the truth about Mack's disappearance, they came to apologize to Mother and me. Lil told us that because she had gone to prison for stealing when she was a young woman, she was hypersensitive when Mack asked her about his watch. It was found in Howard Altman's apartment. We'll never know whether he stole it from Mack's college apartment or took it after he killed him.

Lil also explained what she had found in Mack's room that had made Gus so angry. "It was a silly note making fun of me, saying that I wanted him to take me dancing, but it hurt my feelings," she said. That, of course, was the note Nick had written and then thrown away. Obviously he had been right about the fact that Lil was a bit nosey. When I asked him about it, he said he had crumpled it and thrown it in the wastebasket near Mack's desk. That is why Lil thought Mack had written it.

I'm happy to report that I'm one of the busy Assistant District Attorneys of Manhattan and regularly work with the detectives who started by suspecting me and now are my close friends and colleagues.

Nick and I were married three months ago. We have turned the loft into a charming New York apartment. The Woodshed is doing well. One of our favorite eating places is his father's newly reopened Pasta and Pizza in Queens. I've always said I would have four children, and we're looking forward to having the first one before too long. I hope it's a boy. His name will be Charles MacKenzie DeMarco.

We'll call him Mack.